About the author

Donna Maree Hanson is a traditionally and independently published author of fantasy, science fiction and horror. She also writes paranormal romance under the pseudonym of Dani Kristoff. Her dark fantasy series (which some reviewers have called 'grim dark'), *Dragon Wine*, was published by Momentum Books (Pan Macmillan digital imprint) in 2014. *Shatterwing*: Part One and *Skywatcher*: Part Two are now re-published independently in digital and print on demand. *Deathwings*, Dragon Wine Part Three and *Bloodstorm*, Dragon Part Four were published in 2017.

In April 2015, Donna was awarded the A. Bertram Chandler Award for 'Outstanding Achievement in Australian Science Fiction' for her work in running science fiction conventions, publishing and broader SF community contribution. Donna also writes science fiction romance, with *Rayessa and the Space Pirates* and *Rae and Essa's Space Adventures* out with Escape Publishing. *Opi Battles the Space Pirates* was published independently in 2017. In 2016, Donna commenced her PhD candidature researching Feminism in Popular Romance at the University of Canberra. Also, available is her epic fantasy series the Silverlands, *Argenterra*, *Oathbound* and *Ungiven Land*. Donna lives in Canberra with her partner and fellow writer Matthew Farrer.

You can contact Donna at her blog http://donnamareehanson.com

Or on Twitter @DonnaMHanson and Facebook

www.facebook.com/donnamareehanson

And if you like to keep in touch and hear about special offers, then consider signing up for my newsletter, Wing Dust.

Also by Donna Maree Hanson

The Silverlands (Epic Fantasy)

Argenterra, The Silverlands Book One

Oathbound, The Silverlands Book Two

Ungiven Land, The Silverlands Book Three

Dragon Wine Series (Dark Fantasy)

Shatterwing, Dragon Wine Part One

Skywatcher, Dragon Wine Part Two

Deathwings, Dragon Wine Part Three

Bloodstorm, Dragon Wine Part Four

Love and Space Pirates (Science Fiction Romance)

Rayessa and the Space Pirates

Rae and Essa's Space Adventures

Opi Battles the Space Pirates

Deathwings
Dragon Wine Part Three

By
Donna Maree Hanson

Dedication

For my friends who make living so worthwhile

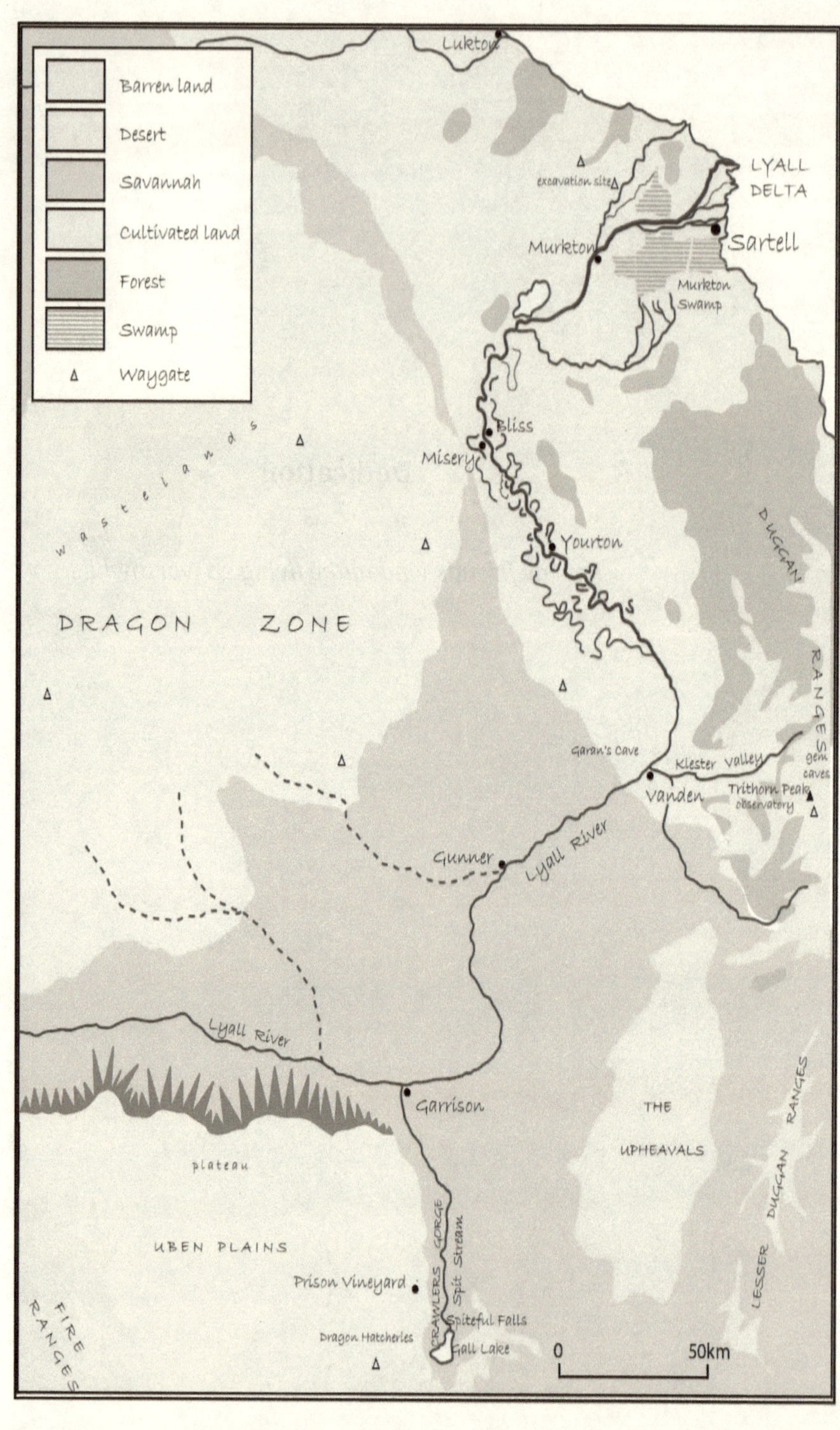

Barren land
Desert
Savannah
Cultivated land
Forest
Swamp
Waygate
Luktou
LYALL DELTA
excavation site
Murkton
Sartell
Murkton Swamp
Bliss
Misery
Yourton
Wastelands
DRAGON ZONE
DUGGAN RANGES
Garan's Cave
Klester Valley
gem caves
Vanden
Trithorn Peak observatory
Gunner
Lyall River
Lyall River
THE UPHEAVALS
Garrison
plateau
LESSER DUGGAN RANGES
UBEN PLAINS
CRAWLERS GORGE
Spit Stream
Prison Vineyard
Spiteful Falls
Dragon Hatcheries
Gall Lake
FIRE RANGES
0
50km

Prologue

Dust particles shimmer in the light of Margra's sun, enveloping the world below in a lavender halo. A lump of space rock turns end over end as it plummets, a tail of vicious fire in its wake. Belle moon's surface erupts as debris is thrown high and another crater is born. The planet revolves on its axis again. Oblivious to its doom.

Part 1

Like blood, a rich drop of wine is licked from the fingertip

Chapter One

WINGS

He was falling.

Air rushed past. Breath stolen. Sharp rocks below. Fear spearing into his lungs, his heart.

A blur of the world around him.

Gercomo opened his mouth to scream. No air. No sound, his mind white with panic.

His arms and legs flailed. He tried to fly.

It was like swimming against the tide, limbs useless, clumsy. A great, burning surge of blood trammeled every muscle, undoing his humanness, remaking him, remaking his mind. Dulling it, smashing it, obliterating it. He sucked in a lungful of air snatched from the wind rushing past.

A guttural cry vibrated against his hardened skin. His own fear haloed him. He struggled to maintain height, wrenching his shoulders, clenching his jaws in the effort to crawl through the air, yet he continued to drop.

Throwing his senses out, the world around him spun and slowed and came into conical focus. Valleys and rifts and eroded peaks loomed large beneath him, all jagged, with the capacity to rend flesh.

He flapped. Wings moved, halting his plummet.

With a desperate heave, he threw more of his strength into his wings until his muscles burned, the sensation as if the flesh was being ripped from his bones. It wasn't working. He was falling, still. But slower, now.

With a last ditch effort, he fought to recall the dance of dragons, remembering how they skimmed thermals and glided above the prison vineyard. Effortlessly they used the membranes on their wings to trap the air and slide. That was what Gercomo was doing wrong. He was fighting against the air instead of working with it. He ceased his struggling and stretched out his arms, no, his wings, and air billowed underneath them. The headlong rush to the ground slowed as the wind caught and gently lifted him. A relieved laugh turned to a screech that was alien in his mouth as he soared higher.

He was no longer falling, but he was too tired to stay aloft for long. Already the muscles between his shoulder blades ached.

Beyond the treacherous foothills of the Duggan Ranges, the desert plain stretched out in a muted pinks, mauves and browns. He tilted his body in that direction, the hues of the landscape strange and his vision distorted while he tried to process a greater range of colors and a spectrum of light he'd not experienced before, a fierce violet glow and other alien ripples of energy that radiated and bent as he turned his head from side to side. He wasn't seeing with his own eyes. It wasn't the same. These were his eyes now. He had to adapt.

The flat stretches of wasteland gave him an uninterrupted view of his surroundings. Yet he could not tell if objects were near or far. At times he thought he could, but his brain was having trouble interpreting the new information.

Drifting lower, the wind grew precarious and, like a cough, the air pushed out from under his wings. In a panic, he tried to maintain his height, to stop himself from falling, and failed. Instead, the clawed foot he extended to the earth clasped emptiness and he rolled and tumbled. Over and over he went, his bones bending and his tendons twisting. Fear and agony intermingled and robbed him of even a scream. When he finally came to a halt, he lay there stunned, pain shafting through every part of him, while he waited to breathe again.

Gercomo uncurled his claw and then dragged a torn wing from underneath his ungainly, scaled body. Every movement radiated hurt and increased his confusion. He no longer had hands that could touch. All he could do was lick his skin. It was then he noticed his size.

He was puny. Even he could tell that he was small compared to the immense dragons. He was hardly larger than a man. What horrible twist of fate was this? To be cursed to exist as a beast, but not a real one, just a semblance of one. Looking down at his body, he knew it was terribly wrong. He was nothing like the huge winged beasts that overflew the vineyard. He was pitiful. What if another dragon found him? They would know he was different, alien. Instinctively he understood the danger. With one wing dragging in the dirt, he scrabbled across the stony ground, scooping loose earth with his claws as he waddled, driven by the need to hide before Margra's sun set, bleeding the sky of light.

The desert was barren and there was no sign of human habitation. Turning to glance behind, he saw that nothing followed on land or sky. The changes in his body had slowed. He found his sense of smell enhanced. As the light faded, the tortuous jigsaw of his vision settled and honed to a rare acuteness. He could see the warmth of the day's sun radiating off the sand. Above, the dark purple of the sky was marred only by Shatterwing glittering pinkly above the horizon. Ripples of red and violet caressed the sky far into the distance. The colors confused him. *Why do I see in this strange spectrum?*

⊃⊂⊃⊂⊃

During the night, Gercomo found a patch of ground, layered with rough, loose sand. A nudge of his snout revealed it was littered with large, round stones, as though a river had once flowed along the plain. Within the soft folds of earth, he found he could wriggle down and cover himself with the sand. Delving deep enough to keep himself safe, he finally allowed himself to rest. After a few hours, pale pink sunlight swept over the horizon. Then as the sun climbed higher, the sand began to warm his skin. The pain eased as if the dirt provided healing. And as he lay there his mind began to relax and to warp. The human concerns began to wane, but a few knots of anger did not disappear entirely. He held on to the important things and would not let them fade—anger, envy and lust. They were what defined him, and they melded well with the animal desires surfacing within him. He was hungry, and he was lonely. He had never needed another person before, but now there was something burning in his blood, something driving like stakes through his brain. He needed kin.

In the late afternoon, Gercomo was rested, but a cavernous hunger had grown inside him. He needed to eat. Needed to move. Simple as that. Thoughts of food, of starvation, began to dominate his mind.

What did dragons eat? Was he a dragon or dragon enough to eat raw burden beast? He lifted his head and sniffed. There wasn't much of anything except dust on the breeze. He would need to search out prey.

The sand dropped silkily from his scaled hide as he clawed his way out of his resting place. Tentatively, he stretched a wing and tested it. It no longer sang with pain yet it was still tender in places, particularly the elbow joint. Fortunately it functioned. In the growing shadows, he stepped confidently, his strange vision still pink and mauve with flashes of vermilion. He remembered there were other colors in the spectrum of light and that the world wasn't nearly as contoured as it seemed now. The small stones around him were so clear and precise, and the distant peaks loomed so large and felt so near he imagined he could breathe onto their slopes. Even these human thoughts of what he'd lost slid to the back of his mind as the need for food took over.

The sun's rays began to cool as night shrouded him. A scent drifted on the light breeze. He turned his head and concentrated. In the distance, he heard something, a *clink, clink*, as if someone was throwing stones against a rock. Perhaps it was an animal, something he could eat. He inhaled, hoping what he smelled was food.

While the aroma called to his olfactory senses, Gercomo zeroed in on the sound, learning with each step how to control his various body parts. The more he walked the more natural his gait became. He was almost elegant as he slowly stepped toward his prey. Ahead he saw that there was a tumble of boulders, spread in a circle like thrown dice. Farther on he could see the mark of flame burning across his vision. Beyond that was a settlement or a dwelling of some kind. But there amid the standing boulders was a boy, tossing stone after stone. Stealthily, Gercomo angled around to get a better view and to see if any adults were about, to see if there were any dragon lances or harpoons. The boy was aiming for a target, a crudely drawn circle on one of the boulders, the outline faint in the dim light emanating from the small fire. *Tick, tick.*

Gercomo sniffed and realized the boy was the food he'd smelt. His stomach churned and saliva filled his mouth, dripped off his tongue. He wanted to surge forward and swallow the boy whole. But he held that impulse in check when he detected a new scent and then heard the sound of a woman's voice. The urgent call was distant but growing closer. The boy paused as if hearing the voice but then shrugged once and kept aiming at the target. So far he had not noticed Gercomo standing behind the surrounding boulders, not twenty paces away.

The boy looked about ten years old, maybe younger. Gercomo blinked and saw that the child had a faint violet glow about him as well as the tantalizing scent of food. Another cry from the woman and the boy laughed and scooped in the dirt at his feet to pick up more stones.

As Gercomo crept forward to within striking distance, the boy stiffened and turned around. With a faint squeak of surprise, the open-mouthed boy stood stock-still. Hot piss wet his bare feet and stained the ground. Gercomo snatched at the boy, grabbing him around his small waist and clasping him tight in his grip. Looking down at the scaly appendage that held him, the child screamed and struggled. Gercomo liked the sound; it made him drool.

The woman's voice was suddenly closer—after a pause, there was a sharp intake of breath from just outside the ring of boulders. A frantic wail cleaved the night.

Swinging his head round, Gercomo saw her jerk as she entered the circle of stones, saw her recoil at what he was holding in his claws and stop dead, her eyes like large dark holes. When he had her full attention, he bit off the boy's head and upper torso and swallowed. Next he ate the remainder, enjoying the crunch of bones in his jaws, the sharp gnash of his fangs and serrated back teeth as he chomped and chomped and then swallowed. His laugh echoed around him, sounding like a roar.

With a guttural scream, the woman pulled her hair and fell to her knees, lost in a moment of grief. She should have run. It would have made better sport. Gercomo threw his gaze toward the settlement, but no one stirred. She was alone and unprotected. The boy's life blood filled his stomach with warmth, spreading out and reaching his extremities with a tingling sensation that enlivened him. Eating humans was good.

Like a dart he lunged at the woman and pinned her against the target her son had painted. She fainted so he let her go. After falling to the ground, she came to, shook her head and began to crawl away. He let her go at first, seeing that she found hope in that pointless exercise. Then, reaching out, he pierced her dress with his index claw and drew her slowly toward him as the cloth fell from her shoulders. With the other claw, he flipped her over and drew a line down her front. The sharp tip cut the skin. A fine red gash opened up. The scent of blood teased his hunger and made his pulse throb. A howl like the lonely wind tearing across the plains rose from her mouth. How he wanted to taste her and yet play with her and draw the moment out. This hesitation was both invigorating and excruciating, priming his taste buds until he drooled hot saliva across her face and shoulders.

The woman struggled and tried to break free. She turned on her stomach and scrabbled in the dirt on all fours. At his screech, his victim shivered and shrieked. He liked her fear, reveled in it. He flipped her over and her screams became music and then she stopped, her eyes wide and staring, though the life had not quite left her body.

When she quieted, he played with her some more, exciting that melody once again from her throat. A bite of her arm was a tasty morsel, raising the tune to a new pitch. As he lapped the blood from her wounds with care, savoring each drop, her voice became low and husky. He began again, this time at the legs. Her scream flowed over him, filling him with joy as he licked at the arterial blood gushing into his mouth. As he gulped down a thigh, her voice grew whisper-thin. Another bite and there was a visceral grunt and then a low moan as her last breath eased out of her throat. Gercomo didn't know if she could see his grin, see how happy she had made him. He had found a new source of power—human flesh.

Chapter Two

VANDEN'S FALLEN

Tumbled rock, blood-smeared fragments of masonry and dust spread around Danton. The main building of the observatory rose above him, magnificent and untouched. "We have to do something about the dead," Danton said as he balanced on a flat slab of broken stone in the remains of the observatory's courtyard. "And then there's the wall to repair."

Not only was there a breach in the wall where the Inspector's siege engine had torn through, there was the debris from Danton's carefully laid explosives, which had blown up the entrance to the courtyard. Such devastation had been necessary to save the observatory from its invaders. With his empty eye socket covered by a patch, the rebel leader turned in a full circle, nodding slowly. This was where the Inspector had indiscriminately sacrificed so many lives to reach his prize.

Danton's young rebel companion, Brill, climbed up behind him, anchoring his feet on two large pieces of rubble. Now that Danton knew Brill better he understood why Salinda had helped this young lad, with his vision of hope for the future of humankind.

"There are so many of them," Brill said as his gaze raked the scene.

Danton looked back down at the debris-strewn courtyard, stained with blood and rent flesh. Many of the fallen were on the pyre ready to be burned, but still too many remained in the rubble. He tried to bring a smile to his lips, but found that he couldn't muster one. He was tired.

Deciding to help the observatory in its fight against the Inspector had ramifications. He found he could not walk away, even though he wanted to do so. Who would have thought his attempt to rescue Salinda would lead him to this place? "Yes, and they are ripening." He brushed the end of his nose with a knuckle and shook his head.

Brill's head angled in the direction of the observatory's elders and tenders, who were crawling over rocks, peering into crannies to locate the dead with their mouths and noses muffled by cloth. Brill's mouth turned down at the corners and dual tear trails wormed a path down his dirt-stained cheeks. "That's not the only problem. The escaping rebels will take away tales about the technology this place possesses." Brill wiped his nose with his shirtsleeve and sniffed loudly.

Danton thought it was more than sorrow that made his young friend's eyes water. The dust and the stench were sufficient irritants to make a herd of burden beasts weep. "You think the Infra-pact rebels will come back?" he asked.

Brill's brows drew together and he shook his head. "No, I don't think so as they have the dragon wine. But it would make interesting information for their superiors."

"Damn!" Danton's expletive made a few elders look up from their task, dark shadows under their eyes. Acknowledging them with a nod, Danton scratched his beard and then ran his hands through his hair. "I didn't think of that. Who knows what damage such a report could do? It could threaten the future of this place. Wing dust!"

Different options ran through Danton's mind. There was no help for it. He could not hunt down every last Infra-pact rebel and silence them. He and Brill were the only fighting men here, and he couldn't imagine that the observatory would condone wholesale slaughter in any case. Thoughts of escaping rebels clouded his future plans. "Our goal is slipping through our fingers."

"The wine?"

"Yes, the wine; meeting up with the rest of the men. I must be dust mad." Danton wiped his forehead with a cloth from his pocket and tucked it back into his trousers. "But right now we need help to clear this."

"Agreed." Brill turned away, nodded to one of the elders and jumped across the gap between two chunks of wall. Calling over his shoulder he said, "I'll speak with Elder Wylie. He's escorting the evacuees back from the caves. I'll ask if he can bring them here as a priority so we can speed up recovery of the dead. And I'll suggest he start on works for repairing the wall."

Danton nodded as he watched Brill's figure recede. "Check with Salinda first. With the Master Elder dead, the elders have turned to her for leadership. Good idea about the wall, though. I may have brought it down, but that doesn't mean I have to put it back up."

Brill paused and looked back over his shoulder. "Doesn't Sal want to leave straight away?"

Danton felt a weight pressing down on his chest and swallowed. Thinking about Salinda was hard. He wanted to stay close to her, but she was with Nils now and that made his feelings redundant, except to him. And there was duty, which was everything to her. It was his duty to recover that wine stash, that much was clear. "Yes...and so do we."

〰〰〰〰〰

The subterranean city of Barrahiem seemed emptier than usual as Nils strode through its desolate, dust-filled streets. White homes stood sad and empty, their walls punctured with dark round holes, like the eyes of vermin. He was the last of his kin. He had been in a prison of sleep for over a thousand years. Now he had to face the future without the succor of his family, without hope.

If not for the lure of dragons, and his desire for knowledge of this new species that had appeared on Margra, he would never have been inclined to explore the world above, the world of the Sundwellers. He would not have rescued Salinda from that witch's pyre, brought her to this secret and sacred place and taken her for a mate. Now he missed her.

A sudden, intense cramp made him falter, made him lean against the balustrade for support. Thus enfeebled, he found he was seized with a coughing fit, until his throat burned. Struggling for breath, his legs buckled, too weak to hold him up. When it was over, the pain subsided to a dull ache, but one that weighted his footsteps and took the spring out of his step. With Salinda still at the observatory, the bond between them was stretched so taut that it caused him physical and mental pain. Thankfully Salinda did not experience it thus. To her their bond was nothing tangible at all, but an ephemeral promise.

Nils understood that his mate's duty lay elsewhere. The battle at

9

the observatory and Master Elder Jalen's death had left the observatory in a delicate state. Salinda could not turn her back on them. Yet, the bond they had formed in the deep lake stretched out through the Ways to where Salinda was, and it hurt.

Burying himself in research appeared to be the single means to salve his pain. With his dying breath, Jalen had spoken of Trell of Barr, Nils's grandsire. The Master Elder had mentioned that he had seen the name in a book. That had intrigued Nils.

In his workroom he found the index markers for his grandsire's writings. A quick scan of the dates made Nils frown. The dates were within the year he had been interred in the sarcophagus and made to sleep away a thousand years or more. He read the final entry.

My heart is heavy this day. My favorite grandchild has been placed in the sarcophagus—a prisoner of sleep. It pains me to know that we will never talk again. It pains me to know that the world he will awaken to will be less than it is now. But in my heart I hope that there will be a world for him to enter again.

The child of my heart has always shared my passions. I remember the light in Nils's eye when he peered through the scopes at Trithorn Peak. I remember the catch of his breath when I told him of the bands of power holding Ruel together. I remember how he touched my hand with his forehead in thanks at the gift of knowledge and experience I had given him. Now I see his face stilled in sleep, as cold as death, caught at the cusp of adulthood.

Barrahiem holds nothing for me now. My kin are mine no more. I turn my back on them, on their ignorance and their fear. They will not heed my warnings, nor will they make any preparations for the inevitable end. I go out into the world above to seek other learned men, Sundwellers who will work with heart and mind to save what they can of Margra. For the failing Ruel will be a global catastrophe that will leave this world shattered. We cannot avert this doom, but we can make something from the ashes.

Nils searched the records again, puzzled. That could not be Trell's last entry. Did his grandsire truly leave his kin, to dwell above after Nils was interred? That would mean that the observatory possibly held the last writings of his grandsire. No, that could not be allowed. All the knowledge must be kept together in the archives. Then he recollected that the old observatory had been leveled, and the present one raised from its remains. He shuddered at the thought of the loss of Trell's thoughts and deeds from the archives. It was akin to having his grandsire's existence expunged from the world.

He left his workroom to return home. When he reached his abode, he realized there was no reason to put off his departure. All he needed was his shroud and supplies and he would see Salinda again and perhaps look about for Trell's writings in the ruins of the old observatory.

♋♋♋♋

As Laidan leaned against the balustrade looking out over the disheveled courtyard, she considered the bodies piled on the pyre and experienced little emotion. Intellectually, she knew she should feel something more. She should be concerned about her lack of feeling, her arid and desolate emotional landscape. But too much had happened.

Her mentor, Thurdon, had been poisoned and he'd thrust the cadre into her unprepared mind before he died, then she had almost been raped and killed, more than once. Then she'd been brought here, chased down by an evil man and his army. Those people on the pyre were dead because of her. She shook her head. *No. No. Not me. It wasn't me. It's not my fault.*

It was too much. She shut it all out. She shut it down. The cadre too. She didn't want to have it or feel it. Now there was an empty space surrounding her that blocked her from empathizing, from feeling sorrow, from feeling anything.

The world was too awful. Its evil had slapped her in the face and there was nowhere to hide. What was the point anyway, of obeying the rules, doing what you were told, if you only ended up dead? You might as well enjoy yourself while you could. That was her new approach to life.

Salinda had her studying mind-numbingly boring texts. They served Laidan well, though, because the more she read, the more distant that seat of unsettling power and thought, the cadre, became. Thurdon's voice had been so loud, so overpowering, that she had been grateful when Salinda had been able to quiet it and give her some peace.

At least she had Brill. He made her light up, made her feel like she was beautiful and important. If she was patient Brill would be finished with the bodies and then he would come to her, like he had promised when they rendezvoused in the closet. She would make him come to her. She would make him promise. Brill always kept his promises.

⊂∽⊃∽⊃∽⊃∽⊃

Garan thought that a late lunch of cacti porridge, soft bread and some mulled dragon wine would wash the taste of death from his mouth. He was wrong. Everything he ate and everything he touched tasted of rotting corpse. When he closed his eyes, images of the faces, the bodies, the blood, the severed limbs were always there. He could not shift them from his mind. They appeared in the dark shadowed corners and dwelled in the depths of his dreams. They would plague his mind forever.

He would hazard a shooting star that he was not the only one who had not slept or who was similarly discomfited by their duty. Unease and despair were in the air around him, like a sob held in check. The observatory was grieving. They had mourned the Master Elder but now they mourned Vanden's dead, those who had been sacrificed by the Inspector against the walls of Trithorn Peak.

Even if the observatory's inhabitants remembered the faces of their dead kin, few were recognizable, not from what he'd seen. Faces smashed, skulls caved in, bodies flat and crushed, gizzards everywhere. Blood like paint staining everything, providing a feast for flies. The observatory's inhabitants mourned every single death as if it was their own flesh and blood. Such horror was new to them, new to Garan.

As he chewed and swallowed his meal without tasting it, he became lost in his nightmarish thoughts until he was startled by Salinda sitting down next to him. He gaped at her. She, too, looked like she had had a difficult day. Lines at the corners of her mouth cut worry into her face. She'd been helping the elders restore some order after the attack, working long hours. The refectory doors swung open and Danton and Brill walked in. Garan thought Laidan might have been with them but she was nowhere to be seen.

Salinda looked at Danton, and Garan followed the path of her gaze. He had never seen the one-eyed rebel look so grim. His smile was forced and his expression haunted as he joined them at the table.

Garan's mood plummeted. Danton, who had helped him face the worst moment in his life, the death of a friend by his own power, was now succumbing to the misery surrounding them. Something had to give.

Salinda's hand started to move across the table, then paused before she withdrew it again. Instead, she wished him a pleasant evening. The look they shared with each other spoke volumes. Garan thought the rebel might cry.

Brill appeared in better spirits. Pointedly ignoring Garan, he began chatting to Salinda. Brill had believed Laidan's story about Garan trying to ravish her. Garan bore it best he could. He was to blame. Not Laidan. She did not know any better. It was right that Brill stood by her, supported her through her trials. Garan sniffed once. He would like Laidan to turn to him but he knew that was out of the question. Not with the lithe and polite Brill dazzling her with his gallantry and smile. Garan was an ignorant oaf in comparison.

"How are you feeling now?" Brill asked Salinda. "Less stressed?"

Salinda smiled lightly. "I am feeling more in control, thank you, Brill. And you?"

As his plate was empty, Garan was about to stand up to fetch more food, but he hesitated. Salinda's question had brought a blush to Brill's face. Danton avoided Garan's gaze by twirling an empty cup around in his hand, apparently absorbed in this action. What was going on now? Surely Brill had not been dallying with Laidan? Why, Brill must be exhausted from all the heavy work during the day. Garan glanced at Brill's hands, which were loosely clasped in front of him. The younger man had not bothered to get a meal yet. Brill's fingers were cut and grazed and most of the fingernails were broken. He had not been shirking.

Danton stood up. "Come on, Garan. Let's get some food. There is more work to do before this day is done. Let Brill talk to Salinda for a bit."

Salinda rubbed her hand over her face as if that would wipe away her fatigue, frustration and numerous other ills. Just then, the door flew open. "My lady," said the familiar croaky voice of Elder Wylie as he ran toward her breathlessly. "Forgive me...disturbing your meal. You must come...come to the gallery and see..." Behind him strode Elder Titina, her longer legs easily keeping pace with her fellow elder. She looked thinner than the last time he had seen her. Garan recollected that she had been in the caves supervising the partial evacuation and then had fallen ill. Titina's brows furrowed to form a "V" between her eyebrows and fatigue had increased the wrinkles around her eyes and mouth. With a brief nod to him, she kept her gaze on Elder Wylie and Salinda.

Salinda stood up straight away, shifting her robe out of her way to follow. Garan hastened after them. The anxiety in the elder's voice was acute. Elder Titina followed close behind, her steps unhurried but efficient. Once out the doors, Garan heard people whispering in the corridors. It was like the rush of wind in an empty cave, echoing and amplifying. Something had excited the inhabitants of the observatory. A glimpse over his shoulder showed Garan that the rest of the party had followed them.

Salinda took the steps two at a time. Elder Wylie trailed her as best he could. Once out on the gallery, the afternoon sun near blinded them. The old man led them round to the Klester Valley side. As Garan came up behind Salinda and Elder Wylie, he didn't understand what he was seeing. Then the sound filtered through and that drew his gaze. Beyond the pile of corpses stacked for the funeral pyre was a line of women with stooped shoulders accompanied by ragged, barefoot children. Garan could hear them wailing.

Salinda stood stock-still. "Oh no!"

Chapter Three

REFUGEES

Salinda faced the three travel-stained women who led the mob from Vanden and touched her swollen abdomen reflexively as if to remind herself of the life growing within. Fighting her anxiety, she welcomed them. This was a new complication—refugees. The ramifications for the observatory and her plans sent her mind spinning. Behind them the wailing increased as the people from the observatory mingled with the ragtag newcomers and found others to share their grief. More refugees and their children continued to struggle over the debris of the gates as they talked. Garnering scraped knees and red-raw hands, they lurched forward to gather behind the leaders. With each breath Salinda took, the crowd swelled.

Discerning voices above the general hubbub, she heard questions fly about—*Have you seen my son? Where is my husband? Noddy didn't come home, is he here? Can you help me?* Then the voices of the observatory's inhabitants mingled, and the noise became a cacophony.

Salinda tried to shut it out and focus on the three women in front of her. She could not help but see the devastation in their eyes. It was their husbands and sons piled up ready for burning. It was their lives that had been shattered and destroyed beyond recognition. Her gaze surveyed the ruins of the wall and the partially demolished lower floors of the front section of the observatory. Collateral damage. The dead were piled where all could see. The wall could be rebuilt but the dead could not be replaced.

The refugees' pain and desperation were evident in their clenched jaws and frightened eyes. They reminded her of the downtrodden prisoners in the vineyard. A sudden flashback to the misery she'd witnessed during her time in captivity had her panting, and she rode it until her mind calmed again. It had been but a second. Suffering and death—it was everywhere. It was unstoppable. It was following her around—the terrible deeds of the Inspector. Salinda fought the wave of despair that threatened to crash down on her and let out a long, slow breath. Then, gathering a cloak of calm around her, she looked at the women in turn. "How may we serve you?" she asked the lead woman, who was maybe thirty-five or forty years old, plump with a long grayish-colored skirt, dirty, brown-colored blouse and a threadbare shawl pulled tight around her shoulders.

The woman's hair hung down from a tangled bun. Salinda could see her scalp in places; raw, blood-stained flesh peeked out through the strands. Around the woman's neck were bruises, where it appeared someone had tried to strangle her. A small hand grasped the woman's skirt and a young child stared up at Salinda, her large dark eyes liquid pools of pain. All trace of innocence was gone from the child's face. Salinda was moved beyond words. The sight before her reminded her there was more to this fight than dragon wine, power and Shatterwing. What had this woman done to bring this fate upon herself? Nothing. The child was even more innocent. Both had been born into this world, and that was all. It had to end.

The woman stood straighter, squared her shoulders and raised her chin. She swallowed painfully before speaking. With a twitch of her skirt and a tug at her blouse, she said, "My name is Mandin. We have come here because we have nowhere else to go." The woman's voice was gravelly, perhaps raw from screaming. "The town has been burned and our homes are lost. Do not, we beg you, turn us away."

Salinda's throat was dry. Her gaze roamed the faces around her, once again taking in their sorrow. How could she turn her back on them? What would Mez have done? The cadre hummed in her head, warning her to keep focus. But faced with what was in front of her she lost the struggle between the call of duty and compassion. People were what mattered. Right now she could do something real. Perhaps she could help these people without hindering her cause.

Before she could speak she was interrupted. "I assure you we have no intention of sending you away," Elder Titina said, stepping forward. Elder Wylie nodded, unshed tears glistening in his eyes.

"We want to help you if we can," Salinda added. "You can see that there has been a battle here. Many of our kin and yours lie among the dead. We say to you that this is not our doing. What we did, we did in defense."

The woman's face was stricken. She gestured to Vanden's women and children. "The issue of blame can be decided later. Right now, we require aid. For a long time there has been an association between the people of Vanden and the observatory. We call upon that relationship in our hour of need."

Elder Titina put out a hand to the woman. "The observatory will honor that bond." Mandin looked at the hand, reached out to brush her fingers against the elder's. Her expression was weary, almost beyond hope. Titina lowered her arm, the fingers trembling.

"Thank you." The woman nodded, relief relaxing her features. Her gaze searched behind Salinda and then met Salinda's again. "My son lives here. Do not keep me from him. I have lost so much already."

Salinda's skin grew cold. Surely if her son were in the crowd he would have come forward. Perhaps he was elsewhere working, or still evacuating the caves. Looking about them, the women behind her added their voices to Mandin's and began calling their sons' names.

"Tell me the name of your son and I will call him to tend you."

The woman's eyes tracked the inhabitants milling around. Then her gaze swept over Garan, Danton and the others who had followed Salinda. "Turnet. My son is Turnet."

Salinda heard Garan's intake of breath, and the woman didn't miss it. "What is it?" she asked, looking sharply at Garan. "Where is he?"

Elder Wylie stepped forward, his shoulders slumped, his gray hair lank on his shoulders. "Turnet was a good Skywatcher. But he was taken from us not long ago. I am so sorry." Salinda heard a sob and realized it came from the old elder. His shoulders shook as he tried to suppress it. Casting a quick glance behind her, she saw that Garan's expression was frozen in horror.

The woman retained her composure, though she held her jaw tight. "Husband and son both lost." She shook her head in a dazed sort of way, as if nothing would or could faze her. "What of the other sons and daughters? Can the survivors of Vanden see them? Can they claim them? Now that our husbands are dead we need our sons and daughters to help us survive."

"Of course." She motioned Elder Titina and Elder Wylie forward. "These elders will assist you and your people."

Salinda turned away briefly, taking in the pile of corpses. This close the smell was terrible. Why, the stench must travel for miles. A thought like a thundercloud grew in her mind. She wondered at it.

"We have to deal with the dead," Salinda hissed to Garan and the others. Danton nodded. Perhaps he understood the danger as she did.

Elder Titina had gathered the three women leaders to her. "We should be able to accommodate you all for a short time in the lower hall. It has been cleared of debris. Come this way."

Salinda focused again on the women. Mandin's posture sagged noticeably now, perhaps because she had no further need to be strong. "Thank you," she whispered, before turning to clasp each of her two companions on the shoulder in turn. Salinda found that she admired the woman's courage and her ability to lead others when her hope was gone. Salinda wondered if she could ever muster the same strength.

Before Mandin became engulfed in the crowd Salinda asked, "What can you tell us of the rebels?" The woman turned back and their gazes locked. After a moment Mandin's face changed. It became a hard and angry mask.

"They're gone...but they...they, um...left their mark on all of us."

Salinda swallowed a hard lump. "I see. We shall talk more when you are rested."

As she turned away, a sense of dread and danger filled Salinda. The dark cloud that had built up in her mind coalesced. "Danger!" she cried.

"What?" blurted Elder Titina, her face a mask of puzzlement.

"The dead." Salinda covered her mouth. The power grew in her mind. Then she pointed. "The smell of the dead! It draws them."

Danton leaped into action and he and Elder Titina began chivvying the refugees into the lower hall. "Hurry!"

"What is it, Salinda?" Garan asked.

"Run and take cover." Salinda took a handful of robe and ran. "All of you. Dragons! Dragons come to feed. The scent of the dead has reached them and they are hungry."

Screams erupted as the word spread. Salinda sped back into the observatory the way she had come, Garan and Elder Wylie hot on her heels.

"Elder Wylie," Salinda said as she ran. "Did you find oil? Are we ready to light the funeral pyre?"

"Almost..."

Then the scream of a dragon echoed through the observatory, and was almost immediately joined by three more. "Not good enough! They must burn."

With his longer stride, Garan was ahead of them and ran to a window overlooking the plains. "Wing dust! They are huge."

Salinda made it to the observatory proper and strode to where she could look out onto the courtyard below. A dragon had alighted on the funeral pyre and was clawing at the dead, trying to dislodge some. She stepped back, her hand to her middle protectively. Suddenly the dragon snatched at the top body, gulping it down. Then it took another in its jaws and took wing. Human screams filled the air as this fresh terror ripped the scab off people's grief. Salinda turned to the plains side, her mind awhirl. There was only one thing she could think of to do. Arms outstretched, robe billowing in the breeze, she called for Plu. Her faithful friend, who was always closer than expected, who always seemed to come when she called. What a lucky day it was when she had found him as a hatchling.

Turning back to the courtyard, she saw Garan gaping at her. Brill grinned lopsidedly and then said, "She's called her dragon."

Garan eyes grew round with surprise. "She has a dragon?" Then his face transformed with a stupid grin. "Of course she does."

Salinda turned back to look at the dragons feeding. There were four of them. She could feel their minds. Their thoughts and emotions crawled into her head whether she wanted them or not. How or why she had this gift she didn't have to time to consider. She was dispassionate about the dead being eaten. It was the danger to the living she worried about. Second to that came the feelings of the living and their religious beliefs.

"Elder Wylie," she called. "Get ready to light the pyre. We won't have time for a dedication. We need to burn the dead now."

The gallery rocked, nearly tumbling them all to the ground. A dragon's tail had caught the roof as it swooped in. That made five.

"Garan, run and tell everyone to stay hidden and quiet."

Garan took off like an arrow from a bow. Salinda's mind was full of the dragons' presence. So much so that she couldn't discern whether Plu was close by, whether he was responding to her call. She had summoned him, but would he—could he—come to her aid? Dragons tended to be territorial as far as she had observed. Would these others prevent him?

"What can I do?" Brill asked.

"See if you can get to Danton and let him know we will fire the dead. Plu will provide the flame."

"Are you sure? There are a lot of dragons out there."

Salinda chewed her bottom lip. She watched the dragons eating, saw several of them fly away with a body in their jaws or claws. "They eat and then they leave to take food back to the hatchery. If people keep out of sight they should be safe."

"Let us hope that they do not bring more of their herd with them." Brill's comment was so aligned with her thoughts that she gaped at him.

"Yes. Just so. That's why we need to burn the dead so there is nothing to draw them here. We do not wish to be overrun by a whole herd."

Brill grimaced. "They have no harpoons or weapons to fight dragons here so let's hope we can burn the dead in time."

Salinda unclenched a hand that had been gripping her robe. "For now, we are lucky there are enough dead to fill their bellies. From what I understand dragons do not pass this way very often. It was the stench of the dead that drew them. When that is gone, the danger should pass." Salinda cast about. Where was Elder Wylie? Why was there a delay? The old elder had complained of no oil to sustain the pyre and she had tasked him to overcome that problem. Closing her eyes, she prayed that he had or this dragon problem would escalate.

Brill nodded. "I know. We worked as fast as we could. I'll go now so Danton can prepare the refugees and the observatory's inhabitants for the funeral pyre."

Just as the young rebel ran off, a familiar mind distinguished itself from among the dark mass of need that filled her head. *Burn the dead, Plu*, she called to him in dragon tongue. She caught a glimpse of him as he flew past. The other dragons were too intent on their food to pay him any mind or to fight for territory.

Yet to avoid any misunderstandings, Salinda knew she had to give the dragons an alternative food source, for the moment at least. A strong link formed between her and Plu. She rocked back on her heels at the force of it. It was so much more powerful than it had ever been before. The memory of the Inspector transforming into a dragon came to mind, the mauve flame of dragon essence consuming him. He'd fed her that stuff. A perverted version, certainly, but it was still dragon essence. Had that changed her somehow, made her more open to the dragons' minds? If it had, there was no time to think about it now. She sent Plu mind pictures of the dead littering the streets of Vanden. *Bliem, ger bach hun. Valley, man place by the river.* Then she added an expression of affection and gratitude, *Neun. Neun, my friend. I will see you again.*

Plu spewed flame at the pyre. The low *whoomph* as the flames caught was soon superseded by the outraged shrieks of the dragons that had come to feed who were now driven away. Flames leaped up and became self-sustaining. Salinda realized that Elder Wylie must have overcome the shortage of oil to fuel the pyre after all. She knew his resourcefulness would kick in.

Plu took wing, screeching long and varying his pitch, communicating Salinda's information to the other dragons, she supposed. Then, one by one, the other dragons began taking wing and diving after him and sent rock and damaged walls crashing into the forecourt. Other dragons flew overhead, bypassing the observatory as they followed Plu's lead. It had worked. By the source, it had worked!

Salinda sagged against the railing, panting, her heartbeat gradually slowing. The immediate threat of the dragons was gone. The stench of burning flesh replaced the ever-present stink of rotting corpses. The refugees began to crawl out of their hiding places, chanting as they drew closer to the funeral pyre:

> *By fire ye shall pass, by flame you shall be freed*
>
> *Thus, Magol said and all assembled agreed*
>
> *Magol! Magol! We praise your grace*
>
> *For returning our souls to time and space*
>
> *To join once again with the source of all things*
>
> *In harmony with the universe as it sings*

And the inhabitants of the observatory joined them in farewelling the dead. Wearily, Salinda turned away to find some rest.

A singed Elder Wylie came running up to her, coughing and with tears streaming down his blackened, withered cheeks.

"We used latrine gas, Salinda. We could not spare oil. But the pyre is lit."

Salinda stared at him, mouth agape. "Toilet gas?" She shook her head. "You look like you were caught in the flames. Are you well?"

"Yes, yes. Quite fine now. Those dragons are fearsome creatures up close. We do not get many in these parts. Not since my younger days..."

"Excellent work, Elder Wylie. Be thankful, though, that they are not your daily bane." She kept walking, just thinking about how nice her bed might feel.

Elder Wylie hurried to keep pace with her. "With all these extra people making waste, there will be more where that came from. At least we will be able to cook and keep warm."

Circumspectly, she grinned. "There is that," Salinda replied in a soft voice, still trying to put some distance between her and the elder. She was heading to her room for the rest she so badly needed.

"The elders are meeting now," Elder Wylie said to her back as she walked down the hall. She paused, looked over her shoulder and sighed loudly.

"Will you join us and give us your counsel?" Elder Wylie's voice was hopeful.

Her bed could wait just a little longer. Turning on her heel, she swept the robe away from her feet and walked back to where Elder Wylie stood, then together they marched down the corridor to the Master Elder's office.

Chapter Four

A WOMAN'S BANE

Mandin had heard the words that her son, Turnet, was dead, but did not feel them. The words fell into the pit where she existed in blackness, and did not land. They could not find her heart. They could not reach her. She was lost and there was no light. She had lost everything: her husband to Gercomo, her daughter to the rebels and her son to the observatory. There was nothing left for her. The beating, the rapes, what were they? She had no life, no reason for living—except that her daughter was not dead. Yet.

The dragons had been a shock. After all they had been through to then be terrorized by such monstrous creatures. At first, she had been dumbfounded by the sight of them, huge mauve and green-scaled beasts with gnashing fangs. Maybe once or twice in her life had she seen one in the distance. Up close, the sight had made her knees tremble and her palms sweat. The noise of their screeches had been overwhelming.

When all the dragons had gone, they came out from their hiding places. The funeral pyre was lit—women chanted an ode to passing. Observatory people wiped tears. She joined them as they ringed the pile of burning bodies. It was then that Mandin's control crumbled. The sounds of wailing and woe seeped through her and undid the bindings of her pain. Tears singed her cheeks. They were hot from the heat of the pyre as she wiped at them with the back of her hand. It was there as the dead of Vanden burned that she found the strength to cry.

It did not cleanse her as tears were meant to do. The smoke she inhaled was so pungent with death that her own soul was tainted with it. Perhaps it was fitting. She was dead already. But then not dead, not fit to die.

Past memories of laughter were like the sounds of glass breaking, shattered and sharp, meant for pricking her sorrow, bringing it into contrast with this emptiness inside. There was a need to weep, to rage and to bellow. But she knew that giving in to the urge would break her open, give that seeping, septic wound a means to flow pus. She couldn't do it. To acknowledge the pain, the despair, was to wallow in it, and that would lead to drowning.

The child at her skirts was an orphan. Who knew what the poor wretch had seen or experienced? A homeless, dirty waif, ready to be thrown on the mercy of the observatory. Mandin could not find it in her to give the child comfort. She had protected it and delivered it here. That was all she could manage. The rest of her strength and resolve had to be harnessed for the future. One of the observatory's tenders started gathering up the orphans to feed and care for them. Mandin prized the little girl's grubby hands from her skirt and led her to join the other children. Mandin could not look at her and turned away. She would not look into those desolate eyes, as they reminded her too much of what was in her own heart.

"Will you come and take some refreshment?" one of the observatory's tenders asked her and her fellow refugees.

As they made their way across the broken lower hall, a cold shiver lanced through her body when she crossed the blackened pools of dried blood. It was here the men had died. This place was the focus of their grief.

Later as she stood in the lower halls, peering through the windows at the great stone observatory, she thought of her son. Just gazing upon the building brought back the words in Turnet's letters of days well spent in duty and friendship. She did not begrudge him his happy life. Letting go of one's son was never easy. It hadn't been when he said goodbye as a child. Now there was nothing left to farewell. The observatory had been good to him and now he was gone. Just like that. Turnet had been the beacon she had run toward as she fled Vanden. The one remaining piece of herself and, like a flame extinguished, he was dead.

The elders' genuine remorse at Turnet's loss had gone some way to soothe her. But what comfort was there in her son's death? There was no smile to look forward to, no hug to anticipate, no dark hair or shoulder to pat. No support to be had, no comfort. Nothing. Oh how she hated that word, that sensation of emptiness. Nothing! Now she had nowhere to aim her anger, no one to blame, except herself for not being stronger or smarter.

With a weary sweep of her gaze, Mandin saw the other women nod, their eyes heavy with tears and tiredness as they accepted the observatory's hospitality. There was hope in their eyes. Perhaps their kin lived. Mandin tried not to hate them for that. All had suffered as she had done. Her suffering would continue, that was true. Mandin wanted to turn those feelings of despair and loss into something useful. She wanted to fight back. She wanted not to accept her fate.

Plans were forming in Mandin's mind. She was not going to let this situation be. She was not going to stay here and rot in her misery. She would act. It made pure and absolute sense. If she did not act she would become nothing. Nothing was waiting to swallow her up and she couldn't give in to that. She refused to be nothing and refused to do nothing.

A cloud of dark smoke rolled over her. Eyes stinging, she coughed and breathed in the essence of Vanden's slain.

Part of her lived still. Her daughter was out there somewhere, her beauty marred by pain and disgrace. Dragged away by the rebels to be sold. Yet there was a chance she could save her. Mandin would give her life to find her, to save her and to bring her home. *Great dragons*, she thought to herself as she watched the flames. *Your fire has set the souls of the dead free to join with the source. By my life I pledge I will not rest until I find my sweet Eneit. I will not rest until I have found her alive or dead, but find her I will.*

Later as they gathered for a meal, Mandin mingled. The observatory provided food, cacti bread and watered wine. As she was not destined to die just yet, she must eat.

A one-eyed man with dark curly hair approached her and nodded. Mandin lifted her chin. She would meet this man with pride. A smile lifted the corner of his mouth, but his one dark eye held her. In it she saw pain reflected back at her. This man had known suffering, had seen it once too often. At that brief recognition, she came close to letting her control go. Yet she did not. Instead she let the words flow: The details of the condition of the town when they left. The attack on the crops and how it was dealt with. Estimates of the number of fleeing rebels. What they took. What they destroyed. Mandin had it all in her head. Lastly, she told him of the children they had taken. She told him about Eneit. He listened, he queried and he listened some more. "Thank you," he said. "Drink this watered dragon wine and rest now. I will tell your tale to those in charge and then we'll take action."

Mandin sipped the wine cautiously as it stung her cut lip and burned her sore throat—a throat sore from screaming and the clench of a violent man's hands. Never did she take her eyes off the one-eyed man. "I'll be going after those rebels," she said.

For the length of a heartbeat, the man stared at her and then nodded slightly. "Perhaps you will."

ᏘᏘᏘᏘᏘ

After the meal, one of the observatory folk showed Mandin to some bedding and she looked for a space among the other sleeping forms.

While she looked, Gailen, one of the other women, came up to her and patted her on the shoulder. Although Gailen's hair was askew and her face bruised, she smiled. "He be a handsome man, that Danton, don't ya think?"

Mandin did not smile back. "Who?" She'd found a spot between two women who were already asleep. She went to step toward it but Gailen held her back.

"What d'ya mean who? That man ya spoke to. He's a rebel, they say. The man that saved the observatory. He'll be chasing down them that burned Vanden, ya know."

Mandin looked back at her. "I see. Just the man for me then. Thank you, Gailen. I think I see a place to rest. See you on the morrow."

As she nestled within the bedding, among the warm bodies of the others, she hugged Gailen's words to her soul. If this Danton was chasing the rebels, then she was going with him. Convincing the man of that fact would be her next task. She reflected on what she had seen in his eyes. She didn't think she would have a problem. He understood her already.

Chapter Five

A LEADER NEW

Sunset was a vivid red, a portent, Salinda thought as she turned from the window. As the room filled up, she took a seat at the Master Elder's desk and prepared herself mentally for the meeting. The elders were subdued as they sat huddled around the desk. By invitation, Danton and Brill were present to share information on the situation in Vanden and they stood at the rear of the room, both looking freshly washed. All of the elders and both the rebels had been assisting Vanden's refugees while they took refreshments in the lower hall. All had reports to make.

Salinda leaned forward and studied the faces of the elders as they conversed with each other. Thus cocooned, the room felt small and warm and comforting. Strange to experience such cheer after all the horror of the day.

The sound of the elders' whispers rose and from the words she caught, the situation was dire. She waited a few moments for them to come to order but they didn't. They were unsettled. "Let us begin," Salinda said, not caring if she was abrupt.

The whispering cut off in a breath. Shocked faces regarded her.

"What of the town, the food supply?" she asked, eyeing those closest to her.

Danton put up his hand. "I can give you some word on that." Their eyes met, and Salinda tightened her lips and inclined her head to him.

The murmuring began again, a low rumble. The elders turned in their seats to see the rebel who had saved them. "The harvest is still intact, though the town itself is wasted," Danton said, his tired gaze sweeping the room. The elders must not have liked what they saw there because most looked away or to the floor.

Salinda nodded and lifted an eyebrow in query. Elder Titina put up her hand, taking her cue from Danton. "The harvest is important. The surplus usually comes to the observatory. Obtaining a share of that will assist us greatly. It could mean survival for us."

"I agree the food is important. Yet, the townspeople cannot tend their crops from here," Salinda said. "They would need to return to the town. The crops need irrigation, do they not?"

Titina inclined her head and her eyebrows drew down. "Yes, I believe so."

"The townsfolk will need help to rebuild their homes," Elder Wylie interjected. "As well as to harvest the crops. They have to have shelter if they are to work the fields."

Salinda nodded and rubbed her chin. "Yes, that much is clear. If they return to Vanden it will have to be rebuilt. What we need to do is find a way to help them without disrupting the observatory's work. Brill, what were your observations?"

Brill looked at his hands, rubbed them together slowly, taking his time to reply. The elders quieted, as if sensing that the young rebel was deeply moved. "All of the women and half the children have been beaten and mistreated to some extent, and most of the women have been raped, even some of the children. When the rebels burned the town, Mandin, that's Turnet's mother, gathered them together and forged the plan to escape to here. They lost many on the trek up the valley. About thirty were killed in the firing of the town, trapped, it seems. Mandin had to choose between trying to save them and escaping with the survivors."

Danton added, "The rebels seized ten young girls, probably to be sold as slaves. This they can do when they reach any sizable town. Mandin said the captives' ages range from ten to thirteen. Her daughter, Eneit, is among them."

A collective gasp ran through the elders. Elder Wylie whispered, "Turnet's sister has been taken?" Salinda knew that was a wound close to home. Turnet had been loved by many, and according to

Elder Wylie, Turnet had often talked of the mother and sister he left behind. This was the first time, Salinda guessed, that the observatory's inhabitants had had to face the reality of life on Margra. What it was really like out there with little law and order and no care for the lives of ordinary people. In the observatory, they lived a sheltered and ordered existence, untroubled by the daily chaos that others experienced. They may have heard stories of the evils out in the world but most had had no direct experience of it. Now they knew that the innocent were the casualties. Now it was close to home. The sorrow on the faces of the elders touched Salinda and she was sorry for the loss of their innocence, even though it was essential that they knew the truth. It was only due to a quirk of fate that they had been spared the horrors of the world. Until now, that was. Reality was upon them. They might never be the same again.

Salinda cleared her throat before speaking. "And what of the rebels? Do the refugees you spoke to know where the rebels went? Or what their intentions were?" Her gaze flowed over them, assessing, searching. She wished this crisis would reveal a new leader. It couldn't be her, but no one else stood out yet. In loyalty to the Master Elder, Salinda owed it to the observatory to leave it strong when she left. More than that, they needed to be strong enough to continue the work of protecting Margra from moonfall.

Elder Wylie put up his hand again. "One of the other women, Mart, I think her name was, told me that the women managed to hide a store of dragon wine in Vanden. The rest of the store was taken by the rebels. Some of the rebels left on foot. The remainder went with the barges of wine down the river."

"That is good. There is wine and a potential harvest." This was positive news, but Salinda's mood did not lighten at the thought as so much was still up in the air.

A newly initiated elder called Manton stood up to speak. Salinda remembered that he had been made an elder before the crisis. "It is strange that the rebels did not destroy the harvest. Did they run out of time?"

Danton chimed in. "They tried, but the women saved the bulk of it with their irrigation system and smart thinking. The rebel band sought to terrorize in the short term and didn't stay to see the job done. Also, I think their defeat was a surprise. It was a leaderless, ragtag bunch of men that returned to the town and they left as fast as they could, wreaking as much damage as possible on their way out. They wanted to scare the townsfolk so that they would not be pursued."

Manton's brow creased. "I see. Thank you for explaining." He sat down again and whispered to the elder beside him. Perhaps he remembered that Danton was also a rebel and had cause to understand their motives and actions.

Elder Wylie asked tentatively, "The young girls who were taken, I suppose they were taken for household slaves?"

Salinda answered the old man matter-of-factly. "The girls will be sold for sex slaves or prostitutes and more than likely the rebels will use some of them on the way, despite the lowering of the expected price. If they survive the journey, those girls will be grateful to be sold to a brothel or pimp. Anything would be better than repeated rape and abuse while being dragged from place to place, sleeping rough, no food..."

Titina cried out. "Oh, by the source! You cannot be serious."

"I have lived in the world, madam. I speak with surety because that is the nature of our society. There is no other reason for those children to be taken."

Titina wiped her eyes and wrung her hands in her lap. "Those men ought to be castrated."

Salinda shared a look with Danton. She knew that they would be, if Danton had anything to do with it.

As Salinda looked around at the gathered elders, she could see various levels of shock and horror written on their faces. She decided it was time to change the subject. "Let us decide what happens next. Can we accommodate all these women and children?"

Elder Titina stood, smoothed her robe and looked Salinda in the eye. "No, we cannot. There is another way, though."

Salinda was pleased. Here was someone who was prepared to think strategically at least. "What do you suggest?"

From her seat, Titina picked up a notebook. "I've taken a tally of the women and their skills. Some of them could be useful to us here. There are many single men who could take them as wives, if the women wanted to have them, that is. That way there would be less impact on the accommodation if they stayed."

Elder Manton spluttered. "Are you mad? More women to feed?" Others started talking as if they agreed with him.

Elder Wylie stroked his chin. Salinda knew him to be a practical man, one who had come into his own since the Master Elder's demise.

Titina faced the room of elders. "No, hear me," she said in a loud voice, forcing the others to fall silent. "We would have to send some men to Vanden with the remainder of the women. If we manage this carefully, we could do a swap. Some of the women could be trained as tenders to replace the ones who leave. We have fifty male tenders. We could spare twenty, if they could be replaced by Vanden folk."

"Lose twenty able-bodied men?" the previously silent Elder Tralee roared from his seat. Salinda didn't know this elder well. She recalled that he looked after the mines and was not often in the observatory. "How will we continue our work? We need to mine the crystals."

Elder Wylie answered him. "We only need enough gems for our Skywatcher work at present. There is no need for gems for trade in the short term at least. I think we could cope."

Elder Tralee grumbled into his beard, wriggling in his seat with indignation.

Brill ignored Elder Tralee's continued grumbling. "What about the orphans? Mandin said they had twenty children with no parents living. If the bulk of these folk return to Vanden to start anew, you can't expect them to look after these children too. The orphans will have no shelter, little food and no education."

Titina lifted her head from her notebook. "Test them. If they show talent, teach them to use the crystals."

Intrigued, Salinda asked, "And those not talented?"

Titina faced her calmly. "They could soon take the place of those who will go to Vanden. Or we could teach them skills useful to Vanden so that one day they could make a life there. In the end the observatory would benefit, you see. We depend on their food and other things we cannot make here."

Salinda found it hard to estimate the numbers involved, but she could see from observing Titina's scribbling that the woman was making calculations, then scratching them out and starting over.

Elder Manton added his voice once again to the discussion. "But we are on rations as it is. Who will care for them?"

Again, Titina fixed them all with a forthright stare. "You are forgetting. If we help the people of Vanden care for the harvest, we will all benefit. It will be hard in the short term. It will require sacrifice, but we will adjust and benefit in the future. Vanden has been the source of our prosperity in the past. We have a moral duty to help them now as well as a practical need to ensure our own future."

Salinda threw a suggestion to the group, interested to see whether it would divide or unite them. "Have you considered abandoning Vanden altogether and resettling the townsfolk elsewhere? The plains behind us are uninhabited, and the people would be safe from reprisals in a new village."

Elder Wylie cleared his throat. "Maybe...but Vanden is their home." He looked around the room, at each face in turn. "Their kin are here in the observatory. It would be cruel to send them so far away. We cannot turn our backs on them."

"Yes, Elder Wylie speaks truth." Titina waved her notebook in her hand. "And there's the importance of the river. If we send them away from it, there will be nothing but death for us all. No water, no crops, no life. No, we must help them repopulate Vanden. To refuse them aid would make us no better than the animals that did this to them in the first place." With that said, Titina sat back down.

All was quiet as each person mulled over what had been said.

Salinda's thoughts turned to her own companions. Danton's path was clear, Salinda knew. He must follow the wine. To pick up the rebels' path he needed to go to Vanden. In doing so he could escort those women willing to return to the town. He could also assay the damage and send back a reliable report. Brill would go with him. Though it was clear he was moved by the refugees' plight and wanted to help them, without the dragon wine they were all doomed. Damn Gercomo and his greed. It was all his fault. Salinda balled her fists and then tried to calm herself.

She was reminded of the story of Brill's father and the vicious stamping out of his highland confederacy. Danton had told her that the aftermath was similar to what had happened in Vanden. Brill had been hidden away by his father so he had escaped the worst of the destruction. But unknown to Brill, Danton had been there. He had responded to a call for aid from Prince Hubert of Duval, but had arrived too late. Little had she known when she sent Brill to join Danton that there would already be a basis for a bond between them.

Salinda knew that Danton was in sympathy with Brill's views, though he was more cynical. Life had taught him that. He had seen many attempts at a better way of life thwarted. Perhaps in the past Danton had not believed that humans were worth saving. She shuddered, recalling the looks on the faces of Vanden's refugees. She knew they were worth saving. Looking at Danton now, the tension in his body, the horror that cloaked his eyes, she was certain that he cared and that he would do what had to be done. It was the butchers who had attacked those innocents who were not worthy to walk on Margra's soil.

The collaboration that had saved the observatory had given them hope. That was a feeling that Danton, Brill and she shared in the aftermath of Gercomo's attack: they had somehow managed to protect the wonder that was at the heart of Trithorn Peak, its people and its mission to save the world.

The discussion continued for a while longer. More and more Salinda could see that Elder Titina had a vision and strategy. She also considered Elder Wylie, who knew how to get things done. It was not easy to choose between them. But for the first time since the Master Elder had died, Salinda thought she had viable candidates who could step up as his replacement. For now, though, the hour was growing late.

Salinda stood and the elders stopped talking among themselves. "Let us think on it. Tomorrow morning you will cast a vote, though it appears there is only one proposal of merit. So the choice will be to commit to Elder Titina's plan or do nothing and send Vanden's refugees away."

Chapter Six

A DRAGON'S LAIR

Gercomo loped awkwardly through the night, his senses alive to the dark tide of evening and the rising power of Belle moon.

Never had a meal been so pleasurable. No wonder the beasts found human flesh satisfying. The pounding heartbeat, the scream of fear, the ultimate devouring of life force. It was better than sex. And now, in the aftermath, he felt energized, as if he could run or fly for a year. For the first time he did not fear his dragon form.

Before dawn broke he found another place to nest—a mound of soft sand in full view of the sunrise. Strange, but he could feel the pull of the sun before it reached over the horizon, and Margra's soil was soft and warm like a blanket. Why had he not sensed these things before? Was it a sense peculiar to dragons—to feel the movement of the planet and sun and moon and Shatterwing? Were dragons somehow attuned to the flow of the universe? Burrowing deeper and gouging into the dirt and rubble to cover himself, he reached out with his new sense and touched the lumps of broken moon that formed Shatterwing as it glittered with energy. As that sense of the universe opened up inside of him, he realized that he was part of a much larger existence, one beyond mere flesh.

The sun caressed the sand covering his hide. The energy prickled his skin, sending healing fingers to unknot the muscles and caress his wings back to wholeness. Combined with the meal, the sun invigorated him so much that he wanted to roar. He managed a contented groan as his healing continued.

As the sun rose above the horizon, its rays lulled him to sleep. His dreams were strange visions, cut through with violet and red. Voices called to him but not in words. Memories of his life flitted across his mind as he slept. Salinda once again trod his dreams, bringing him to wakefulness. But she was not there and was no real threat so he let the image of her fade and let the strong heat of the sun stroke him back into unconsciousness.

While he slept, the sun rose and set a few times. He was aware of the coming of the day and night in the same way he was aware that he breathed. He did not need to see it with his eyes. One afternoon he woke from a dream to hear loud explosions reverberating in the air. Rocks fell from the heavens, searing the air with energy. He could almost taste it. When they impacted the meteorites showered the plain with dust. Gercomo lifted his snout out of the dirt, blinking at the spray of energy—violet streaks tinged with yellow raked the sky. He shook his head in wonderment. While he was a human he had never seen such a display. After the shower stopped and the lights faded from the sky, he drifted back to sleep, dreaming of the wonder of the wider universe.

With the next, new dawn he opened his eyes, shook off the surface soil and clawed his way out of his nest. Warm sand fell from his hide in a rush as he stepped free. Stretching his stiff neck he eased it down and then up, marveling at his dragon body's flexibility. Then, as he blinked sleep from his eyes, he took in his surroundings, trying to decide the best direction to take.

Swiveling his head in a full circle, he detected something in the distance, a prickle of awareness coming from the direction of the sun. Reaching out with his newfound dragon sense, he could feel them. Not food this time. Not the feel or smell of humans. No, it was others like him—dragons not far away and approaching fast. He could not distinguish the minds individually, but he did sense their combined purpose. They were looking for someone or something.

Lowering himself flat against the ground, he held still. Then he reached out with his senses and tried to interpret the approaching dragons' intent. Then the emotions in him shifted as his mind began to sync with theirs. Then he understood. They were looking for him, and that realization jolted. Somehow they had sensed him on the plains, and they knew his deeds.

Flee! was his first thought. *Hide! Flee!* It was too late to burrow farther into the ground. Besides, if he could sense the approaching dragons, then surely they could sense him. Staying where he was, no matter how well he buried himself, would serve little purpose. He had to move. Turning in a circle, he tried to decide which way to run. There seemed to be little option. He could not continue straight ahead because that was where they were heading. He would have to head farther north out onto the desolate plains. Gouging chunks of earth with his claws, he lurched along the ground. To fly he needed to gain more speed. It was his only chance. He pushed himself harder, putting his fear to work. Spreading his wings, the air fluttered beneath the membranes and then when he drew them up and down he began to lift off. He could do it. He could fly. He was becoming more dragon-like.

Stroking harder, he gained height, but he needed more distance from the ground if he was going to find the thermals that would speed him on his way. Could he outrun the pursuing dragons? He was small. Maybe that would help. He could hide where they could not reach.

Once he was comfortable with his ability to fly, he used his dragon sense to locate the pack, because he couldn't fly and turn his head at the same time. He was alarmed to discover they were gaining on him and had shifted direction so that they were zeroing in. One presence, he sensed, was particularly strong and dark. It overshadowed the others. He shied away from it. It was like a mountain was approaching, dominant, inevitable and hard. Instinctively he recognized danger. He found a thermal but it petered out so he beat his wings harder, searching for another that would ease his flight.

A loud roar, behind and above him, made him start. He bleated out a groan that sounded feeble in comparison. He was too afraid to give a full-throated growl. That was new. He had not experienced the sensation of inferiority to another being for a long, long time. Subservience did not come easily and fear had an all too familiar ring to it of late. Damn that woman!

The large beast swooped in close, disrupting the flow of air to Gercomo's wings. He lost height and fear made him stumble. He tried to veer left, but the other dragons were there, boxing him in. With a mighty roar, the large dragon swooped him again, keeping his body aligned with Gercomo's. Gercomo lost height and kept sinking lower until he saw that the ground was approaching fast. Again he was swooped, and there was another beast behind whose roar boomed beside him. He was surrounded by at least ten dragons. The smallest was triple his own size. They were forcing him to land.

Gliding lower, he brought himself to the earth, scrabbling on the ground to prevent a fall. The dust kicked up as he landed with a thud, his snout driving into the soft sand. Shaking his head, he managed to right himself and turned to watch the pursuing dragons descend. He backed up awkwardly, shifting his tail to give him greater balance and maneuverability. Yet seeing them approach, seeing the huge mass of them, looming near him, made him quail in fright.

One by one, they landed and circled him, hissing and scratching at the ground with their claws. The largest one, a bull, landed last and placed himself a little in front of the others. Gercomo growled low, instinctively afraid of the larger dragon, challenged by its threatening stance.

Full-bodied musk wafted over him. Angling his body this way and that way, he searched for an escape route. Their eyes followed him and one of the dragons let out a small ball of flame, which billowed close to Gercomo's head—a warning.

The smallest dragon ventured forward, it scales green with stripes of mauve. Gercomo held himself still, wondering what the beast wanted. Without warning, the runt lunged, attacking him with its snout. Gercomo backed off, slightly stunned from the blow to his head.

Advancing still, the little dragon then extended its claws, raking them across Gercomo's neck and head. Reeling from the attack and the ramifications of it, Gercomo fought for balance and tried to think strategically.

Instinctively, he wanted to fight back, wanted to lash out. But he knew he stood no chance against ten of them. If this was what the smallest of them could do, then they were playing with him, baiting him. Nursing his ripped face and neck, Gercomo regarded the largest dragon. That bull alone could rip him to shreds.

The next largest dragon lashed out from the side and clawed his wing. Gercomo roared out his agony. The next dragon and the next, in order of size, attacked him. Gercomo bore it, even though pain radiated through every part of him. What else could he do? He was trapped. The largest dragon had not raised a claw or let out a roar. The bull's black unblinking eyes watched the proceedings. Could the beast be assessing him? Was a dragon capable of rational thought, or intention, or were they reacting to a perceived threat and acting on instinct?

When all but the largest one had attacked him, the dragons

reformed the circle and tightened it, leaving the bull outside and behind them. Then an almighty roar split the air. Gercomo flinched at the sound, unable to prevent his instinctive recoil in reaction to the more dominant beast's presence. Crouching down, Gercomo wanted to inch backward, yet he was surrounded. Then the beasts drew apart, revealing the bull, who thumped into the circle. Gercomo tried to back up but he had nowhere to go. He tried to make himself smaller by pulling in his wings and tucking in his tail. The bull took another threatening step and Gercomo retracted his neck, drawing his head so far into his body that only his snout showed past his shoulders.

The bull was as implacable as a mountain. It roared again, releasing more of its overpowering scent. The other dragons roared together, urging the bull on for the kill. The bull raised its claw and struck. In comparison, the other strikes were mere light dustings. The first blow broke Gercomo's fang. He cringed and whimpered, not knowing how to survive this attack. Then he took a blow to the side of the head that near broke his snout. Another and he groveled in the dirt thinking: *No, no, please, please, spare me.*

The bull did not let up. Using its snout it flipped Gercomo over, exposing his soft underbelly. Gercomo tried to scramble away, but his tail was caught in the larger beast's snout. The bull bit down.

Gercomo was dragged along the dirt by the tail. All he could think of was how much he hurt. Then, as he became accustomed to the pain, he sensed other things. Odd emotions or thoughts surrounded him. *Runt. Strange. Fear. Food.* Carefully, he opened his eyes and saw the dragons following along the trail that his body left in the ground. The bull continued to drag him along, biting down on his tail until Gercomo yelped. Gercomo thought he would lose the tail and wondered if that would make him less able to fly. What was he thinking? He was not going to live through this. He was no match for these dragons.

Closing his eyes he let the pain wash over him. He had survived the transition into a dragon, but now he would not survive being with the dragons themselves. He was a runt. Puny. Strange. He was to be feared. All the stray emotions and thoughts he detected belonged to the other dragons. They were their thoughts and fears about him. Then it occurred to him that they were articulating emotions. Could the dragons communicate? He remembered Plu. That bitch, Salinda, had communicated with him. Why hadn't he bothered to ask? It had to be possible. If he could understand their thoughts and emotions then surely he could find a way to communicate his ideas to them.

One of the dragons walking next to him shot out its snout and bit him on the neck. The pressure did not let up. Gercomo found himself losing consciousness. When he next opened his eyes, he was on the edge of a crevice. Looking down he could see that it was terraced with balconies of stone. Ramps connected the various levels. At the very base, the ground was carpeted with sand and nestled within he could see eggs. This was where the herd lived. He'd stumbled onto their territory. *Idiot!*

The bull shoved him closer to the edge of the crevice and let him see the depth of it. Leaning down on him, the bull forced all the breath from his lungs. He could see the sky stretched above, with a long line of cloud. Gercomo had no strength to move. He lay there mute and still, waiting for the killing blow. The bull butted him viciously, making him gasp for air. Then his body slid over the edge.

Gercomo toppled over, head rolling over tail two times before he hit the bottom. He lay there stunned and in pain. It took a while to realize that he had missed the hatchery. No precious eggs had been damaged in the fall. The sand was deep and soft underneath him and had cushioned his landing. Otherwise he would be dead. But that was not the bull's intention. If he had wanted him dead he would have killed him out on the plain. No, Gercomo had some use. He had been given a reprieve.

A warm rain began to fall. But the cloud he had seen did not have the potential for a downpour. Then he smelled the pungent musk of the bull and knew that he was being pissed on from a great height. That was something he did understand. Female dragons gathered on the rim of the crevice. The remaining bulls joined together and pissed on him too. The females let out high-pitched roars, and Gercomo caught random thoughts of amusement. It would take time to heal and to learn, but one day soon he would turn his situation around. That bull would lick his ass before pissing on him again.

Chapter Seven

FAREWELLS

Laidan poured the last bucket of water into the round metal tub. The gas fire beneath hissed as a little water spilled down the sides. Her bath was not ready yet. She took a sip of watered dragon wine from her cup and savored the flavor, letting it sit on her tongue for a while. She was glad the stench of the burning dead did not reach her room. How could they all watch the pyre and inhale that stink? She had better things to do, like preparing herself for her tryst with Brill. Their previous meeting had been so wonderful, despite being in a cleaning closet and the need for secrecy. The threat of discovery heightened her pleasure. He had promised to come to her again tonight. Her expectations were so much more this time.

She hoped Brill washed before he came to her. Not that it mattered—if his clothes did stink, then there was all the more reason to remove them. Thoughts of Brill had consumed her all day. Unfortunately, she'd hardly seen him. Salinda had made her read books and undertake exercises in her study all day. With nothing but work to do and no one to talk to—the boredom! Salinda treated her as if she was a child. Not one story to illustrate her points as Thurdon used to do, just quick and firm instructions. Salinda's teaching methods made Laidan bristle with indignation. She hadn't asked for the blasted cadre to be shoved into her mind. Why should she waste time trying to use it? To own the truth, it terrified her. That was why thinking about Brill was so much better, so much more relaxing.

While sipping the last of the wine, she saw steam wafting up as the flame tickled the bottom of the tub. Sniffing a chunk of her hair, she decided to wash it too. She could dry it before the gas fire, even if that meant kneeling in front of it. With Thurdon, any kind of bath had been a luxury. When had she become so spoiled? But she'd been washing regularly for the last year or so at least and she wasn't about to give that up. She parted her robe, letting it slide from her shoulders to cascade to the floor. Stepping into the bath, she sighed. What could be better? A long, warm soak and then meeting Brill. She frowned briefly, recalling that Thurdon would never have permitted her to behave in such a way.

With a twinge of sadness, she thought of her mentor, her father. His death had changed her life. She had become a woman and a prize: two things she had wanted, but now she was afraid. Her life was out of control. Only Brill offered her any center of warmth and calm. As she eased into a squat in the round tub and the hot water crept up her skin, she let out a breath. There was no room to recline, but it was hot and nice. The thought of cleanliness and Brill's kisses sent an excited frisson through her body. Throwing her head back, she sank deeper into the tub, making sure her lower body was fully immersed.

Memories of Brill's kisses filled her mind. She ran her hands over her breasts in the way he had done. She wanted more of him—the touch of his hands and to relive the thrilling sensations he caused in her when he was close. It was so much better than being groped by that fat pig, Nulf. Brill's touch was soft and sweet, like his words. And he was surer and more certain than Garan, who could never be clear in what he wanted.

A vision of Garan came to mind, tall, broad with dark curly hair. His eyes had always fascinated her and when he smiled his lopsided grin her anger always melted away. Yet, he did not worship her in the way Brill did. Besides, she'd known Garan for most of her life. Brill was new and exciting. Never a harsh word from Brill, only thoughtful and considerate suggestions and counsel. Brill would care for her always, of that she was certain. Garan was more likely to trample her in a rush to do Salinda's bidding or to shoot down a meteor. Work was more important to him than her comfort.

Later, with her long blonde hair brushed to shining, Laidan opened the door to her room and checked the hallway. It was empty. Naked beneath her clean robe, Laidan carried a small urn of hot coals as she hurried to the closet. The urn would provide warmth as well as soft light. She placed it on the floor and leaned against the rear wall. Earlier that day she had shifted the boxes around and had placed a blanket on the floor. The sound of the door opening drew her gaze and her breath caught. Brill stepped in, freshly bathed and shaved, and shut the door quietly behind him. She noted his freshly laundered shirt and thought him perfect.

Brill was close to her in one step, his normally bright blue eyes dark and intense. "Laidan, you look beautiful. I don't know how you manage it." He stroked her hair with one hand; with the other he lifted her chin. "You are radiant."

Laidan smiled back at him, then took two steps backward, releasing herself from his embrace. Her robe parted and she heard his intake of breath.

"Laidan?"

Shrugging the robe off her shoulders, she stepped back into his arms and pressed herself against him. She lifted her face, and Brill kissed her. He was trembling. At first she wondered why. Was he afraid? Then when her hands slid beneath his shirt, she felt a jolt as if she had set him on fire. His kiss deepened and once again that out-of-control sensation took over as his hands ran up and down her back, sliding along muscle to cup her buttocks.

Breaking the kiss, Brill groaned in her ear. Lifting his shirt over his head, Laidan kissed his chest, working her way down the length of him. Brill was lost to the moment. His legs shook and his hands grasped her hair. She could sense that his control was frayed. Brill urged her gently to the ground, onto the blanket she had placed there earlier. His kisses were hot and teasing. When his mouth found her nipple, Laidan gasped. Surprisingly it hurt at first but then the pain became pleasure. He moved to suckle on her other nipple and Laidan knew what desire was: a throbbing ache between her legs that made her writhe.

Laidan tugged at Brill's clothes, peeling them away so that their flesh could meet. When Brill was naked beside her, she ran her lips over every part of him, licking and kissing as she went. She took pleasure in her mastery, his inarticulate groans egging her on. Brill showed her the sheath and explained what it was for. Her hands shook with anticipation as she helped him slide it on. She was confident where he was uncertain. Excitement filled her up. They were actually going to consummate their relationship. She was going have Brill inside her, and he would love her and never leave. There was a moment of hesitation, of discomfort, and then it was magic.

Afterward, Brill spoke of his pleasure, his wonderment at their joining and his love for her. She had been his first experience. No one was going to take her place. Laidan couldn't resist smiling. She had won this battle. Brill was hers now. When he lay there spent, she found she could not keep her hands from him. Emboldened, she lay on him and kissed his chest, his navel, and then moved lower. With her nuzzlings, she discovered he was ready for her again. Then there was no time for sheaths. Urgent and potent desire drove her on. Straddling him, she lowered herself, taking him inside. He moved within her, again and again, urged on by her knowing hands and needy hips. His face was full of desire for her. By morning, Brill would not be able to leave her. Ever!

☙☙☙☙

Brill was thankful that Danton was asleep when he returned to the room they shared. If his luck held out he might get a few hours' rest before morning and avoid the inevitable lecture. The taste of Laidan was in his mouth and her scent lingered still on his skin. Joining with her had been wonderful and frightening at the same time. She was a temptress. That part of Danton's opinion was true. She had known what to do, where he had not. She had been a virgin, but was not innocent. He was sure he would not sleep, because his mind was so full of the things she had done to him, and the things he'd done to her.

Thank the source that Danton had given him the sheath, otherwise he may have conceived a child. As it was he had to hope that their unprotected second coupling resulted in no complications. He had withdrawn from Laidan before the end, leaving her dissatisfied. The possibility of a child would have made leaving Laidan that much harder.

He crawled into bed, catching the scent of her again and feeling himself grow hard. *Magol curse me*, he thought to himself, as images of her and what they had done replayed. He could not help but stroke himself, reliving the moment of his first release. *What sort of beast have I become?* He moaned his ecstasy into his pillow to muffle the sound. He wanted to stay buried in Laidan's flesh. He wanted to stay with her, always, hearing his name on her lips. Yet he knew he could not.

Even if a way could be found to convince Danton to allow her to accompany them, Brill knew Laidan would be a dangerous distraction. Brill would feel obliged, even willing, to look out for her, and her actions might risk the lives of others. More importantly, she did not share his vision. She was still young and had yet to find her own dream and ambition for the future. It would be wrong to use his influence over her to make her fight for things she might not truly believe. However, there was a lingering doubt in him that Laidan could feel that way about anything other than herself. That cruel assessment gave him pause.

All through the early hours of the morning, Brill tossed in the bed, struggling with his arousal and his conscience. It was time for them to leave. The rebels had gone. The wine must be found. More than once, he entertained the thought of staying and contemplated the ramifications. If he remained he would marry Laidan, and marry her quickly, before it became obvious that they had a clandestine relationship. From what he understood the observatory held firmly to rules about marriage and relationships and he wasn't one to walk away from his responsibilities.

Usually Brill wouldn't have devoted so much of his time to a person rather than a cause. If he was honest with himself, he could foresee the future he would have if he stayed. Laidan would swell with child after child and all his plans for how he could help people and build a better world would come to naught. He knew he could no more abandon his duty and his cause than he could stop breathing. He had to accept the fact that Laidan and he were on different paths—at least for the present.

Glancing in the direction of Danton's sleeping form, he now thought better of what his friend had been trying to tell him. Danton had warned him against getting involved with Laidan. They had argued about it. Now Brill understood. Laidan knew her power and Brill had succumbed, despite knowing it was wrong and that he was going against his own morals. Brill making love to her was going to hurt other people: Laidan when he had to leave and Garan when he found out. Salinda, whom he respected, would also take a dim view of his actions. He was less than he was for enjoying her body in that way. He shook his head and then drew the blankets closer to his chin. What a fool he had been. It was as if he had been possessed by madness.

A vision of Laidan arose and he bit his lip. It would be a bitter parting, a scene he was not looking forward to, but part they must. He hoped it would be soon, because he could not be alone with her again. He would be lost to his own weakness and that frightened him. Previously he had assumed that nothing could ever stand between him and his vision. Now he found that his biggest weakness was his own notion about himself.

Before dawn, Danton woke him, plying him with wine and bread. "We leave today. Just after first light it we can manage it."

Brill took a mouthful, grateful to be woken from his fitful doze. "Yes. I agree," he said after he swallowed. It was dark outside; hardly anyone would be about. He warmed to the idea that he would be spared a painful goodbye to Laidan. "To Vanden first and then pick up the trail from there?"

Danton nodded before taking a large gulp of watered wine. "Yes, I packed some provisions before I went to bed. You all right about leaving?"

Brill's cheeks burned. "Yes, of course I am—would that we'd left yesterday."

Danton nodded, as if he understood, then stood and threw his few personal belongings together and put them in his pack. While he worked, he said, "I am going to say goodbye to Salinda. Then I'll drop by the refectory and see if Garan is there. He was on the night shift so he'll probably eat before he goes to bed. You are welcome to tag along or I can meet you at the Klester Valley gate at sunrise if you want some time to yourself or to say your own goodbyes."

Brill looked around him, emotionally flat, an empty vessel, when only a few hours ago he had been so overwhelmed with love and desire. What a contrast. As his gaze tracked the room he realized there was little for him to pack. Saying goodbye would be hard and it was best not to be alone for that. "Wait for me. I'll come with you."

Danton waited until Brill put his things together and tucked in his shirt. Brill knew he was being a coward about saying farewell to Laidan, but he told himself it was for the best. Then they headed down the hall, treading softly so they did not disturb those who slept. A few tenders and Skywatchers were about now. Danton headed up the stairs to Salinda's room. The rebel was bristling with energy. Brill noticed that the cloud of dread and despair that had been hanging over Danton's head was gone, shucked. The rebel leader was once again a man of action. Brill, too, found that with each step, and each breath, his old sense of purpose was returning.

Nearing Salinda's door, he detected a hitch in Danton's stride. Then Danton grinned and boldly reached out and banged on the door, as if saying goodbye to her meant nothing. Now that Brill had himself loved, he understood Danton's anguish better. Yet he could not understand how Danton could bear to be so close to Salinda without wanting to touch her. There was a lesson in that, Brill thought—control and duty. Two things he had forgotten in the last few days.

Salinda opened the door quickly after Danton's knock. Perhaps she'd been expecting him. Her face was drawn, showing her fatigue. Yet there was a sparkle in her dark eyes. "Come in," she said in that rich voice of hers. Her tone reminded Brill of the first days at the vineyard and how kind and tender she had been. With shame he remembered how he had scorned her in his ignorance, not realizing the courage and the strength she had. Nor had he known about her power then. His internment at the vineyard seemed like a hundred years ago. How much he had grown since then.

In the dark of the room Brill sensed the presence of the strange creature, Nils. In the air, there was also the scent of recent lovemaking, a scent with which he himself had become familiar a few hours before. He hoped that Danton could not smell it, but knew that the older man would. Danton was no fool.

Salinda lit the gas lamp, its yellow ripples of light dispersing the dark. Nils loomed tall, thin and pale on the far side of the bed, his alien features glowing faintly in the light. Without his shroud, he appeared large and real. Brill envied him his capacity to render himself near invisible. A shroud would be useful for stealth, useful for a rebel.

"Greetings," he said with his accented voice. "Salinda tells me you are leaving."

"Yes, right now actually," Danton replied, his gaze lingering on Salinda.

Brill nodded in agreement, lost for words. He took in the scene. Salinda with her Hiem lover, father to her unborn child, in the room with Danton, the man she still loved. Danton hid his feelings well. Salinda, Brill thought, was less capable of doing so. Her lips trembled and tears gathered at the corners of her eyes, but it was the way she looked at Danton that betrayed her heart. Her eyes glittered with interest and her gaze traveled over the length of him.

"Well then. Let me wish you well." She embraced Danton and hugged him tightly. Danton hesitated, eyes on Nils. Salinda pulled back, glanced up at Danton quickly then moved to Brill.

As she hugged him, Brill said, "Thank you, Salinda. Thank you for everything. Please tell...say that..."

Salinda gazed into his eyes and nodded. "I will say what has to be said, Prince Brill. My thoughts go with you both. I know you will win through. We will meet again."

Then releasing Brill, she gestured toward Nils. "Nils has brought you these."

Nils bowed his head and stepped forward with some silvery-gray cloth in his arms.

"It was Salinda's idea. She thought they would be useful to you both. Provided you do not overuse them they should have sufficient power to last for one week of continuous use, and much more if you use them sparingly."

Brill looked at the bundle in Nils's arms. "Hiem shrouds!" The very thing he'd thought would aid them and Nils had provided it—pre-Shatterwing technology. His heart fluttered with excitement. The shrouds provided an array of possibilities to them. Brill tried to calm himself as Nils explained the care and workings of his gift. Luckily, Danton appeared to be taking it all in. Brill was having trouble keeping his spirits from soaring. The shrouds would make them appear near invisible, a tactical advantage that their opposition would not expect.

They took their leave of Salinda and found Garan exactly where Danton had said he would be, in the refectory staring at a plate of cacti porridge. Garan stood when they entered and clasped Danton's shoulder formally. "Did you hear that we spotted a herd of dragons flying toward Vanden during the night?"

Danton straddled a chair, not quite willing to relax, Brill thought.

"No. I didn't. Is that usual?"

"No, but after yesterday anything is possible."

Danton frowned. "I hope they have left the town before we arrive."

Brill smiled. "Perhaps Salinda will come with us and send them away with her power."

Danton shook his head. "No. Her place is here with Nils. Our concerns are not hers. Besides, I think you overestimate her control of the winged beasts. Plu has been her pet since he was hatched. Only he does her bidding."

Garan's gaze flicked from Danton to Brill. "You're leaving now?"

"Yes," Danton replied. "We've come to say our farewells. I know we will meet again, Garan. Look after Salinda for me. Listen to her well. You two look after the big stuff. Brill and I will do what we can with the small stuff."

When Garan looked confused, Danton pointed to the heavens, and Garan nodded in understanding. Yet the color of his eyes was subdued. "Many work to that aim, Danton. If we all do our part, a way will be found. I look forward to seeing you again, no matter the circumstances. You have been a true friend to me."

Garan turned toward Brill. Brill was uncomfortable under the other man's scrutiny. It occurred to him that Danton saw true. Garan was a good man and one with a heart. Brill knew he had betrayed him. He had taken Laidan and nurtured her love for him at Garan's expense. He'd taken the gift of her womanhood and was leaving Garan to deal with the aftermath. Garan was the one who would be with her from now on. He could see now that his own actions had been badly done. His elation was beginning to wear off; he did not feel so all-powerful anymore. "Forgive me," Brill said.

Garan's eyebrows flew up in surprise. His gaze flicked to Danton's, and a question formed on his lips. "I don't understand. What am I to forgive you for?"

Brill grasped the other man's forearm and squeezed lightly. "Let's just say that I could have been a better friend to you." He let go and stepped back, feeling more emotion than he expected.

As they made their way to the Klester Valley gate, past the pile of ash and bone that was all that remained of the funeral pyre, Brill saw someone standing by the rubble, hair wisping about her round face. One of the refugees.

Her shoulders straightened as they approached. Brill cast an uncertain look at his friend. "Danton?"

Danton stepped toward the refugee woman and faced her square on. "Well met, Mandin. What can we do for you?"

"I am coming with you."

Before Danton could reply, Brill blurted out, "No, you're not."

Danton raised his hand for silence. Brill held his tongue and tried not to frown.

His stance relaxed, Danton spoke to the woman. "Why would you wish to accompany us? The way is long, hard and dangerous. You have a home in Vanden. The observatory will help you put your life back together."

The woman's expression hardened. Her bruised neck flushed pink and purple. "Vanden will be my home again when I have my daughter with me. The only way I can achieve that is finding those who took her."

"We are rebels too. What say you to that?" Danton kept his expression bland.

"Yes, you are rebels. But now I know that there are rebels who fight for good. You seek those who did this. If I come with you, I will find Eneit and free her if she is alive. I have nothing left in this life but that. Understand?" Her unwavering gaze spoke of determination.

Danton sighed. "I do understand. If you came with us would you obey orders and travel without complaint?"

"Danton...I don't think..." Brill's gaze shifted between the two. He couldn't seriously be considering bringing this woman with them, could he? The memory of Squab came to mind. Had that rebel once been a woman like this? He shook his head in wonderment.

"Not now, Brill. Mandin must answer."

"Yes, I would. I vow it on my life and that of my daughter."

"Then you can join us."

Brill sucked in a breath and frowned at both of them. Danton ignored him and smiled at the woman. Some of the tension seemed to drain out of Mandin. She grimaced once. Brill couldn't call it a smile. The woman then bent to pick up a cloth with her belongings in it. Apparently she was ready to leave.

Danton took one final look around the courtyard. "Let's get to Vanden, then. The observatory will send couriers to take back our report. Right now we need to move before the trail is lost."

Danton hitched his pack higher on his shoulder and set off. Brill followed closely behind, occasionally looking over his shoulder to see if the woman followed. What would Laidan say when she found out they'd taken a woman with them while she was left behind? What was in Danton's mind? Did this woman have a use? Perhaps his entire rebel band had been recruited in this way. Eyeing Danton's back, Brill kept pace with him, all the while burning to speak to him alone

Chapter Eight

A HARD ROAD

The town of Vanden was exactly as the refugees had described it, thought Danton as he strode down a street strewn with debris. Rows of small houses and shops, burned-out or partially demolished. Turning his head he assessed the damage: shattered walls, broken roof tiles, household furniture deliberately smashed spilling out of doors or littering the street. Interspersed with the larger pieces were personal possessions: cups, plates, lamps and shredded clothing. Some houses were just shells, blackened stumps of smoldering timber and piles of rubble. A breeze lifted the remains of a shirt and blew it until it caught on the jagged edge of a table. Who knew whether the owner was dead or not? Danton stopped himself from thinking about it. He had already let emotion guide him when he had stayed so long at the observatory, helping them longer than he should have. Now it was time to focus on the task.

The acrid taint of smoke permeated the air. It caught in his throat, and he paused to cough. Wiping his mouth with the back of his hand, he checked his comrades' whereabouts. Brill was scouting down one side of the street, venturing into smaller cross streets and alleyways. Occasionally, the lad would wave an all-clear as he ducked back up the main street before darting down another debris-choked alleyway. Danton had sent Mandin down the other side. He turned full circle, trying to pinpoint exactly where she was. No point in losing his new recruit before he had even trained her. Mandin's knowledge of Vanden had been useful and accurate as far as he was able to verify. They had chatted as they made their way down Klester Valley, and she had been able to describe the Inspector's occupation of Vanden in great detail.

Apparently her husband had been a trader before being drafted into Gercomo's service. Mandin had a good eye and ear for detail as well as a good memory. Combined with an excellent intuitive sense, she was able to creditably interpret the actions of others—in this case, Gercomo, the Inspector. These were useful traits for a rebel. The information she gave confirmed his own assessment of the man and gave him some insight into the quality of the rebels he was dealing with. While the caliber of the rebels was not a comforting thought—they appeared to be well-trained—he had no complaints about Mandin and her usefulness so far. He was impressed by her potential, considering what she had been through, the type of life she had led and the small chance she had of achieving her stated aim of rescuing her daughter. It was not his business to dissuade her though. There was a possibility she would succeed and he would not take away the hope she had in her heart. Meanwhile, she would be useful to him, a decent recruit if she stayed for the longer term.

As Danton continued walking down the street, he saw no sign of life. The collateral damage was fairly significant. A few of the buildings had sections that were salvageable, but it would be a large undertaking to make the town habitable again. Thank the source they would be long gone before that task commenced. It would take precious months. It wasn't that he didn't feel for the people of Vanden. He did. But that wine, that precious dragon wine, was getting further and further out of his grasp. The longer he was apart from his men, the more vulnerable he, and they, were. They needed his leadership and protection. He needed their support. He could not afford to fail. Not for any reason. Above all, Salinda needed him to succeed, for in dragon wine there was hope. Hope for many. The essence of the dragons in the wine was what allowed humans to live. Without it they would perish. The importance of the wine was not widely known but Danton believed it. Salinda certainly did. The Inspector also—why else had he hoarded it at the prison vineyard, kept it hidden and then tried to sneak it out? Someone wanted that wine for themselves and be damned with the rest of the human race. Danton could not let that stand. He must get that wine.

A breeze gusted dust and tendrils of smoke wafted ahead of him on the street. The absence of life felt eerie. The absence of death was equally disconcerting. There were no bodies. Mandin had assured him there had been plenty of dead people. She had even pointed out places where there had been particular groupings, but all that remained were bloodstains splattered on walls or darker pools of clotted blood where body parts had littered the streets. As the others continued scouting, Danton headed down to the river's edge, to the place where Mandin said the salvaged dragon wine had been stashed. It was important to retrieve it and re-secure it in a safer location. The townsfolk had buried it near the banks. One heavy downpour and the river swell could uncover it and wash it downstream.

The old mansion house where Gercomo had made his headquarters was now a burned-out shell. Behind it, Danton found the marked trail left by the Vanden women. He had to admit that for a hastily planned departure, Mandin's trail-marking had been excellent. If she had not told him the clues to look out for ahead of time, he would not have found it easily by himself. The trail looked as much a part of the general chaos as the debris-strewn main street.

The river oozed by, looking pale gray and dead. Danton jumped down the embankment, where the sand had been compacted to serve as the underbelly for the pier, and completed the short walk to where Mandin's marker was placed. The spot where the wine was stored was undisturbed. With a quick glance around to check the damage to the pier and the rubble lining the river, he knelt and started shoveling the earth with his hands. Soon grainy river sand was piled up around him, and he had uncovered the tip of the first of the casks. He grinned and wiped the sweat from his forehead. One small part of a much larger hoard, yet it made him feel good.

A whistled signal alerted him to Brill's approach. He eased himself out of the hole and peered over the embankment, where he caught sight of Brill with Mandin trailing a little behind. Even from this vantage point he could see that the woman had been crying, as her face was smeared with soot. Danton guessed she had been going through the ruins of her home. His gaze skipped to Brill. He noted the young man's posture and frowned. The lad had taken to ignoring Mandin. Danton thought it would take some time for Brill to adjust to her presence. Danton had every confidence in him, though, and expected he soon would not only accept her but welcome her.

"Uncovered them already?" Brill asked as he jumped down beside him.

"Some. There are more, though. I could use your help." With a nod, Brill knelt and went to work uncovering the other barrels of wine. Mandin took a less direct route to the site of the stash, walking to where the embankment was not so steep and backtracking along the river's edge. Avoiding Danton's eye, she ambled up to them and began immediately to dig. Working in silence, it didn't take long for the three of them to uncover all the wine casks.

Lined up on the bank, Danton counted them. "Twenty!" At first he was thunderstruck. Then he threw back his head and laughed. "By the great dragon's holy ass! Twenty!" He couldn't dampen his grin as his gaze swept over a sweaty Brill and a bedraggled Mandin.

Jumping down beside Mandin, he slapped her gently on the shoulder. "You did well. This is no mean stash of wine."

She nodded once and sniffed. Then she stared bashfully at the ground as she rubbed the sand from her hands against her skirt. Brill climbed up the bank to stare at the wine casks.

"How did you transport it here?" Danton queried her.

Again, Mandin looked up, emotion staining her cheeks red. She glanced at Danton and then climbed up the embankment so she could peer over the top. Danton followed her and saw where she was pointing. Brill also looked where she indicated. "With that." She was pointing to a piece of wood jutting out of the ground.

Danton frowned, not hiding his puzzlement. Mandin heaved herself over the top of the embankment and made her way to the piece of wood. Curious, Danton followed and stood behind her as she squatted in the dirt. With a few sweeps of her hand, she had uncovered a wheel. Danton heard a step and realized that Brill had followed. When he saw what she was doing he finished extricating the wheel from the sand. Mandin scouted around and found another one. While she was uncovering it, she described to Danton where the other parts of the cart were hidden.

Within half an hour they had recovered the pieces of the cart and had nearly finished assembling it. The cart was an ingenious design in that the parts fit together and were held snug by bolt and pins. These had been expertly hidden within the ruins of the town so that they appeared little more than scattered wreckage. Danton's admiration for the townswomen and Mandin's quick thinking rose steadily. He noticed Brill's thoughtful expression and guessed the direction of his young friend's thoughts. Then they began the task of re-situating the wine stash so that it would be safe and available to the returning refugees. As they worked Danton suggested to Mandin that the town use part of the dragon wine to barter for goods and labor from the observatory. Brill then gave her instructions on how best to water the wine so that it would last as long as possible. Mandin nodded. "I'll leave a message for the others. I'm not staying here. Don't think you're leaving me behind."

"Of course...I wouldn't have it any other way," Danton replied. He had given her an out, and she hadn't taken it.

Brill raised an eyebrow at her outburst. Danton caught his look and Brill lowered his head and avoided meeting his eye. "So where should we put the wine?" Danton asked.

After a lengthy discussion, they chose a suitable storage spot. When the last of the casks was stacked near the old pier, against the half-wall of the mansion that remained standing, they piled up loose planks of wood and earth to disguise it once again.

Danton found a spot in the shade and lowered himself to the ground. The sun was setting, layering the sky with vivid reds and pinks.

"Brill, look for the trail of those who left on foot. I'll write a report for the observatory. The first Vanden contingent will arrive tomorrow. I want to be long gone by then." Danton did not want to be drawn into the salvage operation and resettlement. If he was here, they'd be tempted to ask him and he'd be tempted to say yes.

"With the information Mandin gave us I should be able to pick up the trail easily enough." Brill took off after a quick nod of acknowledgment to the woman.

Brill was soon out of sight along the river's edge. The woman wiped soot from her face and tucked wisps of hair behind her ears. "Mandin, while I prepare this report for the tenders would you prepare instructions for the refugees? I think they would take advice from you more readily than outsiders. Let them know they have some bargaining power."

"I will," she answered. Danton thought she would move off as he began to put pencil to paper. After a few minutes he noticed she hadn't moved. Out of the corner of his eye he saw Mandin rub the dirt from her hands and study her various cuts and scrapes. Repeatedly her gaze traveled up and down the deserted streets. Looking up from the report he was writing, he asked, "What is it?"

Mandin frowned at him and then shrugged. "When we left here, the streets were littered with the dead. I wonder where the bodies have gone. I haven't seen one in any of the ruins."

Danton shrugged once. He knew what had happened to the bodies. He'd seen the dragon droppings. Perhaps Mandin did not recognize them. Danton weighed up whether he should tell her straight out, and then with another shrug decided it was no use trying to spare her the harsh realities of life. "Dragons ate them, I expect."

Mandin reeled back, disbelief written on her face. "What? But..."

Danton pointed behind her. "If you take a walk down to the intersection and look to the left you'll see dragon dung on the street. There are more piles of it near the remains of the outer wall too. It is dark gray in color now, but fresh it looks green. It pays to know these things when you are a rebel. Dragons may cross our path again."

Mandin glanced down the road to the intersection and gulped noisily. She hesitated as if she was tempted to take a look rather than take Danton at his word. He didn't mind either way. Then she turned back to him. With a sigh he looked up, raising his eyebrow.

Mandin shifted her weight from foot to foot while staring at the ground. He waited, scratching under his chin, while he looked up at her.

Her gaze flicked upward. "Is it true? I heard rumors at the observatory that the Inspector...well, that he changed into a dragon."

Danton chewed on the end of his pencil while he nodded. Then he took the tip out of his mouth and answered. "Yes. It is true. I saw it with my own eyes, and I still don't understand it."

"But...how?"

Danton angled his head down and wrote another word in his report. He had to consider how much he told her. He wasn't lying when he said he didn't understand it, but he couldn't help being cautious. "I don't know how...Something to do with dragon essence, something the Inspector had made and drunk. Salinda had seen him drink this and seen the effects. She wasn't completely sure but she thought it may have helped him transform or forced a transformation. The dragons are powerful beasts themselves and trying to ingest their concentrated substance was likely too much for the human form." He shrugged at her aghast and disbelieving expression. "I know...I said I don't understand it. It had something to do with that and power—the power of the observatory and Salinda."

"Power?"

"Magic might be a better word." He scoffed and rubbed his hair off his forehead.

Mandin frowned and scratched her scalp, jostling her bun. "I see."

"Mandin. I've told you something that could be dangerous to know and to tell. Be cautious. Salinda will leave the observatory, and as you don't know where she will go, I don't think you knowing can harm her. I want you to be careful all the same. Agreed?"

"Yes, of course. I understand completely. Well, I don't understand what it all means, but I do understand about keeping quiet." With that she turned, shook out her shoulders and wandered down the street, presumably to look at dragon dung. Danton suspected that she didn't believe him. He didn't blame her. If he hadn't seen it, he wouldn't have believed it either. Only in knowing old Mez, Salinda's mentor, did he realize that there were greater mysteries that couldn't be understood or explained by simple men like himself. Danton trusted what he could see and feel and do. He'd seen things he couldn't explain, but he accepted them without too much deep thinking—that would only warp his mind. After a few minutes, Mandin returned and took up her report, scribbling like crazy. Danton grinned. The sight of dragon turds could be rather daunting to the uninitiated. He'd seen his share at the prison vineyard. He'd been up to his elbows in it. More than a lifetime's share of dragon shit.

Brill rounded the corner as Danton put the finishing touches on his report, which gave the new arrivals an idea of where to start with the salvage operation and a coded message of where to find the wine. As a rebel he was quite expert at re-using materials and making the best of destruction. Danton had no idea about the crops so he would leave that to someone else.

"I found the trail," Brill said as he ran up, slightly breathless. Danton stood and checked to see if Mandin was nearby. She was. He waved, and she hurried over, breaking into a cumbersome jog. Danton bit his lip. He knew that after a week of travel her fitness would improve. For the moment he must be patient. Her attempt at running took a lot of effort for no more speed than a brisk walk. Danton sighed. It was going to be a long road ahead.

When Mandin arrived, gasping for breath and hunched over, Brill continued.

"There are tracks following the river. There are about ten rebels by the number of the boot prints. I guess they are sticking pretty close to the shipment. There were smaller prints. Hard to tell for certain, but maybe nine sets."

"Nine? But that would mean one is..." Mandin's dark gaze traveled from Brill to Danton.

"Dead," Danton finished for her. "Maybe. With that many prints it's hard to judge accurately. It could be eight, could be ten. With captors like those rebels the outlook isn't good for those girls so the chances are that someone will die the longer we linger here. Belle Moon is full so there will be sufficient light for a few hours, so I suggest we make a start now."

Brill looked around the town, his eyes haunted. "I agree. Some distance between us and the town will make me sleep better."

Danton placed his report and Mandin's in the agreed spot and then dusted the dirt from his hands on his trousers. He glanced down at his apparel. When he'd left the observatory his clothes had been clean. Already he looked as if he had been a month on the road. Thoughts of life at the observatory arose, which led him to think of Salinda. He had to put those feelings away. Their lives were separate now. He had to let go of those emotions. He thinned his lips to hide his frown as he looked at the others. "Ready?"

After a quick check of their gear, and a quick top-up of wine, they headed for the riverbank and the trail Brill had found. Danton was conscious of the woman following on behind. He could hear her, sucking in breath after painful breath. She was older and less fit than he liked, yet he kept up a steady pace. Stubbornness would keep her going; it was up to Danton to husband the woman's strength and to maximize her usefulness.

Brill looked askance at him, indicating that they should travel faster. Danton shook his head and slowed his pace marginally. Mandin had the potential to be useful so there was no point in pushing her to the point of exhaustion. It was a question of balance, of obtaining more than one goal. Brill had a lot to learn about people and leadership. The lad was good but needed further seasoning.

As Danton surveyed the trail, he noted the tracks and signs left by the departing rebels and occupied his mind thinking about Brill's situation with Laidan. He knew the boy had snuck out again, even after they had argued about the girl. Laidan had won Brill's innocence but she'd lost him to his cause. Danton would have been surprised if Brill had chosen to stay with Laidan. Thank the source the lad hadn't asked to bring her along. That would have been an impossible situation. He was sorry for Laidan really. She couldn't help being beautiful and so needy. She was in a bad place mentally and it was going to take time and care for her to heal. Salinda was better equipped for that than Brill could ever be. The lad was subdued as he scouted around but was bearing up well. Danton made up his mind to help him get over it. A first love would be hard to forget, perhaps never forgotten, but Brill would come to terms with it eventually. Danton thought about his own love for Salinda. That hadn't waned at all. Maybe he was being overly optimistic about Brill's circumstances. But Danton had never had sex with Salinda. It was perhaps his greatest regret that he hadn't. She had wanted to but he'd been so damaged by the Inspector's brutal sexual assault and beating he couldn't bear it. There had been so much shame and self-hatred back then.

Looking across to Brill, he suspected the lad was already regretting his entanglement. It was a good call on his part to leave when they did. He would never let on that it was Brill's deepening relationship with Laidan that had made him decide to depart at that moment.

After a signal from Danton, Brill headed off to continue his scouting away from the riverside into the surrounding scrub land. It paid to keep track of things: discarded items, disturbed areas where somebody may have stopped or camped. About an hour later, Danton and Mandin found signs of a camp. They stopped and stepped cautiously in case someone remained.

"Look for anything useful they may have left behind," he said to Mandin. Danton circled the camp, taking slow steps. He saw where the rebels had sat, saw where they had tied the girls. There were splashes of blood at the base of a tree. He snuck a glance at Mandin, glad that she hadn't seen it. Danton swallowed a lump in his throat and tried not to think about the fate of the young girls. What was Mandin going through as she thought about her daughter? Danton didn't even want to consider the girl's chances of getting out of her predicament unscathed. A shrill whistle from Brill and Danton knew there was trouble. Mandin was squatting down near the remains of a campfire. She looked up at Brill's signal. "What is it?"

"Not sure. Wait here. If we are not back in ten minutes continue downriver. We'll catch up with you."

Mandin stood, nodded and wiped a hand across her sweaty brow. Her breathing was still ragged and her face flushed. Giving her a small task would allow her to rest. "I'll continue to scout around," she said

Danton ducked under some branches and angled back to where Brill's signal had come from. Tree roots pierced the soil of the forest floor, making it difficult to sprint. He let out an answering whistle and Brill sounded again, letting him pinpoint his position. Danton adjusted his direction. After rounding a group of three trees, he found Brill squatting at the base of a lone tree, shifting leaf matter with the tip of a stick. The stench wafting from the undergrowth gave Danton a clue as to what the lad had found.

As Danton drew nearer, he saw what was partially buried by the leaf litter. It was the body of a girl. Naked, her body hacked in places, the girl had died horribly. He noted the long, dark hair matted with blood. The swarthy skin of the girl's face was bruised and cut. He committed the image of her to memory and noted her general size and shape. He would tell Mandin when he thought he could, although he hoped this wasn't her daughter. Her misery would probably undo him at this moment. Danton stood up, leaving Brill staring at the corpse. Danton wanted to make sure that the bastards who had done this paid in some excruciatingly painful way. There was nothing there to reveal who in particular had performed this foul deed. He could only take revenge against them all.

He walked up behind Brill and squeezed the lad on the shoulder. "Let's go. We don't have time to bury her. If we keep moving we may find them before they kill any more."

Brill stood, a sob rocking his chest. "I can't leave her like this." His words were forced through a tight throat. With the back of his hand, he wiped away tears.

Danton nodded. "I know it's hard. We don't have time for a pyre and even if we did, it would alert the rebels to our pursuit. Cover her with more leaves and branches. That should help protect her." Danton knelt down beside him. "Here, I'll help."

They made a pile of leaves over the girl's body, covering her completely, then placed branches over the top so that the structure resembled a small hut. Brill said a few words about finding the source, and they backed away. "I feel so bad about leaving her like this."

Danton sighed. "I know...Maybe when we pass this way again." He knew what they had done wouldn't protect her from foraging animals, but it made Brill feel better about leaving her.

Brill sniffed. "Yes, maybe."

In silence they made their way slowly back to Mandin at the rebel's camp. Danton could not speak of his fear that the girl might be Eneit, and he was certain that Brill understood what they might have found. When he and Brill entered the deserted rebel camp, Mandin was standing with her back to them, staring out at the river. At their approach, she turned slowly, looked at their faces and said nothing. Her expression was quiet and still, as if she was holding her fragile self together. Danton found that he respected her restraint. He doubted he could have maintained such poise at such a time. She must suspect, but she didn't press them. Danton gave her a nod and led the way out of camp. The trail was easy to pick up and so they followed it in silence, listening to the river as it gouged its way toward the sea and the cool of dusk settled on them.

Chapter Nine

SEPARATION ANXIETY

It was time for Salinda to leave. Her few possessions were already stuffed into her pack, which she hefted on her shoulder. Closing the door to her room, she headed down the corridor, recalling the earlier scene in which she had packed Laidan's gear away while the girl looked on, sniffling and wiping tears from her cheeks as Salinda revealed that Brill had left at dawn.

"I don't believe you," Laidan had cried shrilly. "He wouldn't leave without me."

Salinda had remained unruffled by Laidan's stormy demeanor. "Yet it is true. It is done. He is gone."

The look on her face when she understood Salinda was speaking the truth was one of absolute devastation. "But he..."

Brill's departure had given her the edge she needed to sway Laidan to accompany her to Barrahiem. "You will come with me now. There's no reason to stay here and I need you."

Wringing her hands, she paced the room. "I can't believe Brill didn't say goodbye. If he couldn't take me with him, at least he could have said something. When will I see him again?"

Salinda patted her on the back and said soothingly, "Who knows when you will see Prince Brill again. I have a feeling we will all meet again in the future. For now, I hope he and Danton are successful in their quest."

Laidan stopped mid-sob, hands covering her mouth. Then after a beat, she dropped them dramatically and demanded, "Why did you call him Prince Brill?" Her chin came up. "Are you making fun of me?"

Salinda narrowed her gaze. "No, of course I wouldn't make light of your distress. You really do have a strange opinion of me." She cocked her head to one side. "Didn't he tell you that he is Prince Brilliant of Duval? He is a rebel now that his father was ousted."

Laidan gaped, caught between surprise and a sob. Salinda watched her battle it out. When she recovered, she exclaimed, "A prince? How could he keep such a secret from me? I could have been a prin—This is terrible...Why did he not say? I don't understand why he wouldn't take me with him."

Bowing her head, Salinda shook it slightly, gathering all her patience together for one last attempt at explanation. Then meeting Laidan's gaze she said, "It would have made no difference if he had stayed or left. You would come with me regardless. The cadre is more important than our individual needs. Have you not been listening to me all these weeks?"

Laidan drew herself up to her full height. She topped Salinda by a hand span. "By making Brill leave, you have given me no choice at all," she answered saucily. "Why couldn't I have gone with Brill and learned to use this thing in my head at the same time?"

With resolute firmness, Salinda explained things as she saw them. "Because Brill has better things to do than pander to your needs. And I have better things to do with my time as well."

"But we love each other!"

Salinda sighed, long and slow. "Now Laidan, be reasonable."

Laidan sucked in a huge breath, throwing out her chest. "Reasonable? I don't know how I will bear it without him. You are relentless. You never leave me alone. You are worse than a curse!"

Salinda had a slight inclination to pity the girl, but when Laidan had begun to moan irritatingly, that inclination had died a premature death. So it was with a light heart that Salinda entered the refectory and noticed that Garan was ready. He was such a pleasure to deal with and so full of potential that Salinda almost gasped with wonder when she looked at him. To her inner eye he had a glow about him, something she had never come across before. When he glanced her way, she saw with her normal sight that he was a bit haggard around the eyes, which was normal, she guessed, for someone who had worked the night through and had no time for sleep.

Her gaze encompassed the assembled party. Smiling, she murmured a greeting to the elders who had answered her summons. With a nod to Garan, Salinda observed that he reapplied himself to eating breakfast, ignoring the goings-on around him. It was his last observatory meal, so she thought it best to let him enjoy it. She doubted Barrahiem would supply him with his favorite foods.

Salinda looked over to the servery and saw Laidan leaning against the wall and staring at a plate of food. It seemed she had no intention of eating it. The girl was paler than usual and thinner as well. Salinda found it hard to be sympathetic and a frown gathered on her brow. She had to stop comparing Laidan to herself at that age. Their lives had been completely different, and Laidan was finding the current circumstances hard to bear.

Hearing a light step, Salinda was recalled to the presence of the gathered elders. Elder Wylie had stepped up to her and bowed. "You are not leaving us?" he said in his familiar, croaky voice.

Salinda smiled and clasped the old man's shoulder gently. "I'm afraid I must. But you are all ready and able to continue on without me." She guided Elder Wylie toward the gathered elders. "I have no power here, except that which you have given me by listening to my advice. Even as I leave, I can give you a couple of recommendations on how to go on."

There was a general outbreak of protests from the gathered elders. She raised both hands, gesturing for quiet. "Please, listen. I am honored by your faith in me." Right then she did feel touched by their desire for her to stay and guilty about leaving. Repressing a sigh, she said, "I will be back in the future. I must come back to help you fight this rogue asteroid heading into the Wing. If there is any will in me at all, it is to find a way to combat that. I have a strong feeling that there is an answer out there. If it exists, I will find it."

She was tempted to mention the store of knowledge held by the Hiem but decided against it. Nils would not like them to know of it. What they didn't know couldn't hurt them. "Among you are elders worthy of leading you. I suggest to you two names and two ideas. Elder Titina is worthy of the position of Master Elder, and in this role she could be assisted by Elder Wylie. Then in the future if there is some mishap you will have someone to step into the role if necessary.

"Master Elder Jalen did not have a successor named or trained. I recommend that in future you should always have someone ready to follow on. All important tasks should be taught to others so that nothing is left undone in times of need. There are challenges ahead that will be greater than the ones we have faced. We need to prepare for them in the best way we can." She paused and made eye contact with the elders in the front row. "Once again I thank you for your friendship and your aid."

The elders separated and began to talk among themselves. In the break between Elder Wylie and Elder Manton, she saw Elder Titina smiling broadly. Salinda had not seen her appear so happy before. The older woman came up to her and took both Salinda's hands in hers. "Thank you for having faith in me."

"No thanks are required. Will they vote for you?"

Titina glanced over to the gathered elders and nodded. "I think they will. The suggestion of Elder Wylie as a second is a good one. Since Jalen's death, he has come into his own. I always thought him rather vague, but now he is so decisive." Titina eyed the old man until Elder Wylie turned around and grinned. Salinda thought she saw him wink. Perhaps her suggestion would lead to more than a leadership hierarchy.

"I have learned a lot from you, Salinda. I hope we meet again soon. Your company and counsel will always be welcome."

Salinda returned her smile and released the older woman's hand. "Thank you. I wish you luck. Running this place is hard work. You may not thank me when we meet again."

Elder Titina bowed once, still smiling widely, and moved away so that Salinda could say her farewells to the others who had gathered behind her. A twinge of sadness twisted in Salinda's gut momentarily. She realized that she would miss this place and its good and altruistic people. It was a stark contrast to the vineyard, and even her childhood memories of Sartell.

With all the goodbyes said, Salinda, Garan and Laidan took their leave. Salinda was free of worry for the first time in weeks as she headed out the last gate to the winding path that would take them to the valley floor and the entrance to the caves. Nils lurked in the shadows not far down the trail. It was odd, but she had detected his presence before she had seen him. Was that the bond Nils spoke about? Was it growing stronger or was it his nearness that made her more aware of it?

No time now to consider such things. She greeted him solemnly, offering her hand to him. He touched it briefly before turning to lead the way down the path. There was a hint of happiness in his alien expression. But his posture and step revealed to her how happy he really was now that she was coming home. Her hand drifted to the soft swell of her stomach. The child had grown in the weeks she had spent at the observatory. Dropping her hand, she glanced behind her at the two young people and then turned her mind to her footing on the rugged track.

Nils walked steadily and quietly as they made their way down the trail to the caves. Garan talked about the caves, pointed to ones where the gems were mined and mentioning others he had scouted. Between Laidan and Garan there was a frosty reserve. Salinda was not eager to pursue the reason for the unease between them, although she suspected its cause. Laidan had spread rumors that Garan had tried to rape her, which was not true. Garan knew about the stories circulating but was feeling so responsible and guilty that he would never dream of taking Laidan to task over them. He was too fond of the girl. Laidan had been complicit in that brief sensual interlude, but had chosen to attack Garan's good name rather than face her own disgrace. Salinda shook her head. She was certain the issues between them were bound to come up in the next few weeks. There would only be the four of them in Barrahiem, after all. Plenty of time for all kinds of simmering tensions to come to the boil.

After a while, Garan eased ahead on the trail and walked side by side with Nils, to avoid accidental contact with Laidan, Salinda suspected. Nils began asking him about the cave where the Way Gate was located. "Are you able to access the remains of the old observatory from that cave? Surely the old Way Gate opened near the original construction."

Garan slowed and cocked his head to one side, considering. "I have not looked too closely at it. Previously I had only ventured into the first part of the cave, up to where the light ends. Until we exited within it I did not know the Way Gate existed, so I have never looked for the remains of the old observatory nor stumbled on it."

"Do you know much about the old observatory? Is there a particular place where relics from there might have been placed? My own inspection of the Master Elder's possessions revealed little."

"Relics?" Garan paused.

Nils slowed down. "Yes, relics. Items, records, books dating from the earlier observatory, from before Ruel fell."

Garan shook his head, glanced behind him toward Salinda. "I do not know. The Master Elder might have known but he never confided such to me. I thought all the old stuff was in the Master Elder's study." He continued to walk along, with Nils keeping pace.

"Jalen had a number of items of interest, but he mentioned others. Perhaps we could go looking for the ruins one day?" Nils suggested.

Salinda frowned. She wasn't quite sure what Nils expected to find. No doubt he would fill her in when they had time alone.

Garan smiled and nodded. "Yes. I would like that. It would be amazing to see what's left of the old observatory."

They stepped off the path into the shadowed gully and headed for the cave mouth. Nils stopped, his robe swirling about his legs. He held out his hand to her and Salinda smiled in response to what she saw in his expression. There was so much happiness in his face. She'd never thought to see it there. He was bringing her home again.

Chapter Ten

INTO THE DEEP, DARK PLACES

In the gray space within the Hiem Travel Ways, Garan stared raptly at the substance surrounding them. Even so, he was always aware of Laidan, trailing behind Salinda. It annoyed him that he was always aware of her and he wished that he could get her out of his system. These days she was always upset and moody when he was around. Garan had hardly seen her in the days before their departure so he suspected it was the incident where the Master Elder had found them that was still bothering her. He knew there was a nasty report about his behavior and he knew it must have originated in Laidan but he could not believe that she was capable of such character assassination so he refused to believe it. His skin could still feel the warmth of her and his lips the soft touch of her mouth. Had all of the familiarity that had grown between them disappeared as quickly as a meteor shot down by the observatory?

Brill's leaving had saddened her, for sure, but that was not Garan's fault. Although it upset Laidan, Garan found Brill's absence lifted his spirits. He had not missed the rapport that had sprung up between the two, or Brill's greater charm and manners and how Laidan responded to them. Was this pining after Brill serious? Garan ground his teeth as that thought jelled into certainty with each step he took. Just how close had Laidan and Brill become? A sigh escaped him and he tried to push the thought away. They could not have become intimate. Not the honorable Brill. Besides, the rebel had been so busy with recovering the dead and the general cleanup that he could not have had the energy to dally with Laidan. With a nod to himself, Garan put the thought of Brill and Laidan out of his mind and paid attention to Nils and the Hiem Travel Ways, both of which fascinated him no end.

The construction of the Travel Ways was remarkable; it was astonishing that they existed at all. They were ancient and alien, built with a technology that may as well be magic to his mind. It looked like there was a wall, but his finger found something else—a spongy texture that tingled against his fingers on contact. While the Ways disguised distance, Garan noticed the passage of time. His stomach growled loudly in the quiet and the lack of sleep was starting to make him stumble.

"We will stop for a rest now," Salinda said. Garan lowered himself to the ground wearily, putting his head on the cold, marble-like substance that passed for the floor of the Ways. He must have fallen asleep because some time later, Salinda was poking him in the shoulder.

"Wake now. Take this." Garan rolled onto his elbows and took the flat cacti bread and the water she offered.

Laidan sat on the opposite side of her, knees bent, sipping water, but her serving of bread sat ignored by her foot.

Salinda must have noticed. "Eat that, Laidan. I don't want you fainting. We have a while to walk yet."

Laidan lifted her head, speared Garan with a look and then took the bread. "I don't even want—"

"Enough," Salinda said, cutting her off. "I've heard it all before. You will find a lot to wonder at in Barrahiem. Consider this visit a unique gift. Besides me, you two will be the first humans to witness the marvel of the Hiem and glimpse the past we lost when Ruel split."

Garan nodded and finished off his food, keen now to get moving. This underground city of Barrahiem might provide answers or, in the very least, broaden his understanding of power in all its shapes and forms. The Hiem had technology, some of which Nils still used and understood. He might even learn more about himself and the power the crystals had awoken in him.

On the move again, Nils set a quick pace, his white hair faintly aglow in the dimness. Salinda had said Nils was eager to return home and it appeared she was not wrong about that. After pumping Garan for information about the ruins of the previous observatory, the strange being seemed to tremble in excitement. When the Hiem paused to check on their progress, his silver eyes glowed eerily, making Garan shiver. Nils was alien enough in the observatory surroundings, but in his people's domain, his true distinctiveness was obvious. Just imagining a whole race of Hiem, walking these paths thousands of years ago, made him question his view of the world. Garan was not repulsed by Nils. Yet Garan found he was conscious of his presence, especially when he happened to draw too close, because the hair on his skin would stand up. It was as if there was an energy about him that Garan responded to unconsciously.

Although Salinda had explained Barrahiem City to him, Garan found it hard to comprehend. It was an old city, older than the observatory, yet it was where a whole race had died, many unburied and unburned. He wondered what that meant for their souls and their return to the source of all things. Nils did not think the absence of burial rites mattered too much. The Hiem had always buried their dead in Margra's warmth. So the fact that the city was within Margra's soil was sufficiently funerary. When Garan had seemed puzzled, Salinda had added, "There is little for Nils to do now. His kin have long turned to dust. Do you really have no conception of how old he is, and what he has lost?"

What could Garan say to that? Nothing; he did have no idea. Shaking his head, he had kept walking. Garan barely understood the world around him, even the small portion he had experienced. It irked him that Laidan knew more about what life was like on Margra than he did. That was his burden to bear. It certainly was not Laidan's fault.

"Here we are," Salinda said, pointing ahead. "This is the Way Gate that will take us into the city."

Garan squinted but could see little to indicate a marker. Yet when they walked up to where Nils loomed ahead of them in the dim light, he saw the painting on the wall, and could pick out the ornate carving in stone marking the doorway. Just like the ones they had seen when they first entered the Ways while they were escaping the Inspector's men.

Nils faced them, blocking the path. His cream and blue robes rippled with movement. "Before I allow you to enter Barrahiem City, you must swear an oath of secrecy."

Laidan stood next to Salinda, frowning. Garan coughed once. "I am happy to swear."

"I wish you to swear not to reveal anything about the existence and working of the Ways to anyone. About the city you must not even mention its name. The treasure of this place is a particular thing. It is not in jewels or art or in sustenance. It is information and technology. These are to be kept intact. If they fell into the wrong hands—"

"Which are the wrong hands?" Laidan asked, suddenly taking an interest.

Nils glared at her, his voice dropping a tone. "Hands like those in power above. I may be a recluse, but I have ventured out. I have seen what rules the minds and hearts of men. The man who was transformed into the semblance of a dragon was one example only."

"Oh?" Laidan replied before chewing on the end of a strand of her hair and staring at the floor.

"I swear I shall not reveal anything about this place or what is within it," Garan said.

"I'm not going to swear. I don't even want to be here."

Garan was horrified by Laidan's outburst. Not by what she revealed so much as the manner in which she spoke to Salinda and Nils. She really had changed since they had returned to the observatory. She was not the Laidan who had come to comfort him that night when Turnet had died. She was out of control. Garan bristled. "Laidan! You should not speak to Salinda or Nils so," he chided. "Thurdon taught you better than that."

Laidan turned her anger on him. Her face twisted with rage. "Who asked you, brute! Thurdon is dead. He can no longer judge me. I am in charge of myself."

"Laidan," Garan said, with an edge to his voice. "You shame Thurdon and yourself with this childish—"

Salinda reached out to pat Garan's hand, and he fell silent. "Now, now. Let's have enough of that. I understand your choices have been limited, Laidan. But it will serve everyone better if we didn't complain about it all the time. You will find that none of us had much choice in our present circumstances."

Laidan bit her lip, flicked her gaze dismissively over all of them. "I will swear then." And so she repeated the words. Garan was still reeling though. Why was she behaving this way?

As Garan walked through the Way Gate, he wondered if Brill and Danton had been required to make similar oaths. They, at least, knew about Nils and the Travel Ways but had not seen the wonders of

Barrahiem. Yet they knew of its existence and knew its name. There had been so many chores to do before they left Trithorn Peak that any number of things could have happened with the two rebels without Garan's knowledge, so he left off fretting about it.

The other side of the Way Gate did not appear too different from the Way they were in. When Nils turned on a light, Garan found that instead of the gray nothingness of the Ways, there were smooth, dull walls. Garan touched one with his fingers and it was definitely stone. At his feet was rubble and dust.

Nils took the lead, explaining as he went. "We must travel this stair for an hour or so. The closer gates have been damaged and do not function. Soon you will behold the wonder that is Barrahiem." He paused and looked over his shoulder. The look Nils shared with Salinda was filled with joy. He really was excited to be bringing her home with him.

Now, on the verge of seeing an underground city that had been built before Ruel had split, Garan found his mind was still full of Laidan. Yet he couldn't blame her for her opinion of him. He was a brute, big and clumsy, especially in comparison to Brill, who was more the gentleman. What did Garan know, except what he had learned from books? His rescue from Vanden had been fraught with mistakes. That Laidan was saved at all was due to the assistance of the rebels, Brill and Danton. No wonder she thought more of Brill than she did of him. Garan's pace increased and soon he outstripped the women and drew closer to Nils. It was then that the Hiem came upon the stair. He lectured them all on how to descend safely and led the way. Salinda placed herself at the end, leaving Laidan to follow close behind Garan. The stairs were steep, leading them down into the depths of Margra and toward the city of Barrahiem.

Garan expected another door before they would see the city proper. However, the roof above the stairs gradually rose and leveled out so that the stairway began to sink in a cavernous chamber. The surroundings brightened at the same time and Garan found that he barely noticed when Nils extinguished his lamp. As he had been concentrating on keeping his footing, Garan was surprised when he looked up and saw that Nils had paused on a landing. The Heim waited patiently, gaze glued to Garan's face. Then Garan took in the vista around him. Sloping down to the edge of a large, dark lake was a city. It appeared to be carved out of one piece of stone as each building rose from the surface to nestle between, above or next to its neighbor.

Ornate swirls carved into the cornices could be seen through the doorway ahead, and the walls glowed with a fine web of light all their own. It was a plant, Garan could see. Garan ran a finger along the growth closest to him. Small nodules emitted light.

"That is the shuwai," Nils explained. "Within the city itself there are lamps, though these are fewer than they were." Nils's silver-colored eyes passed over him, and Garan was moved by the sadness he detected in them. "Once the glow of the city lights reached far up into the stairway. I remember that I had to blink away the glare. The city was so full of life and light then."

Garan found he could not move from the spot. Laidan elbowed past him and made her way down the stairs after Nils. This was a city from the world before. It was a marvel even after all these years had passed. Garan found it hard to process, even to breathe.

"Salinda..."

Salinda stood by his side and breathed deeply. "I know, Garan. If this is what the Hiem cities were like, what were our own ancestors' cities like? Imagine it. If we can get Nils in the mood, he might read you an account of a visit to one of the greater cities before Ruel fell."

"Truly? At this moment I realize how little I know of the world. And you say Nils lived back then, more than a thousand years ago. What a wonder it must have been."

Salinda nodded, a smile playing about her mouth. "A remarkable man. That's Nils. And he can help us find a way to fight the rogue asteroid too. I'm sure of it. He doesn't know how yet, but I am certain the answer is here within the vaults of knowledge he guards. The cadre hints at it."

Garan tried to absorb that information. The cadre was an alien thing to him, a concept he had heard about, but not quite understood. "And Laidan's cadre? Can she master its secrets yet?"

Salinda moved past him and put her foot on the first stair before pausing. She swung her dark braid over her shoulder and peered up at him with her brown, almond-shaped eyes. "We are making slow progress, Garan. I am hoping that now Brill has gone she can focus on other things...well, actually I am hoping she can focus on the cadre specifically."

She turned and walked down the stair. He followed after her, not daring to ask what he feared to know. "So do I."

When he was abreast of her, she spared him a quick look. "You needn't worry about Brill and Laidan. Brill is much too dedicated to his cause to take a wife. She is young. If she had an infatuation for him, she will get over it. I kept her busy and hopefully out of trouble until he left with Danton."

Garan nodded. Brill was young too, possibly too young to consider the responsibility of a wife. Then again, Garan was only two years older, and he would marry Laidan right then if he could or if she wanted it. He was sure he could do his work and have a wife too, despite what the Master Elder had warned. Sure, she was angry with him now, but she could be so nice and sweet, and she was so beautiful Garan's heart had almost stopped when she first smiled at him. If only she would smile at him now.

By the time they had caught up with the others, they were in the entry to the city proper. Here the ornate carvings and murals abounded. Laidan had obviously overcome her pout, because she was exclaiming excitedly over the beauty of the place to Nils. Garan thought he detected in Nils a hint of pleasure at Laidan's praise. A quick glance at Salinda's mouth spread in a smile made him think that he hadn't been too far wrong in his guess. She was beaming happily, a light in her eyes as she watched Nils and Laidan. The sight of Nils acting so normal allowed him to relax. Now less anxious, he would be able to explore this place and learn. Just then, Laidan turned toward him, and after looking so radiant and happy, her face became an angry mask. He looked away, wondering whether it was just his presence that repelled her or the fact that he was not Brill.

As they walked through the city, with its empty houses and earth-tinged odor, Garan nicknamed it to himself, the city of the dead. The thought that so many had died here seemed more immediate and more real now that he was here. He couldn't really explain why. Perhaps because the city was closed in.

On the surface of Margra the wind and the rain and the years had eroded the presence of those who had died in the millions. It made the evidence of their existence less. Here, it was as if the Hiem had walked the streets only yesterday. The echoes of their lives abounded in their houses, and their artworks adorned the walls. It was not easy to forget.

They continued along a wide pathway bordered on one side by a filigree fence. Garan's gaze traveled between the rows of houses as they passed. Nils explained that the grouping of homes were called nodes that in his time had been occupied by family groups. He saw that pathways were clear of debris, except for the layer of dust. Gateways to the nodes of houses were richly carved, each with its own distinct design but still harmonious overall. Perhaps the same hand had etched out the pattern. He wanted to ask about it but he thought that might be a little too personal, a little too difficult for Nils to answer.

Nils was silent as he walked, as if the place overbore him to such an extent that speech was a desecration. Salinda moved closer to him, placing her hand on his elbow. Garan frowned and kept walking along behind.

Laidan, now enlivened by her arrival in the city, turned her attention to the Hiem and his despondency. "What's the matter?" Laidan asked as she swept her long hair behind her ear. Garan was glad that her mood had lifted to such an extent that she noticed what was going on around her. Nevertheless, he winced at her apparent lack of tact.

Salinda held out a hand to Laidan and beckoned her closer. "Nils is wary of bringing you here. He even had trouble adjusting to my presence. He is worried about the repercussions. If his people were alive they would not approve."

"Are we not welcome then?" Laidan asked.

"It is not that. Many of the things you will see here, artifacts from the Hiem and the Moon Binders, the archives, and the abodes of the Hiem, have not been seen by 'Sundwellers' before," Salinda explained.

"Sundwellers?" Laidan asked.

"Moon Binders?" Garan said at the same time.

Garan drew closer, keen to hear Salinda's explanation. "Sundwellers is the Hiem name for our forefathers, the people who lived above before Ruel split. It is best you know this now. Nils does not believe we are as worthy as our forefathers. Consider this when he says things that you may find insulting. Ignore it. That is his way."

"Oh?" Laidan glanced at Nils, who had continued to climb, though slowly. Garan suspected that the sound of their voices would have carried anyway, and Nils would not be ignorant of Salinda's words. He had not contradicted her.

"And Moon Binders?" Garan reminded Salinda.

Salinda frowned. "Ah...them I don't know much about. But Nils tells me that they built this city originally, and they were responsible for much of the technology and many of the artifacts that are within and below the city. I do not know if they left things on the surface too. They were either dead or departed when Magol and the first settlers arrived on Margra. It is said that it was they who bound Ruel in bands of power, hence their name."

"Bound Ruel in what?" Garan was surprised. He had not heard this tale.

Salinda laughed lightly. "I know it is hard," she said as she resumed her ascent "We cannot see Ruel as it once was and the stories we have are littered with inaccuracies. But Nils tells me he saw them with his own eyes—red bands of power, binding the moon together. It was the snapping of these that destroyed the moon and created Shatterwing."

Garan's mouth dropped open. "Such power. It barely seems possible that a moon could be held together with...I don't know what you call it." He took two strides and was then abreast with Salinda. "The mass, the calculations. No one at the observatory would have considered such a thing feasible. And you say Nils saw that?"

Salinda patted him on the forearm. "There will be time to talk of this and more later."

Laidan walked past them, lifting the hem of her gown so that she could take longer strides. Pausing for a second to take in the view around her, she spared Garan a pointed look and then turned away to follow Nils. They had passed along a wide balcony that afforded views across the dark lake and were now climbing up a hill.

So many new concepts. Garan fell in behind. He tried putting the thought that the city was underground out of his head. It was as if the city was a weight in his mind. Being underground had never bothered him previously, as he had often explored the caves around Trithorn Peak. But now he found he longed for open spaces, to take in the sunset over the Duggan mountain range from the peak, to feel the wind whip up his hair and cloak. Perhaps it was because they were so deep underground that he knew he would not be able to find his way out. It was not merely a retracing of steps as it had been when exploring caves.

There was something else within the city that affected him. That weight was definitely there; he could feel it growing. A presence? A feeling? He shrugged it off. Perhaps he needed to rest. It had been a long day, after all. He had not slept much except for a nap in the Ways and the muscles in his back and legs were aching from their long walk.

When they reached the Barr node, as Nils referred to it, Salinda stood next to a small round door and invited them in for tea.

For ease of communication, they decided that Laidan and Garan should inhabit two little houses in the same node as Nils and Salinda. It seemed odd that with a whole city to inhabit Nils would want them so close. Garan supposed Nils had his reasons, and they overrode the Hiem's need for privacy. "I have prepared abodes for you. They are similar so feel free to choose," Nils said, inclining his head. "But first you will share some refreshment with us."

"Thank you," Garan replied, casting his eye on the other round houses before approaching the door to Nils's and Salinda's abode. "Refreshments would be most welcome."

Laidan went ahead of him. The odd doorway gave Garan pause. He tried to squeeze through the short and narrow opening, but thought he was too big for it. For a moment he was stuck, then with a final grunt he was through. Once inside, the space was large enough, but he feared the daily reminder of his own awkwardness and bulk would be dispiriting.

"The door is that way for cultural reasons," Salinda explained as she offered him a place to sit.

"Cultural reasons?"

Nils answered. "The small doors remind us to be humble."

Garan nodded and rubbed his elbow, which he had caught on his way through the door. "I will be reminded often then."

Salinda chuckled and then looked him up and down. "Yes, I had not thought. Will you manage, do you think?"

Garan grinned. "Yes. Or I will need to diet."

Laidan made a quip about wanting to see that and Garan's head shot up. Was that the beginning of friendly banter?

Then after a meal of dried fruit and some desultory conversation, Salinda suggested they get some sleep.

Nils let Laidan choose which abode she wanted, leaving Garan to take the remaining one. Laidan chose quickly and slipped easily through the doorway to go to her bed. There was little difference in the houses. Garan stared at his own abode for a while and took in the general surroundings. He noted that the light stayed the same whether it was night or day, and wondered if he would be able to sleep. After wiggling his way through the doorway, he unpacked his things and undressed. He found a washroom, and when he had sluiced the dust from his body, he settled down into the bed.

Garan lay awake for some time, staring at the smooth walls and ceiling and watching the play of the soft, bluish light filtering in through the windows. Already he was missing the observatory. He missed his friends. He worried about his duties and the watch on the rogue asteroid. When Salinda was done with him, he would go back. When he had learned all that he needed, and Salinda understood the nature of the power of crystals, he could relax.

As Garan closed his eyes, he told himself to think about the day of his return so that he would feel comforted. But then other thoughts intruded, exciting his mind all over again. He considered all the things he could learn in Barrahiem, and the mysteries that Nils could show him. Even then he had new ideas and information swirling around in his mind, teasing him to wakefulness. Then he knew, with a trace of sadness, that he would not be the same man when he returned to Trithorn Peak. At least, he hoped he would be a better and wiser man.

☙☙☙☙

Laidan rolled over on her bed and cried into her pillow. She could have been a princess—someone special, someone people looked up to. Instead she was here. Even though this city was the most amazing sight she had seen, she could not be happy with her predicament. It wasn't fair. It was never fair. And it was getting worse.

Before bed, Salinda had told her that she had to work much harder on her exercises. Laidan had already put her best effort into the dull and repetitive things Salinda tried to get her to do. Try as she might she couldn't touch the cadre. She hadn't been able to since that night when they fought the Inspector. Something had snapped. She had tried to tell Salinda about it, but the daft women acted as if Laidan had been speaking nonsense. If that wasn't enough, Laidan was conscious of the way Garan looked at her. It made her skin crawl. She wanted only Brill's gaze—Prince Brill's gaze. Why did Garan have to be the one with all the power? Why couldn't it have been Brill? Then they could have been together in this awful place, and one day they could have been rulers of Duval. If only Brill would come back to her.

Her pillow was moist with the tears of her frustration. She was sure she could make Brill do anything. He was pliant and willing when she put her mind to it. But now he was out of her reach...it was all too hard.

Her body still remembered Brill's caress. She ached with the need to feel him touch her again. She wanted to re-live that wonderful feeling when her heart pounded and her womanhood throbbed, as she experienced blissful release. It was so much better than the fear and the trauma of her previous experience at the hands of Lenk and then the bandits. Once Thurdon died, her world had exploded. Her protection was gone. Her sense of the world was obliterated. She had become a thing. A scared creature who crawled from a bad situation to a worse one. In Brill's arms she felt whole, repaired. Now she would never feel unbroken again. Brill was not there to be with her, to comfort her. Would anyone else make her feel the same way? Then she remembered hiding with Garan, pressed up so close to him and feeling excited by the amount of wine she had taken and his, large, firm body. She had liked Garan then. He had kissed her in such a way as to make that feeling burn inside her.

Unfortunately, thinking romantically about Garan was out of the question. She was so angry at him; she couldn't even try to picture lovemaking with him. If he had done the right thing in the first place, she would not be alone in this bed right now. He should have put her first instead of wallowing in his own grief. She still smarted from the dressing down the Master Elder had given her. She piled all the blame on Garan, the inconsiderate brute. If she was to be denied her newfound pleasures with Brill, she would make sure Garan paid the price. He would wish he had never ever tried to kiss her. He would learn that he was far beneath her and that thinking of her at all had been the biggest mistake of his life.

Chapter Eleven

TO SARTELL

Brill woke before the sun was fully up. He lay in the crook of the branches he was perched on, listening to the river as it slowly oozed past. The occasional fish leaped clear of the water, leaving ripples in its wake. In the next tree, Danton still slept. Turning to look over his shoulder he saw that Mandin had already climbed down from her sleeping place. Danton had not mentioned the body to her, and Brill dared not breathe a word of it unless Danton gave him leave to do so. What if it was the woman's daughter?

They had traveled a fair way, only stopping well after darkness had fallen. The woman had been so exhausted it was all they could do to feed her and help her climb into a tree to sleep. The ground was too uneven to lie on comfortably as the tree roots furrowed the soil, breaking the surface all over the place. Not only that, but within the clefts and hollows lived creatures called mineus. They could deliver a nasty bite but tended not to climb. Danton had suggested the branches as an alternative. It also made being stumbled upon by other people less of a danger. It was easier to go unnoticed in a tree.

Brill climbed down and heard Danton stirring. He went to relieve himself, casting his gaze around for Mandin. Where had she got to? The sound of crunching roots and leaves alerted him to her approach. After washing by the river's edge he came up beside her and squatted down. Mandin had been busy gathering food from the nearby scrub and riverside. She had gathered nuts from the trees and young fern shoots from along the banks. There was enough food for all of them to have a reasonable breakfast. "I didn't know those nuts were edible," he commented after she passed him a handful.

"They are better roasted. Do we have time for a fire? They will be less bitter."

Brill looked up and caught Danton's attention. The rebel leader nodded before heading off to the river to clean himself up.

Brill grinned. "Looks like we do, but make it a small one."

Mandin nodded once and went to round up dry wood and kindling. Brill saw that she was very quick, having already scouted around for materials.

By the time Danton returned Mandin had started a small fire and was positioning the nuts in the outer ashes. She looked calm and relaxed and gave no sign of her exertions of the day before. Brill found his respect for her growing. He had to admit that Danton knew what he was doing. He wondered how he could learn to assess people in the way the rebel leader did. It was a reminder once again that he had a lot to learn.

Danton squatted near the fire and stared into space as he began to munch on a fern shoot. Mandin watched him silently for a few minutes. Then, with a quick sideways glance at Brill, she asked, "Will you tell me what you found yesterday? I can bear it."

Danton sucked on the fern shoot a little longer, and Brill knew he was weighing up the situation. Brill lowered his gaze to his hands and played with his fingers, his heart heavy.

"Tell me what your daughter looks like," Danton said suddenly.

Mandin swallowed once. "She has short dark hair and fair skin. Her eyes have traces of green in them and for a young girl she is quite well formed. I mean, she has the beginnings of breasts."

Danton reached forward and picked out another fern shoot. This one he ran along his teeth while he thought things through. "We found a body. She had long hair and dark skin. She had not begun to mature. She was small and thin."

Mandin's gaze was riveted to Danton's. She let out a slow breath, as if she had been holding it for a long time. "Sounds like young Sindia. Mellie's daughter. She was only nine years old. Did they..."

Danton nodded and tears welled in Brill's eyes. The image of that ravaged body, left to the insects and creatures of the scrub, filled his mind. Would that they'd had time to burn her and set her spirit free to return to the source. But Danton had been right; they couldn't risk the delay or the possibility that the pyre would be detected. The shame of her death and lack of decent burial would stay with him a long time.

Mandin asked no more questions. After they had roasted all the nuts and eaten them, she put out the fire with river water. Danton gave them all a ration of dragon wine. The power of the wine thrummed through Brill's veins. More and more he was becoming sensitized to its power. It was more noticeable the less wine he had. The layers of skepticism were almost completely eroded. He had seen too much now to deny what Salinda had told him so many months ago. That humans needed the dragons to survive and that dragon wine was necessary for them to live.

They headed off, keeping to the river and following the trail of the rebels. With her local knowledge, Mandin was well placed to show them what was edible. Every day she became more and more resilient and less tired. Despite himself, Brill was warming to her.

Then when they neared the town of Yourton, they lost the distinct trail of the Infra-pact rebels in the increased traffic along the river. Here footprints were many and the trail was trodden into the river mud.

They spotted the town of Yourton as the sun poked fingers of light over the horizon at dawn a few days after finding the dead girl. In Yourton, Danton sent Mandin into town to scout around. Danton gave her money to buy provisions and a change of clothes for herself. It had been her idea. Mandin was less likely to be identified as a rebel than the men, and more likely to hear gossip if she went alone and perhaps hung about in the markets.

☙☙☙☙☙

Mandin crept through the streets of Yourton as the early sunlight dribbled light over the cobblestones. Noises of the morning surrounded her, growing louder and more frequent—a mother calling a child, the clink of a burden beast's hooves, a hammer clanging. A man pulling a cart of dried dung to market turned the corner ahead of her, the cart wheels rattling. Smoke from dung fires wafted along the streets in wispy, pungent streaks. It was strange walking through a town again after what had happened in Vanden. Yourton was larger than her home, but it wasn't only that. There were intact houses and the normal, everyday sounds of people within them.

From memory the market opened early before the day grew warm and the insects came to attack the meat and the fruit. Stepping into the shadow of a doorway, Mandin put down her backpack and checked her clothes, tugging her skirts and rearranging the gathering to hide stains. Using a bit of spit, she smoothed her stray hair and reformed her bun. Before they set out from Vanden she had secured a clean apron for herself. Difficult when your house had been sacked and burned. Yet there had been one under a pile of smashed furniture. Town and village people wore aprons. Clothes were not easy to come by generally, so keeping them clean was necessary. With one last check of her clothing, she was able to continue her mission. She was not elegant but at least she was respectable. A slight grin showed on her face. Mission...she was a rebel now, bent on finding those girls.

The coin Danton had given her made the pose of searching for produce in the market more realistic. Yet first things first: she would seek out a seamstress. There was bound to be something more suitable for cross-country travel than her homespun, country skirt.

Tables were being set up. A few of the stallholders looked up at her approach. She knew she was being assessed and tugged her backpack higher. She looked too poor to be propositioned by the sellers. That was a relief as she didn't want to draw too much attention to herself. She was already a stranger. Outside the bakery was a table spread with freshly baked rolls. The smell of yeasty bread lured Mandin to assuage her hunger.

"How much?" she asked the baker's boy who had returned to the table with a pile of coarse grain loaves.

"How many?" he asked.

"One of those bread rolls." She pointed to the steaming pile.

He carefully placed the batch he was carrying one by one on the table. Then he selected one for her.

"One tinker," he said as he held out his hand for the coin. The other held the roll, ready to be handed over. The lad was suspicious of her.

Mandin probed the coins she held in her hand for the little coin the boy wanted. The bread roll was neither cheap nor expensive. She deposited the coin in his outstretched hand and snaffled the bread roll in her own. Walking away, she inhaled the scent of it and picked the bread apart small piece by small piece to lengthen the pleasure of eating it.

She wandered around, looking at the stalls as the plaza filled up around her. Her first hope of seeing the girls for sale was soon dashed. There were no slavers in evidence. Nor was there any sign of slaves inhabiting the town. Most people were dressed as she was in village attire, though some were dressed more richly or in city clothes.

Slaves usually wore rags and had leashes around their necks. She could see no one like that there. Vanden had had a few slaves so she knew what to look for. Danton had filled her in on the rest.

Brushing breadcrumbs from her fingers, she spied the seamstress she had been looking for. Hanging above the woman's stall was an array of secondhand clothes. Mandin did a walk-through of the other stalls before approaching. She needed to check if there was any competition. That was important for her bargaining power. She nodded to a few stallholders as she passed by their stalls of hanging pots, mounds of fruit, chunks of meat on hooks. Farther on, she found a middle-aged man with a large stomach who also sold secondhand clothes. She asked him if he also did repairs or allowed trade-ins. It was her intention to trade in her own clothes to reduce the price of the ones she wanted.

"Cash is all I take, mistress," he said without looking at her as he rearranged clothes on hangers and unpacked others.

Appearing to be casual in her intentions, Mandin made her way back to the stall of the seamstress, sliding through the bustle and flow of the market. An old woman carrying a basket slipped by her, without touching, without looking. A child ran past with a wooden whistle, blowing high-pitched sounds. Other women picked over the fruit stall, carefully selecting morsels. It was so normal and yet alien to her. Vanden hadn't been as it should for a long time, not since Lenk killed his brother and took power. Now that she looked around, she found she craved normality—the simple, hard life of eking out an existence without the stress of warlords, rebels or a prince's ambitions. It was a dream, though. This town would have similar issues, tyranny in some shape or form that she couldn't see because she was an outsider. If she lived there, she would come to understand it in time. Now her life had irrevocably changed, just as she had changed.

Around the campfire the previous night, Danton had talked to her about what he had seen in his travels and the dire straits the world was in. She believed him, even though it was all too dreadful to understand. If she spent any time thinking about it, she wouldn't want to live. All she could do was focus on what was in front of her. All she could do was find Eneit and save her. That was all that was in her power. It was her only remaining purpose in life.

Saving the world—that was impossible. Brill had confirmed Danton's words about the state of the world. He seemed bent on doing something about it. The lad had a way about him. If you listened to him long enough you could believe that he could redeem the world and that it was worth doing so. Never before had someone made her realize how much her life was centered on herself—her aim had been surviving her life in Vanden and caring for her family. Wider issues had not made an impact on her until she was faced with the loss of everything. There was no hiding from it anymore. Her young daughter was to be sold into prostitution. She had no choice but to face the world and battle the evil that threatened to swamp everything.

Mandin found herself standing alone in front of the stall. The crowd she had been mingling with had dispersed. Had she been daydreaming?

"Mistress?" The seamstress was an ancient, wrinkled old woman, with hooked fingers and bent shoulders. "What can I do ya?"

Mandin stepped forward, her gaze assessing the clothes hanging above and around the stall. "Well...I am seeking a new set of clothes. I want to trade these." She tugged on her skirt. "They are dirty but the cloth is good. They were new last summer."

The old woman peered at her, squinting as she looked her up and down. "An' what clothes would you be wantin' then if these'n not good 'nough?"

"I want trousers, like a man, and a shirt too. I want them brown or pale green so I don't stand out."

"An' where ye goin' if ya wanna look like that?"

"That be none of your business...but I'll tell you." She leaned in closer, realizing the woman was more likely to loosen her tongue if Mandin did so first. "I'm traveling to the capital."

"Really? Ya mean downriver to Sartell?"

"Well, that's the only capital there is, isn't there? Or is there something I should know?" Capitals did move. There may have been a revolution or some such. "Did something happen?"

The old woman laughed and flapped a dismissive hand. "Nah. I can see yer up to my tricks." She started to sift through the piles of clothing she had. "Mmm. I might have somethin' that will do for ya. Although I'll have to do a bit a' mendin'. Do ya 'ave time to be measured? It may take a while. A few hours at least."

"I've got the time if the clothes are right...and the price is reasonable considering the exchange."

They bargained on price for another ten minutes. Mandin was surprised at how wily the old woman was, and how chatty. After submitting to being measured for a pair of mid-brown trousers and a slightly lighter-colored beige shirt, she rearranged her clothing. The old woman put aside the clothes she had chosen, and Mandin was preparing to leave when the old woman called out to her. "Ya know," she said, "if ya want a new look ya should get a haircut. Try Maisie."

Mandin's brows furrowed. A haircut? An excellent idea. She would not have thought of it. Scandalous at home to cut one's hair. But home was no more. "Maisie?"

"She a granddaughter o' mine. She's not set up in the market, mind. She be on Nestler's Row."

"Daughters." Mandin sighed loudly. "I be lookin' for mine."

"Really? How young she be?"

"My daughter is about ten years old, but she looks older, poor thing." Mandin cupped a hand near her breasts.

"Yes. I know what ya mean...girls that are pretty and look older are in for a heap of trouble."

"Been any trouble like that around here?"

The old woman tilted her head and studied her. Then she looked around casually, but Mandin suspected the old woman didn't want to be seen talking to her. "Best ya get yer hair done," the woman said in a loud voice.

Mandin nodded, understanding the message. Out here in the market, people would notice. In a place where women got prettied up, no one would notice the gossip. "So Maisie cuts hair?"

"Yes, and other stuff too to make ya look pretty. Though ya be wantin' none of that wearin' men's clothes. Maisie likes to talk a lot and so do her clients."

Mandin tugged on her bun. She hesitated. It would be like cutting off her old life. The old woman was right. What point was there in dressing like a village woman now? Who cared? She'd be dressed like a man so she may as well cut her hair and look like one too. It would be easier to look after on the road, for starters.

The old woman was good with her directions and the town's layout had a certain kind of logic to it. Maisie's place was fairly easy to find, even when Mandin took two wrong turns before an old man sitting in the sun with a hat over his face corrected her. The houses were numbered but not in order.

In the center of the town there wasn't a prince's mansion; instead there was the governor's residence. All the streets radiated out from it in concentric circles. Laneways and larger roads dissected them like wheel spokes.

The door to Maisie's place was short and thin, more like an afterthought than a proper entrance. When Mandin went inside she could understand why. The room was large and had another door, which presumably led to the rest of the residence. The street door had been cut in later to give the family privacy. The building workmanship was poor. Mandin hoped the haircut was going to be better.

There were three other women sitting in chairs waiting to be served. One had wet hair and another had mud piled up over her face. Mandin was taken aback at first and then she realized it was some kind of beauty treatment. She shook her head. It was probably river mud scented with oils. What astonishing things women would do in the pursuit of beauty!

"May I help you?" asked a girl, who looked no older than sixteen. Mandin's gaze lowered and she noted the lass was at least six months' pregnant.

"I'm looking for Maisie; her grandmother sent me here for a haircut."

The girl's eyes lit up. "Oh, Nani? That is so good of her. I'll give you a special price."

Mandin smiled, knowing the special price was probably the normal price that everyone else paid. She couldn't imagine the girl's regular customers putting up with discounts for out-of-towners.

"Thank you. I'd appreciate it."

Mandin took her seat to wait her turn. She listened to the desultory conversation around her and worked her way into it as skillfully as she could. "Nice town you have here," she commented as the woman under the mud mask was revealed. She was younger than Mandin and didn't look in need of beauty treatments.

"Why, thank you. We think so. Are you not from around here?"

"I'm just passing through. But I've been here before, trading. No slaves in evidence here. Makes the place seem prettier and tidier."

"Yes...there are a few, but people tend to treat them well."

"The other week we had a nasty lot come through trying to push some young girls on us," the woman with the wet hair interjected.

The woman having her faced cleaned of mud shuddered. "How scared people were. Such desperate men."

"No luck selling them then?" Mandin asked carefully, her gaze shifting lazily across the room. She needed to appear disinterested.

"No. We're a respectable town."

The wet-haired woman smiled knowingly.

It took a great deal of control to keep up the facade of disinterestedness. Mandin fought to keep her hope from soaring and her expression bland. "Sneak one in, did they?" she asked casually.

The smiling woman nodded and touched her nose. "Not common knowledge, I dare say. But I heard they sold one of the girls so that they could buy passage to Sartell."

"I suppose they were well-used little slatterns," Mandin prompted.

"Not that I heard. Don't know who bought the girl, but my Jinny did say she saw a new girl at the well near Governor's Lane."

The mud mask woman stood up and was readying herself to leave. "I wouldn't pay too much heed to Finzy's gossip. It was on the other side of town and it was the grain merchant, Cressley, who purchased her. He needed some help sewing sacks for grain."

Finzy, who was obviously the woman with the wet hair, lifted her nose and turned her face away. It appeared the two were rival gossips.

"Are you ready now, ma'am?" Maisie asked. "How would you like it done?"

Mandin sat in the chair offered and told Maisie that she wanted her hair cut short to make her look younger. She found it hard to sit still, because she was dying to find the merchant to see which of the Vanden girls had been sold. It was too much to hope it was her Eneit. The girl was too young and pretty to be sold to a merchant for manual labor. It was to Sartell she was bound, Mandin was sure. Yet she must speak to this girl as she should have some word of her Eneit—some inkling of hope to keep Mandin on the trail.

The seamstress had her clothes ready when she returned to the market in the early afternoon. In a makeshift closet Mandin changed out of her clothes and exchanged them for the new ones. The pants were quite tight. They hugged her bottom more than she had expected. *How come pants do not look like that on men?* she wondered. The old woman explained that she had made the trousers adjustable at the waist, just in case she needed to pull them in tighter. Tighter? Her shirt was a short tunic, which was snug too. Pulling it over her generous breasts was difficult but she liked how it looked. Luckily the seamstress liked to talk, too, and so after completing her transaction, she gave Mandin some very precise directions to the merchant Cressley's place of business and residence.

Mandin waited until sundown before she approached Cressley. She was able to fill in the time by buying supplies and her knapsack was full. So was her stomach. Some kind of meatball in sauce was the culprit. They had been cheap but filling. Cressley was locking up his shop when Mandin approached. The man was around fifty and his nicely trimmed beard was speckled with gray. He did a double take when she walked up and greeted him. She no longer looked like a village woman or a local.

"What can I do for you?" he said pleasantly.

"I wondered if I could talk to you about the girl you bought." His brow furrowed and he looked around, ensuring that they had not been overhead.

"How did you hear about that?"

"This place has some effective gossips." She held his gaze. It was time for her to tell the truth. She sensed that nothing else would work with this man. "I'm on the trail of a number of girls who were stolen from Vanden farther upriver. We have tracked them here."

"We?"

"Me and some friends of mine. One of the girls is my daughter." She described her daughter to Cressley, and he shook his head. "Not the one I have, and can't say I've seen the one you describe. They brought them out one at a time. They were all so pitiful I picked the halest-looking of the three."

"Do you know how many they had and where they were bound?"

He was shaking his head again. "No. I saw three girls and no more.

None of them sounds like your daughter, I'm afraid. Can't say I heard Torrens and Beck mention any place specific they'd be headin' but there's only one place they can go downstream. Sartell."

Mandin nodded as she listened and memorized the names the rebels had used. Danton would need that information. He was right about the destination. "Can I speak to your girl? I don't wish to interfere, but perhaps she can tell me something about my daughter."

He gazed up at his sign, avoiding her gaze. "I'm not sure. Don't want you upsetting the lass. It has taken us all this time to settle her down. Barely spoke a word or ate anything for days after we took her in."

"Please," Mandin said, surprised to find she was on the verge of falling to the man's feet and weeping. "It could be the difference between life and death. Those bastards are taking them to Sartell to sell as prostitutes. You have saved this girl from that fate. Please help me save my daughter from the same."

His gaze was full on her then. "Very well, but only a few words. At the first sign of distress, you leave. I'll go and speak to her first. She may not agree to see you."

Mandin nodded. "It will be as you say. I thank you."

᥆᥆᥆᥆᥆

After Mandin had departed that morning, Danton began cursing roundly.

"What is it?" Brill asked.

"It's Merl. He should be here but he is not." Brill didn't know the specifics, but Danton had split his band, some to follow the wine while others were to meet up with him later. Danton had said it was need-to-know only, and Brill had agreed. No man could resist torture for too long before he broke; Brill knew that from personal experience. If you knew nothing you could betray no one.

"Perhaps he went with Stinger and the others after the wine?"

"Maybe, or perhaps he went after the first load that never went to Vanden. I don't like it. He would have left someone behind to meet us if he'd gone on, or he would have left signs if he hadn't had anyone to spare, but there is nothing. I know we have been an age. Maybe they gave up on us." Danton shook his head and furrowed his eyebrows. "But that's not like Merl. What could have happened?"

Brill raked his gaze over their surroundings. "When I go out again searching for signs of the rebels, I'll take care to look for Merl's signals. A different set of eyes might help." Danton's men used particular patterns of rocks and twigs to leave messages. If Merl had had to leave in a hurry, he would have followed that routine and left something behind. "If he's left a sign, I'll find it."

Danton's expression lightened and then he nodded once, before crouching down and keeping an eye on the happenings around them.

Keeping out of sight, Danton and Brill kicked their heels on the east side of the town for most of the morning. Later, as the heat of the day forced many to shelter indoors, Danton sent Brill to scout around the pier, instructing him to find out what the various charges were for a berth on one of the barges, and their departure times. The rebel needed to remain hidden due to his distinctive one eye. Danton hadn't said that they were going to take a transport downriver to Sartell, but Brill thought the rebel leader wanted to be prepared for any contingency. Both Danton and Brill thought the rebels would head to Sartell, because it was the best place to sell the girls. The city was renowned for its slave markets. Though he had visited Sartell on occasion, Brill had yet to see one. Once or twice he had visited as a prince, and therefore the seedier part of the city had been denied him. With a frown, he recalled the last time he had visited as a rebel prisoner. He'd not seen much then, either. It was all a blur of pain and bewilderment.

Brill walked along the river's edge, skulking around the piers and barges made of rusted metal and rotting wood. Amid the grunts of the haulers and the smattering of gossip of the overseers, he could discern nothing of interest. He listened in on many conversations and all seemed to be ordinary. Trying to remain circumspect, he asked a few questions but as he was an obvious outsider he didn't learn much. He was reluctant to head back to Danton with nothing to say of the rebels or his men. As he had been gone for a few hours he thought it best to check if Mandin had brought word. It was late in the day when he found Danton scratching at the scar tissue round his empty eye socket and staring into space. He turned his dark eye toward Brill.

Danton didn't say a word when Brill shook his head.

Near sunset, Mandin had still not returned. "Are you sure she will come back? Maybe she has found her daughter or a safe haven and no longer wants to track down these rebels."

Danton scowled at him and then with a heavy breath let his face relax. "You have to learn to trust. Mandin may not return until tomorrow for good reason. It is likely she is on the trail of some information and has to work harder to find it. Source forbid that she is in trouble. For all we know the rebels have holed up there and might have recognized her."

Brill understood Danton's censure and the rightness of it. "How will we find out?" Brill asked, not being able to meet Danton's gaze.

Danton looked longingly at the town as lights came on in the streets and windows.

"If she is not back within an hour of sunrise tomorrow, you will go in and find out what has happened. From memory Yourton isn't backward or a witch-burning place so it should be relatively safe. Mandin said she has been here before to trade so she was fairly confident that she could scout around without arousing too much suspicion."

Brill nodded and pointed at a derelict-looking barge in the process of being loaded. "We could get passage on that. The owner's prices were reasonable and he has room. He leaves at sunrise tomorrow."

"We only go on the river if we find the rebels have. I don't like the prospect that they might have. The river is too well watched—particularly on the regular trade routes. Sartell levies taxes and the customs officials are very zealous at collecting. Only someone with the Inspector's connections could get around them. I guess this lot either has those connections or they'll avoid the river and its officials altogether."

Brill nodded his understanding. "So the rebels could head all the way into Sartell or deviate on the way, thereby making their trail harder to follow."

"My thought exactly. They may go on foot or travel on the river part of the way. Then if I were them, I'd take an alternative overland route. Either way we'll have to be ready to identify and then pursue the correct route when and if it comes up. The river branches out into a delta about a day's ride downriver. There are five main channels deep enough for boats and barges. We'd need specifics on what water course those rebels took. Our best chance is if they split here and some continued on foot. Following the ones on foot will lead us to the other rebels and the wine stash eventually."

Brill stood up and dusted the mud from his trousers. There was maybe another hour of light. "I'll do another scout around then. Just to check the lay of the land." Danton opened his mouth to say something but Brill added, "I need to work off my fidgets."

Danton nodded, a smile quirking the corner of his mouth. "Yes, you do that."

ᴄᴊᴄᴊᴄᴊᴄᴊ

Brill sprinted along a well-worn path along the river's edge, hoping to make it farther than he had last time. He had found no trace of the rebels, and that worried him. Danton did not have to voice his fear—that the rebels had bought passage downriver, taking the girls with them. If they had, it meant that the Infra-pact rebels did indeed have connections in high places and they could pass through river customs with impunity. That would complicate things no end.

Later as Brill made his way back to Danton's resting place, clouds obscured the moonrise and he had to take more care where he placed his feet. His had been a fruitless search for clues.

He heard voices as he approached and breathed a sigh of relief when he saw that Mandin had finally returned. In the light of the campfire, he saw she had swapped her village skirt and blouse for what looked like men's clothes. Her hair had been cut to a short bob, too. It made her look younger and fitter. She looked more like a rebel than a village woman now. Brill grinned widely at her.

"Mandin says the rebels left here two days ago on a river barge. They had eight of the girls with them. One was sold in the town to pay their passage. Mandin says the girl was bought by a merchant."

"Did you talk to her?" Brill asked.

Mandin nodded. "She says she is fine and that the men didn't touch her. But I know she is lying. She is too scared to say what really happened. The merchant's family is treating her well, at least. She sews sacks for grain. I think she is traumatized and shamed by what has happened to her. She begged me not to tell her family where she was, only that she was dead. I didn't have the heart to tell her that her family was gone."

"Did she tell you anything about Eneit?" Brill asked. When he saw Mandin's expression he wished he hadn't. Her face crumpled and she let out a dry sob, as if there were no more tears left in her.

"Yes," she managed to get out. "She is alive. That was all the girl would say. She seemed so fragile I thought it best not to push her."

Danton scratched his beard. "We have the names of the rebels—Torrens and Beck. At least, the names they used here. There is no point in continuing on foot. We must take the passage Brill has found us in the morning. We will have to pick up the trail in Sartell."

Brill stepped forward to take the money Danton proffered. He and Danton had pooled what coin they had. It was enough. "I'll go and finalize the deal then," he said. Brill touched Mandin lightly on the shoulder. "We will find her. We will." Then he broke into a sprint and headed for the pier.

Part 2

Look for truth in other places because in wine there is only need

Chapter Twelve

A SOURCE OF POWER

Nils made haste to leave his abode before Salinda began teaching Laidan. He found he could not bear to be a witness to their interactions again. There was too much emotion and way too much noise for his liking. The conversation he could already hear began with: "I don't understand, Laidan. You could touch the cadre before. What has happened that you cannot do so now? I really don't see how you could lose the ability."

When he entered the main room, Laidan was standing with fists clenched. "It's not as if I don't try. I'm telling you, I can't do it."

Salinda put down a pot of Pardu tea on the low table without any of her usual calm. "Don't want to do it, more like," his mate replied with more bite that he had heard before.

Laidan burst into tears and collapsed on the sofa, arms arranged theatrically. Salinda sat down beside her, leaned over her knees and buried her head in her hands. Nils hesitated, unsure in this new situation whether he should leave or offer assistance. Coping with a mate was one thing; coping with a mate and a student quite another.

Nils crossed to the door, thinking it proper that he leave before he was noticed. Unfortunately, when he looked back, Salinda caught his eye and shook her head. Variations of this scene had played out every morning since the two young people had arrived. Salinda motioned for him to leave and he did, squeezing through the small doorway, once again reminding him to be humble.

"Oh, Nils, before you go," Salinda called after him.

Nils wriggled back into the room and drew himself up to his full height. Laidan ignored him, still engrossed in sniveling into the fabric of the sofa. Salinda grabbed a sack from the kitchen.

"You forgot this. Also, Garan..."

"Yes?"

"You were going to keep him company today."

Nils nodded. The boy was interesting, so this would not be a hard task. Nils considered that he had coped well with the intrusion of two extra persons into his life. They were not Hiem but he found them acceptable. He was drawn to Garan, who appeared to be quiet, thoughtful and very respectful. The young man showed promise, and as Salinda was so occupied with Laidan, Nils hoped to offer an invitation to Garan to enter the archives and explore the vaults today. He was sure Garan would enjoy the experience.

Portable lamp in hand, Nils waited by the door for Salinda's permission to leave. She had asked him to return so it was only polite to ensure that she was finished dealing with him. Laidan let out a renewed wail, which ceased when Salinda handed her some tea, which the girl took and sipped. Laidan's face was blotchy with red spots and her nose looked swollen from her tears. The girl drew in a ragged breath but didn't start leaking again. Salinda turned her head toward him and nodded. That was the signal he needed. He bent his head and eased out through the door, leaving Salinda to teach the girl what she could.

Nils was fascinated with this cadre Salinda and Laidan possessed. He did not understand it, but that did not mean he doubted its existence or even its importance. Nils had also witnessed Garan's power. He did not understand it either, but aspects of the use of crystals resonated with him because they echoed the use of technology of the past. The opportunity to discuss the Master Elder, and a particular book that the old man had mentioned as he died, also weighed in favor of the invitation to spend time with Garan. Jalen had mentioned a book written by Nils's grandsire, Trell. So it must be somewhere in the observatory or in the ruins of the old. Perhaps the boy could reveal something of his treks into the caves. Nils's own attempts had failed to uncover anything of use. Nils had high hopes of coaxing the boy on an excursion with him to the ruins of the old observatory.

Outside the abode, Garan was squatting beneath the long, draping strand of shuwai, apparently studying the peculiarities of the growth.

Nils approached, then quietly waited to be acknowledged. Still oblivious to Nils's presence, Garan stood up and circled the growth until he was facing Nils. After starting, he said, "Forgive me. I did not notice you standing there."

"What do you see when you look at the shuwai? What is it that fascinates you so?" Nils asked.

Garan angled his head to take in the shuwai growth again. He chewed his lip and then turned back to face Nils. "I'm not entirely sure. There is less light here than I am used to, but I think I see tiny creatures living within these filaments." He touched a strand carefully to show Nils what he meant.

Nils drew closer and peered at the shuwai that Garan was holding. "The creatures are known as shu. It is their droppings that sustain the lichen and allow it to glow. A symbiosis—one cannot survive without the other."

Garan let the growth go. "I see. It makes me wonder why it does not grow in the caves near the observatory. It would make mining crystals easier and traversing the caves more interesting. There would be so much to see with the light it gives—colors, formations, hazards..."

Nils kept his gaze steady. He needed to engage the boy rather than remaining aloof. This advice had been sagely provided by Salinda while they held each other in the night. "How do you take light into dark places? You explore caves yourself, do you not?"

"Yes. I have done. I use these." Garan reached into his pocket to show Nils a handful of broken pieces of crystal, which were a dull mauve. In among the larger pieces were small fragments.

Nils peered at the shards and then leveled his gaze on Garan. "You ignite them somehow with this sound you make, this articulation of power?"

Putting the broken pieces back into his pocket, Garan nodded. "Yes. Like in the scopes, only these are less powerful, and depending on what sounds you use the glow can be weaker and more sustained. Instead of an explosive release."

Nils found that his interest was piqued. Unfortunately, he could not make the sounds the young man made, nor could he see himself in a position to use the power of the crystals. The gift to do so was inherent in the boy. "If you are finished with your examination of the shuwai I would like to invite you to join me. I would show you a small section of the archives, depending on how much time there is available to us."

"Salinda does not require me?" His violet-colored eyes were dim in the light of the shuwai. Only in the sunlight did their color bloom. His brows were drawn low over his eyes, a sign that he was concerned, thought Nils.

Nils gestured with his arm in a wide arc, indicating the direction they should take, and answered, "Alas, she is still playing the battle of wills with your young friend and feels you may impede matters. I do not understand your ways well. Even so, it appears to me that things will reach an explosive point very soon. Your kind do not have the Hiem way of deliberating."

"Laidan can be difficult." The smile returned to the young man's face after a slight shrug. "I hope Salinda copes all right with her."

"Yes, I have noticed that peculiarity about Laidan often of late. It makes me grateful that fate brought me Salinda and no other female. She is...how can I say this...clever in how she handles me. I am conscious that she does so but I find I do not mind it."

Nils descended with Garan, stopping occasionally to answer Garan's questions. The functioning of the streetlamps, in particular, attracted the young man's attention. "It is such a shame that they are failing. If only we could find a way to fix them. Then the city would glow as it did before. Then your heart would be a little lighter, perhaps."

Nils was taken aback by the Sundweller's perceptiveness of Nils's state of mind. Was it intuition rather than observation? His suggestion, too, spoke of altruistic motivations. Why would Garan be interested in doing such a considerate deed for him? Until it was mentioned, Nils had no inkling such an idea would appeal to him or how apt it was for his situation. It could change his sorrow and grief into something else—remembrance or reverence. A kernel of joy suddenly ripened and spilled out warmth inside of him. Was it possible? Nils was no technician, but the instructions for maintaining the lights were definitely written down somewhere and there were plenty of supplies for the repairs.

With a brightness in his eyes he lowered his head. "I like your idea and would like to explore it further if that is all right with you." The boy nodded and smiled shyly. "Now, if you come with me I will take you on a detour to the manufacturing area. It is not as interesting as the archives but we will find the necessary resources, one hopes, to decide if it is worth attempting to repair the streetlamps."

Nils had not ventured to the manufacturing area since his

awakening. He had little affinity for machines and equipment. The items he needed for his shroud were in good supply in his family's storage and archival area. The storage area where he was taking Garan had been a communal one and was large.

The door opened without difficulty. It had not been sealed with care as some others in the lower vaults had been. Garan's gaze grew keener as the door slid away. This was a most impressive space. The rear was not well illuminated as the overhead lamps had failed. There was limited shuwai to provide even the most basic level of light. Yet there was much in the first section to attract the young lad's attention.

"What are these?" Garan asked as he inspected a row of shelves, his hand ready to pick up a power unit.

"Please do not touch anything. I cannot be certain that there is nothing dangerous to your inquisitive hands. How would I explain your demise to Salinda?"

Garan's eyes widened and he withdrew his hand slowly. "Not easily, I dare say. I will be careful. I cannot promise that my hand will not stray where it should not. I have never seen anything like this in my life. You say this equipment came from before Ruel split—pre-Shatterwing?"

Nils let his gaze range over the shelves. "Yes, you could say that. Here are the remnants of a much more advanced world, its artifacts now lying useless and their purpose no longer understood."

Garan whistled to himself as he continued down a row while Nils stood by, considering his plan of action. All he had to do was discover the logic of this place. Lekuhl clan had had responsibility for this storage area. It was not a clan he had associated with previously. Who knew what arcane patterns they used. They were not archivist by tradition but a clan of maintenance workers and engineers; not well respected like his family had been.

A quick inspection of a few rows told him that he had no chance of understanding the filing methodology. Equipment seemed to be placed randomly—power units next to sweepers. He decided to check up on Garan, who had disappeared down one of the aisles.

When Nils located him, Garan was inspecting a pile of expended lamps on the floor between two rows of shelving. Nils blinked. Such disorder was disconcerting. No wonder he had had no desire to enter this place previously.

Before Nils could protest his actions, Garan had pulled one of the units apart and was laying out the components in front of him. Nils knelt and turned on his portable lamp, useful in a city whose technology was crumbling into decay, so that Garan could see better.

Considering the boy had not seen such technology before, Nils could not withhold a reprimand. "Why are you doing that? I told you not to touch things. You were fortunate that it did not harm you."

Garan grinned at him. "I am fine. It does not work so I thought it would be safe. If I break this down we should be able to deduce how it works and find the replacement parts on the shelves. This appears to be a power source of some kind." His finger prodded a sealed black cube and then he jerked his finger back. "'Tis still active."

"What do you mean? I did not see anything." Nils nudged the cube with his own hand and detected nothing.

He peered at Garan, wondering what was going on in the boy's mind. Garan reached out and touched the object again and hummed. Nils frowned. Could it be that the power Garan appeared to be able to wield was compatible with the energy sources used by the Hiem and the Moon Binders before them? How could that be? Who would have shared such mysteries with the Sundwellers? Trell? No, he would not have betrayed what it was to be a Hiem. Someone else? Or could it be similar by accident? Yet Nils found the thought disconcerting. He thought of his grandsire. Would Trell have shamed his family so? Was that why his last writings were hidden? If his kin had known of such a betrayal, that would have given them sufficient cause not to accept the works into the archives.

Garan looked up and regarded Nils silently, his dark brows forked above his nose.

"That is interesting. It must have a crystal inside of the cube. Nils?"

Nils nodded, unable to vocalize his thoughts.

Shrugging, Garan returned his attention to the components of the light, nudging them apart with the tips of his fingers and examining them closely. Garan grunted once or twice as he manipulated the parts, picking up a couple to view them at close range. This drew Nils's attention back to what the lad was doing. "Did your people mine crystals?" Garan glanced up at him as he spoke.

"Not that I know of. I believe the Hiem created the substance which powered these lamps. Perhaps the makeup is similar to the crystal you are used to working with."

Garan shrugged and began to reassemble the lamp. When the last piece of lamp was put in place it began to glow.

"What did you do? Did you put more energy in it?"

Garan scratched his head. "I do not know. Maybe this one was not exhausted. Let me try another."

Nils left Garan to his tinkering and went to survey the other shelves. When he saw parts that looked familiar to those Garan had identified, he gathered them up and piled them next to the boy. He supposed he should find a better place to work, but for now Garan appeared content on the floor.

After gathering sufficient for a morning's work, Nils returned to Garan's side. "So what have you discovered?"

In the lamp light, Garan appeared wild eyed. "I can re-energize the power source by touching it. Without even making a sound. 'Tis not my humming that excites the crystal within. 'Tis me, just as Salinda suspected."

"This is a good thing, is it not, to understand the nature of your gift?"

"Perhaps, but it changes everything I have ever known about myself. It throws me off center a bit. I ask myself, why me? Why now?" Garan stood up and ran a hand through his hair.

Nils stood too and was apprehensive about the change in the boy's demeanor. Was it that much of a shock to learn he had power? Nils tried to think about how he would feel but could not quite manage it. "Perhaps it is the power itself that has changed you. Remember how much power you used that night with Salinda? Maybe it is the tool which has altered the wielder."

Garan gazed at him, eyes watering in the light beaming from the repaired units.

"But will I ever be the same again? Does it change who I am?"

"I have slept through the demise of my people and the annihilation of Margra as it once was. I find that I am still me. I cannot escape from who I am. I adapt, slowly. But I find that what I sense about myself is unalterable. Perhaps it will be the same for you. If you stay true to what you believe."

Garan nodded slowly. "That's the hard part. My experience is limited. I know little of the world or even about myself. How do I truly know what I want and what I should do? What I believe?"

Nils reached out gingerly and touched the boy lightly on the shoulder, as he had seen Danton do to the other lad, Brill. Garan did not react, just focused his intense gaze on him. Nils removed his hand, slowly drawing it back as he spoke. "Yet, you have something within you, a peculiar characteristic. I do not understand it. If I had not seen it myself I would not credit its existence at all. You have a good heart. That is how Salinda describes you. Now we know you have the potential for great power also. You must be ready to use it when the time comes. However, for now I think the task of fixing the lamps will be a means for you to understand and learn more about yourself. Later, we will talk about the caves beneath the observatory. I find that I am fascinated with your account of them."

♋♋♋♋♋

Garan labored for many hours on the lamps while Nils left to study the archives. Garan found it a bit disconcerting that a touch of his finger re-energized the crystal within, if that was what was really inside the power cell, the words Nils had used to describe the component. Nils seemed to accept this blatant use of power, but Garan could only wonder at it. Studying his hands, wiggling his fingers, he came to accept that something was inside his own flesh. He speculated about what it would be like if one day it were possible to recreate the lamp's mechanism at the observatory and somehow harness the power cell so that light would burn for years and years. Then his mind strayed to other applications, and it seemed to him that the possibilities were limitless. Why, they could once again become the technologically advanced world they had been before Ruel fell. They could feed and house people, make living easier.

Then his burgeoning extrapolations of the benefits of technology to the people of Margra smacked into a wall: his oath of secrecy. He was bound not to divulge information about what he saw here in Barrahiem, and that was that. There was no way around it. Perhaps one day, when Nils found he could trust those living above, he would allow some of the knowledge to pass to them. For now, all Garan could do was learn as much as he could and labor with the lamps. He found he did not mind the work, the solitude or the time to think. After a while he developed a rhythm and soon he had quite a few lamps laid in rows illuminating the shelves around him.

Occasionally, when Garan took a break, his gaze lingered on a strange mechanism haphazardly placed upon a shelf. Standing up to ease the strain in his lower back and knees, his attention was diverted by a second mechanism, equally fascinating, now sparkling in the greater illumination. Nodding to himself, he decided to take a look at it when his task was done.

As he worked, he once again sensed that presence. He couldn't quite place it anywhere concrete but yet it drew his attention all the same. He shook his head, trying to shake off the impression, but it would not budge. Concentrating on the work at hand allowed him to let it sit there, dark and hollow, and pretend to ignore it.

When Nils returned they began the task of replacing the lamps along the pathways. Nils wanted to start with the Hall of Elders and work out from there. Garan could see that replacing the whole of the city's lights would take a long time. As they placed the lamps, they removed the dead ones and piled them up, ready to be taken back to the manufacturing area to be repaired. A quick touch of his finger to those still functioning made them brighten noticeably.

Nils's expression relaxed. His silver-colored eyes rested on the lamps and then he stood, regarding the large basin in the center of the Hall of Elders. "This was the sacred lamp. It was never left untended, and the flame never waned in my time. When I awoke from my prison of sleep it was as you see it now. Dead. It was the final proof that my kind were really gone. If we finish our task, then we will light this lamp last of all. And then I will know that my people's spirit lives on."

Garan gave the sacred lamp a cursory once-over. He had a feeling that it functioned differently from the other lamps. He would need to take time to study it before he could attempt a repair. A glance at Nils told him it was not the right time to ask questions, though, and besides, Garan was tired. His stomach growled noisily.

His hope that Nils had not heard the embarrassing rumble were soon dashed when Nils exclaimed, "Forgive me. I have neglected you and now you have not eaten for a long time. We will go to the gardens and collect food. You may find a lairn apple or two to take the edge off your hunger while I prepare a meal. Come."

Following Nils from the Hall of Elders, Garan kept pace with him as he made his way to the gardens. Garan found his thoughts straying to Salinda and the child she was expecting.

"Nils, when your child is born, you will be able to teach it how to maintain the city. Then your grandchildren will continue on after you. The sacred lamp may never go out again."

Nils slowed his pace and his shoulders slumped. Garan paused as the older man turned to face him with those strange eyes of his reflecting the yellow spectrum of the lamplight.

"It is a nice thought. Thank you for speaking it—so much optimism in the face of doom. Even if the world survives, I do not expect that I will. I do not expect to even see this child of mine."

Garan was taken aback. "Do you wish for death? I thought that you and Salinda..."

Nils sighed and resumed walking, his gaze roaming about him, face haunted by memory. "In those first days and hours I did wish it. Yet to do myself an injury is contrary to my people's beliefs and, alas, my own. Then when I ventured out and encountered dragons and Salinda, things began to change for me. Salinda is now my bond mate. I cannot live without her. But for her the bond is weaker. She could live on after me. I fear that my fate is to perish along with Margra."

"Are you saying that if she dies, you will die?"

"Yes."

"And you believe the world is doomed anyway...that there is no point to anything we do, that even your child has no future?" Garan stood stock-still, letting the thoughts jell. Could anyone get up each morning believing such things?

Nils stopped beside him and looked at him sideways. "You put it rather bluntly, but in essence, that is what I believe."

Garan reached out to Nils, hesitantly. Nils may have touched him once, but Garan understood that there was danger in reciprocating too overtly. Garan touched Nils's hand briefly, squeezing the long white fingers. Nils was very still during the exchange. "Nils. Believe me. If I can help you survive what is to come, I will. You have too much knowledge, too much importance to think this way."

Nils raised the fingers Garan had squeezed and examined them as if they were some strange gift. Then, lowering them, he asked carefully and sincerely, "But if we are all doomed, what then?"

Garan let his face relax, let the tension slide out of him as he responded. "I cannot accept doom yet, Nils. There is too much chance involved, too much life here, for it to die. You'll see. Wait until the city lights are finished. When they shine once more it will fill your heart with hope."

Nils's expression lightened a little. "Let us hurry then so you can eat."

Chapter Thirteen

TO BE A DRAGON

Gercomo cowered at the base of the hatchery for many days. His injuries prevented him attempting to leave, even if the bull and his cronies allowed him the opportunity. The section of the hatchery he lay in contained warm, soft sand. Again with each sunrise, the energy of the light, warm sun renewed him, built his energy. Yet, hunger bothered him increasingly. All that was nearby food-wise was the eggs, maturing in the sand.

Gercomo saw that the eggs were not guarded very closely. Surely they would not notice one egg missing. It was afternoon and the corner where he lay was shrouded in shadow. The healing warmth of Margra was fading. Moonrise was still a few hours away. In the distance roars and screeching filled the air. Some males were fighting over a mate or territory.

Gercomo had seen eggs laid over the days. Some females exuded enticing strong scent. At first Gercomo had found the smell repellent. The more he lay among the nests, the more he became accustomed to it, the more enticing it became. Perhaps his dragon body was adapting to life as a dragon.

The sound of the fight above ceased abruptly. Gercomo lost interest as the herd settled down for the afternoon. He was disturbed at sunset when a female climbed down to lay her eggs. The apparent victor from the fight climbed down with her to assist in their burial. He had won the right to mate with this particular female. The corner of the bull's left wing leaked blood. To see one of the bulls that had so battered him injured gave Gercomo a thrill. Gercomo climbed on all fours to get a better view. The bull noticed him and growled low. Gercomo stood his ground. The injured bull would be easy to take was the thought that crystallized in his mind. The bull strode forward, putting himself between the female and Gercomo.

Hisses sounded from above. Gercomo looked up to see dragon heads lining the rim of the hatchery. They were watching. Another defeat may be the death of him. He could taste their anticipation. Perhaps not today. Gercomo stood still and blanked his thoughts. Maybe demonstrating he wasn't a coward would suffice for now. The male continued posturing while the female squeezed out her mottled purplish eggs. She had laid three. Gercomo's hunger surged. He would eat those eggs.

Abruptly, the male was shoved aside as the female lunged at Gercomo, spitting snarls and hisses. Gercomo was taken by surprise. Why was she attacking him unless she had sensed his thoughts? Before he had time to get out of the way, the female turned and flicked him with her tail. Once again he was knocked over and he fell against the wall of the crevice. She was on him then, biting down on his neck with a steady pressure. Not allowed to kill him, he thought. A growl and she released him. Then her nostrils flared and she inhaled, moving her snout lower to his penis. Her hot tongue licked. Gercomo froze.

A roar from the male and she backed up. He sensed a thought from her: amusement. She was laughing at him, at his size. She returned the male's roar, apparently unperturbed. Derogatory thoughts radiated from him too. All around him he sensed their ridicule. He rolled onto his front and buried himself back in the sand. *Soon*, he thought, *soon*. But then he kept his thoughts to himself. There was no point in alerting them to his plans. Not that they could understand the intricacies of them. Their understanding was too simple for that.

With one eye on the mated pair he watched while they scaled the walls. He had her scent now. He could trace her nest. She would never find her eggs again. *Quiet, quiet.* He must not broadcast his thoughts. Other females came to rotate their eggs and settle for the night. Once again Gercomo felt trapped. No food. No chance of escape. A cool breeze dusted his hide with sand, which smelled of dragon piss.

꧁꧂

Another week passed and all his wounds had healed. The bull who had bested him leaned over the lip of the crevice and roared. Gercomo, startled from a doze, backed into a corner. The bull roared again. He was being summoned. Did that mean he was free to go?

Gercomo began the slow climb up the side of the crevice, copying the way the other dragons heaved themselves up and down. His claws dug into the soil, sometimes releasing it to spill down to the floor below. After dragging himself to the surface, he lowered his head and inched forward, bringing himself carefully before the bull.

The bull roared and flame billowed over Gercomo's head. All he could do was duck and hope that dragon flesh was immune to flame. It was hot but the fire did not damage him. The others, male and females and hatchlings, gathered around him. Expectation was heavy in the air. What did they want from him?

I mean you no harm. I cannot help what I am. It is not by choice I am among you. He thought these things, felt them and tried to push the concepts out of himself so that he could be understood. The bull lifted his fore claw and slammed it down. Gercomo flinched and lowered his head, burying his snout in the soil. The bull turned slowly. The others pulled back. Gercomo stayed still. The bull lumbered away. Then the others turned and went about their usual tasks. Gercomo was free from his prison. He wasn't sure whether that meant he could leave or not. It was more that they were prepared to tolerate his presence. He watched the bull break into a run, stretching his wings for flight. Then his bulk began to lift and he heaved out a bellow that rattled Gercomo's remaining tooth. He had to be five times the size of Gercomo. That didn't mean that Gercomo couldn't dominate him. He just had to find a way.

Chapter Fourteen

IN THE ARMS OF INTRIGUE

In Sartell, Danton reveled in the steam wafting off the large pool and the firm hands massaging his neck. Toola's brothel was the best rendezvous point he had ever devised. Toola didn't ask questions, always a good thing, and the general goings-on provided plenty of cover.

After Mandin had gotten over her shock at being brought to a house of ill repute, she had found she got on well with Toola, who was, after all, a good woman. While growing up he and Toola had been good friends and had gotten up to lots of mischief together. Although technically his cousin, Toola had always been more like a sister to Danton. He would never forget how much he owed her. That time when she risked her life to save his. It had been a childish prank turned bad, but one with serious consequences. She had covered for him and had been beaten as a result. That was before the government of the time fell and their family lost everything. Danton had gone into the army and later deserted. Toola had been sold as a prostitute to a very exclusive brothel. It had been her choice to have her lips dyed red. The quality of husband she could have attracted had lowered with the change in status. She had judged that prostitution gave her more control over her destiny.

Danton thought her choice appeared to have worked to her advantage. Now she ran this place. Danton didn't know how she had managed it. But as she had always been trustworthy and sympathetic to him, he always came here when he was in the city. It was his most reliable rendezvous point because people were always coming and going so it was easy to blend in with the other clientele. Toola also serviced a lot of traders from out of town—in particular rich ones from the prosperous cities of Lukton and Ferndale. This gave her access to information, which, if given enough reason, she would share.

Danton's men liked this place too because Toola let them have free use of her girls provided they treated them well and the girls were willing. He laughed to himself. Perhaps that was why his men were so loyal to him—maybe it was nothing to do with his leadership skills at all.

These days the red dye on Toola's lips had faded and was disguised with makeup, so she could pass for a respectable woman. Rarely did her girls use dye to mark their profession in her establishment. Toola only allowed it if the girls wanted to mark themselves, and usually they were the ones who worked in the public tavern. These girls lured the patrons and kept the barkeep honest and hardworking. His pay, Toola told Danton, was based on the return the establishment made. So he treated the girls well and kept a good bar.

The exclusive girls were kept in reserve and worked in the bathhouse where Danton was now, rather than the bar. He liked to think that they were the special ones, the most beautiful and graceful. Within the steam rooms and thermal tubs, the girls could choose their patrons. A network of private rooms completed the complex, which was deceptively large relative to the street frontage. Toola was expanding her interests, he surmised.

The complex had a few secret entry and exit points, all of which served Danton's purpose as well as Toola's. There was always some fine outstanding citizen who didn't want to be caught with his dart stuck in a warm and moist target of ill repute. He wondered if that was how Toola kept her connections and maintained her business through each successive change of government. All of the nobility and the civil servants had probably availed themselves of Toola's girls at one time or another. And Toola would use that information. Toola was nothing if not shrewd.

Another advantage of the brothel was that the bathhouse backed onto a rather exclusive men's club, a polite name for a place where men came looking for other men and boys. Thankfully, that club had its own smaller bathhouse and steam rooms. Danton could choose to ignore what happened across the back laneway. Not that he was prudish; he just didn't like the exploitation of children. Yet Danton suspected that Toola had her hooks in there as well. Perhaps she even owned it, though he would have to re-evaluate the status of her wealth and connections if she did. Boys were more expensive than girls. Such was the way of the world.

Toola's girls were clean, well looked after and were whores by choice, or so he understood. None had been forced into service, but if their financial circumstances left them no other option, they had chosen Toola's establishment. Her reputation was that good. Danton had no qualms about tasting Toola's wares, although the opportunity to do so had been rather rare to date. It had been many years since his last visit. A lot had happened since then—the prison vineyard, Mez, the Inspector and Salinda. He hadn't been with a woman since the time the Inspector had violated him and paraded him in front of his guards as a pet. Trauma and shame had worked to stem any intimate encounters. Although he had loved Salinda and desired her, he hadn't been able to consummate their relationship at the vineyard. At the time his pain had been too raw. And so they had parted, she to remain at the vineyard with Mez, and Danton to re-form his rebel band. Yet in his heart he had always thought that Salinda and he would get together. Now it was too late for that.

At present, he felt as if he had been in the desert for a long, long time. He had also been thinking about Salinda a lot, and he really needed to wipe that slate clean, if he ever could. A little relaxation worked wonders in washing away the memories of the last few months. There had been so much death and despair. It was really time to think about something else. Like the things these women were doing to him. If only sex and not war was the order of the day, every day, perhaps Margra would be a better place.

Even as he relaxed and groaned his pleasure as Jewel massaged his scalp, he couldn't put business from his mind. Several things puzzled him. There had been no sign of Merl and the fourteen other men he had sent after the wine at the rendezvous just shy of Yourton. Added to that, he had sent Squab off to rendezvous with him here months ago, before he and the rest of his men had traveled over the range to save Salinda from the vineyard. He'd separated his force as a conservative measure. Sending Squab had been another tactical move; he'd known she would keep a low profile and protect his men at all costs. Squab had seen a lot and was one tough woman. Yet there was no message from her, either. That meant he had to bide his time. More than half his men were unaccounted for. Squab was either in trouble or being very cautious. But the latter possibility was worrying. Toola's establishment was good cover, and if Squab didn't think it was safe to contact him there, then there had to be a good reason. That made him even more uneasy.

Leaning back, he let Jewel extend her massage to his chest. Her co-worker, Felisha, rose out of the water from between his legs, and he sighed expansively. Life was very good indeed.

Brill wasn't being massaged, nor had he let a girl near him in the bath, which was why Danton had both girls tending him. Brill was fixated on his morals. "How can you do it, Danton? These girls are whores," he whispered, his outrage clear in his tone.

Danton groaned. Couldn't the lad see that he was relaxing? "I noticed that." Giving Felisha a little peck on the lips before she submerged again, Danton sighed. Felisha was excellent at underwater massage. "They are good at their jobs too."

Brill stared at Jewel with an expression somewhere between horror and intrigue. "Be serious. I thought you loved Salinda. How can you be unfaithful to her memory? How can you cavort with these women?"

Danton frowned. "Salinda's not dead, you know, just otherwise occupied. And for the record, we have never been lovers. There was potential, expectation, perhaps, but not commitment. She was not bound to me nor me to her. I care for her deeply. Love her, if you will. But that has nothing to do with this."

"Of course it does. How could you stand before her now and profess your love if the opportunity arose?"

Danton found a smile pulling at the corner of his mouth. "Quite easily. I am not in love with these girls. Besides, I think you may have noticed that Salinda is pregnant. One has to engage in sexual relations for that to occur. I am fully reconciled to the fact that Salinda sleeps with Nils."

"I realize that. But she is doing her duty. It is different."

"No, it is no different. Am I not doing my duty? Besides, life has few pleasures and Toola is a good friend, as well as family. I don't want to insult her hospitality. Nor should you."

Brill looked around guiltily. "Do you really think she would take offense? Has she never met a faithful man before?"

Danton threw his head back and laughed, startling Jewel. The girl slid into the bath next to him and began rubbing his bicep. "Faithful? Are you married? Did you exchange a vow with Laidan?"

Brill's face was red. It was caused by the heat or anger...maybe embarrassment. "No. Of course not."

"Then what is your problem? It is one thing to have ideals for yourself. It is another to force them on other people." Danton began to caress Jewel after patting Felisha on the head before she submerged again. He was finding it difficult to concentrate on Brill's dilemma. The girls' ministrations were rather enjoyable, after all...and distracting.

"I have no problem. I don't wish to sully her memory. That is all. Is it wrong to believe in something and convince other people of it?" Brill was half out of the water and his fists were clenched. He was as riled as Danton had ever seen him.

"So you have taken her to bed. I thought as much. So much for your beliefs."

Brill colored and looked away. "I do not wish to discuss it. That is a private matter and nothing to do with you."

Danton chuckled. "If you gave her no vow and you left her behind, how is it any different from what you might do with one of the girls here?"

Brill clenched his jaw. "Are you saying that Laidan is a whore?"

"Not at all. You treated her like one, though."

"I did not." Brill lowered himself back into the bath. He glowered at nothing in particular while water lapped his chin.

Danton let Brill hold on to his denial. He would see the truth of it soon enough. Brill would not want to face the fact that his morals had faltered, but now that they had, he must readjust them or leave them behind altogether. That was part of growing up. He had to let go of his father's ideals and find his own. Danton had no quibble with Prince Hubert's philosophy in general, but it was difficult to follow in a world gone mad. In a community like the Highland Confederacy, it could work and lead to general happiness and contentment—in theory at least. That would never be known now. The Confederacy was destroyed and Brill the only remaining adherent.

Danton leaned back against the side of the bath again, letting both girls soothe his skin with their soft hands. "So now that you have tasted the joys of a woman's flesh, surely you want to do so again. It is not easy to give up once you've begun."

Brill looked askance at him. "Well, I...er...that's different. I care for Laidan. To engage with these girls...well, it is nothing more than pure...lust."

"I see, so you don't feel lust then? I'm happy for you. If you don't mind, though, I'll get on with it. Life is too short and I'm getting old and ugly. It's been years since I've had the chance to indulge in lust of any kind."

Toola entered that section of the bathhouse at that moment, gliding along the walkway dressed in a floral wrap that tastefully clung to her assets and disguised her flaws. With her was a young woman who looked about Brill's age. She was dark skinned, with almond-shaped eyes slanting above her cheeks. Her teeth were even and white, which created a brilliant smile. Brill tensed beside him. Danton eyed the girl casually. Mentally he compared her to Salinda, given their similar coloring, but there was something missing for him. Salinda herself, he thought as he looked away and concentrated on the interesting and teasing things Jewel was doing to his abdomen.

Toola squatted beside the edge of the bath, smiling at Brill and stroking his hair in a motherly fashion. "As none of my best girls suit the young master," Toola said, "I thought one of my newer girls might. She is not schooled, but she is keen to please."

Toola fixed her gaze on Brill, who stared blankly at her and then glanced at the young girl. He swallowed hard, and Danton couldn't suppress a grin. Toola was good. She had the boy pegged precisely. If he couldn't be tempted by expert flesh, give him something innocent and vulnerable and he'd fall right in. After all, it was what Laidan had done to snare him. Toola had told Danton once that all men had their breaking point. Her job was to know what it was and how much pressure to apply. She even kept a few very nimble boys in her employ so that she had ready tools to shape her customers. It was a matter of principle for her to ensure that Brill partook of her wares. Then he would owe her. She had assessed the former royal within five minutes of him entering her establishment. She probably knew his blood line better than he did.

"Master, would Lexia here suit you?"

Brill glanced at Danton and swallowed again. He looked as if he had been hunted and now found himself in a corner with no way out. Danton took pity on the lad and suggested quietly, "You don't have to… you know. Just let her look after you. Otherwise Toola will think she has lost her touch." Danton flashed him a smile.

Jewel and Felisha were beginning to take exception to each other as they vied for Danton's attention. With a look of determination on her face, Felisha dove under the water again. It was becoming more and more difficult to concentrate on the lad's issues. Danton turned away from Brill, luxuriating in the feel of Felisha working her way up his thigh. It felt so good. He wished the lad would take off and leave him alone. Felisha was taking her underwater massage very seriously. For a while he let his mind drift while his body became more and more aroused. The warm steam wafted over his cleanly shaven face and dripped down his neck. Jewel began to lick his sweat. It really was too much.

Once again his attention was snared by Brill. His young friend was smiling at the girl. "Thank you, Toola. You honor me with your thoughtfulness. I'd be happy for Lexia to join me."

Finally! thought Danton. *No more need to justify myself. Let him use her or lose her.* It made no difference to him. Toola sent him a look and a smug smile before she turned and left.

While Brill looked on, the girl, Lexia, peeled off her skirt, revealing long tanned legs. Then she slipped her blouse over her shoulders before easing herself naked into the pool between them. She had the same innocent stare that Laidan had, full of worship and desire. Danton could almost hear Brill's resolve cracking as the girl politely asked if she could ease the tension in his neck muscles.

Now that Brill was taken care of, Danton could pay serious attention to Jewel and Felisha. Climbing out of the pool, he invited them to dry him off and show him where he could continue to relax. He only hoped he wouldn't be too tired afterward. Already fatigue weighed him down. All told, the journey had been hard, and his muscles were sore. After leaving the barge, they had scouted around for a sign of the rebels for days until they gave up and came here. And they attracted too much attention from the customs officials while they were doing it, so hiding out here in Toola's place was the best bet. With his eye patch, he was distinctive.

He enjoyed the girls and the large bed, and he was very soon asleep.

He awoke a short time later, only to toss and turn as his mind became absorbed by other worries. He wondered how Mandin was getting on. The Vanden woman had objected to them staying in a brothel, the very type of place she hoped to rescue her daughter from. Yet from the first Toola had taken a shine to the woman and was pampering her somewhere in the complex.

Sitting up, he found the light. The girls had left him alone, but there was a glass of wine and a note from Toola on the table by the bed. There was news from Squab. Toola had learned from her spies that his deputy had made it to Sartell and had checked in at the brothel twice, looking for Danton and the others. Toola said in her note that she hadn't recollected to tell him because his deputy had not identified herself. Toola made it her business to know what was going on and had put two and two together. If Squab had word of his men, she hadn't been confident enough to leave any messages. This was a good course of action, in case Toola was infiltrated. Although he trusted his cousin, he knew that torture would loosen anyone's tongue.

Danton's room was toward the back of the complex, adjacent to the tunnel entry that would allow him to flee, if necessary. He had that exhausted, replete feeling that a good bath, two good women and a safe house could give. As he lit the small lamp, he wondered if there was anything he could do for Toola to return the favor. She had outdone herself this time. Before he could think of anything appropriate, he flung himself back onto the mattress, luxuriating in the opportunity to rest, and fell into a deep sleep.

He did not know how long he had slept before he was shaken roughly. Danton sat up, alert, with blade in hand. He saw the outline of a squat body.

"Squab?"

"Yes, it's me," she whispered hoarsely, putting her hand over his mouth to prevent speech. "Come up to the roof garden so we can talk."

Danton groped for his trousers and slid into them. He followed Squab's bulky shadow outside and up the stairs. Shatterwing, occasionally obscured by scudding clouds, sprinkled light across the heavens.

"Thank the source you are safe!" Squab said with a feral grin when they reached the roof. "I was beginning to worry."

He kept his voice low and quiet so it wouldn't carry. "Same here.

Are you well? The others?"

"I have a few questions first. You sent no news. Where are the men who went with you? Toola says it is just the two of you and some woman."

"It's a long story. Have you heard from Merl or Stinger?"

She shook her head. Danton cursed under his breath and chewed his lip. "Have you heard about the wine stash?"

Again she shook her head. She was behind in information. That meant none of the men he'd sent after the wine had made it this far.

"You'd better fill me in," he said.

"First, who is the woman and what happened to the others?"

"I lost Didly and Twil at the vineyard to an Infra-pact rebel bomb. I sent Merl, as deputy, to meet me near Yourton to let me know what happened to the wine stash that the Inspector and his rebels filched from the vineyard. Later I sent Stinger after a smaller stash of wine. He was to touch base with Merl and then continue after the wine. I was hoping that you would know more."

Squab frowned and scratched behind her ear. "And the woman?" she prompted.

"The woman with me is a refugee from the town that the Inspector destroyed. She is bent on finding her daughter, who was taken to be sold as a prostitute, we believe. Mandin is tough, hard-working and very determined. You'll like her."

"So she's not this Salinda you were keen on saving at all cost?"

Danton bristled at her tone, which had layers of implied blame. Then the thought occurred to him that Squab had no reason to speak that way, unless she...*No*, Danton thought. Not possible; Squab liked women. "No, though we did find Salinda eventually."

Squab looked around, checking that they were alone, and then edged closer and dropped her voice. "Danton, I need to warn you. There have been some changes in Sartell since you were last here. Be careful. There is treachery everywhere. Even those close to you may be tainted."

A trapdoor behind them opened and one of Toola's staff popped his head out. A sense of unease grew in the back of Danton's mind but he shook it off, not quite prepared to believe that Toola would be so direct in spying on him. "Perhaps we should meet elsewhere to talk. Later on this morning?" he murmured.

Squab nodded and slipped him a note with her address on it. They headed down the stairs and re-entered the corridors, where Squab slipped away without saying anything more. Although happy to see her, Danton was disappointed with the encounter. She had twenty-five of his men hidden around Sartell. The other half were still unaccounted for. Danton didn't like the feeling he was getting. It tasted of loss and despair and he didn't like it one bit.

Chapter Fifteen

TWO MINDS THAT NEVER MEET

Salinda went for a walk, leaving Laidan to rest. She needed to take a break from the girl as her frustration was flowing over and that was not a good thing—not productive, anyway. Who would have thought that a young girl like Laidan, who had traveled with a carrier of the cadre, could be so difficult and so troublesome? Salinda had to grin when she thought about the old man, Thurdon, and how he must have borne a heavy burden, dragging that girl around the Stoli continent and keeping her out of mischief to boot.

Salinda walked along the terrace that overlooked the deep lake, her hand resting on her abdomen. The baby continued to grow, as did the hope in her heart that somewhere in this city they would find the answer to the impending catastrophe, some higher learning that could help the observatory blast a rogue asteroid from its path of doom.

Teaching Laidan to master her cadre was a key part of that. The cadre held knowledge. But she was thwarted. For some reason the girl had lost the ability to touch the cadre. Could it be that it had rejected her? What had the girl done to warrant that? Surely she had not had the opportunity to do anything stupid while her control over the cadre was so fragile. The reverse could be true too: the girl might have rejected the cadre. Salinda thought this more likely, as it had been rather rudely thrust into Laidan, and she'd been given no preparation. Furthermore, possession of it had brought nothing but peril.

If she had rejected it then it would not be a surprise. So little was known about these things. If the art of caring for, carrying and using a cadre had been documented in the past, Nils would have said something by now. All of Salinda's conversations with him since he learned of their gift had revealed that it was a mystery to him. He had not heard of a "cadre" before Ruel broke apart and they were definitely not the product of a technology that Nils knew about or understood. If they had existed in his time, cadres must have been as rare as they were now.

So, she thought at her cadre. *What is going on with Laidan?* As the cadre warmed within her mind, she let it come forward. Then it responded; the minds of those who had gone before whispered to her. Laidan had rejected her cadre, had rejected the life she was brought up to. Only that could sever the tenuous connection she had had with it. Salinda queried further. The manner of the transfer had also compromised Laidan's ability to absorb the connections and take the cadre into herself. That was why her exercises were useless. When Salinda had quieted Thurdon's presence, she had severed the most important connection between the cadre and Laidan. Salinda had cut off the presence of the one person the girl trusted.

Salinda cursed herself for a fool. But what could she have done? The girl had been in agony and their need had been great. Even the brief exchange she had had with Thurdon's essence had given her access to more knowledge and power. Staring down at her hand, she brought the fire to it as he had shown her. Letting it fade away, she looked out to the lake's dark surface and listened to the water lap gently against the bank. As she watched and listened, thoughts of what she had to do crystallized in her mind.

It was time to release Laidan from her burden and take the cadre from the girl.

It was not news to Salinda that Laidan had grown progressively more self-obsessed and insipid along with it. Admittedly it wasn't all the girl's fault. She had not trained to receive the cadre and to have it thus thrust into her mind was likely to have damaged her sanity or at least impinged on her emotional stability. Coupled with the flight from rebels, bandits and near rapes and then the siege of the observatory, then perhaps it had been too much. But the girl had had care and support for weeks now and still there had been no improvement. No, the girl was worse, mooning after Brill and being totally dejected and unfocussed.

Salinda tried to dredge up a smidgen of sympathy. At the prison vineyard, Laidan would have been used up within a week. The girl needed some lessons in survival. For all that, Salinda cared for her. Laidan had been spared many of the realities of the world that Salinda had not. She had grown up cared for and loved, even if the material things in life had been scarce. Thurdon had been a remarkable man. Salinda wished she had had the girl's opportunities. Laidan was as Salinda could have been had things been different.

After Salinda returned to her abode she prepared a meal. While she worked she went over how she was going to broach the subject with Laidan. Nils and Garan did not make an appearance, so they ate without them. Salinda was relieved because that meant less distraction and aggravation from Laidan.

The young girl lay around on the sofa, absently nibbling the food Salinda had prepared. On the sofa opposite, Salinda swallowed another mouthful, suddenly not at all sure how to broach the subject now that she was forced to do so. Laidan was so pretty, so fine featured and pale. Her looks alone inspired softness and gentleness. They were a rarity these days when everyone's bloodlines were mixed. Sometimes the genetic dice would throw out some odd combination of looks, hair, eye and skin color. Garan was olive complexioned and had violet-colored eyes. She, herself, had dark hair and eyes and light brown skin. But they were all human, no matter what the surface showed. Nils alone was something else, something special.

Her conscience troubled her as she gazed at Laidan. Licking her lips and twisting her hair nervously, she considered her options. How could Salinda be so cruel, so focused that she was prepared to hurt this girl to take away something so precious from her? No, she had to stop that line of thinking. Salinda thought the cadre precious. Laidan did not. But the cadre did make Laidan special and Laidan was vain enough to resent losing her specialness. She was prepared for the recriminations from Laidan, and she thought she could cushion the others from the fallout. However, she found it hard not to put herself in Laidan's situation. If it had been Salinda who was to be told that she could not keep her cadre, she was sure she would have died from heartbreak.

Just the thought had her hands shaking. Straightening in her chair and lowering her hands to her lap, she said, "Laidan?"

The girl had her eyes closed. She lifted her hand to her forehead.

"What? Have I done something wrong? Again?"

Salinda leaned down to twirl the teapot by the handle, around and around on the table between them. "No dear. I need to talk to you. It is going to be a long talk." Salinda paused. There was no point in prevaricating. "I've been thinking about the trouble you have been having with your cadre. If I can piece together what has happened to you then I can help."

The girl clenched her fist. "I like the cadre the way it is. Quiet! I don't feel it now and that's good."

Salinda leaned forward slightly, leaving the teapot alone. "No, Laidan. It is not good. The cadre you hold is special, made for a purpose. It is needed now. It is needed to help us fight for the very existence of Margra. Surely you don't want us to fail."

Laidan climbed into a sitting position and sat with her head forward, hair spilling over her shoulders and face. Her voice came out muffled. "Not really. I mean, I'd be dead too, wouldn't I?"

Salinda gentled her voice. "You have said you like the cadre just as it is. Laidan, what if I were to take it from you completely? You could be free of it, of the responsibility. Would this be agreeable to you?"

"Take it from me?" Laidan stared into space for a few minutes. Then her gaze met Salinda's. "Will it hurt?" She was like a frightened child.

Salinda could not repress a shrug. "I cannot say. I have never attempted to transfer a cadre before. I will need to prepare if we are to do it."

"Transfer it? Who to...not...him." Laidan grasped the edge of the sofa with both hands.

Salinda kept her gaze on her, watching, assessing. "Yes. Garan is the logical choice. Thurdon told me he intended the cadre for Garan. As you do not want it, I cannot see how you can object."

Laidan flinched as Salinda said the words. There was no easy way to say them. Laidan sat there with her mouth open, digesting it. Then she looked out the window and said, "But if you give it to him, what use do you have for me? What will I do here?"

Ah, thought Salinda. *We get to the heart of it.* "We will think of something to keep you occupied. There are other ways you can be useful."

Laidan glared at her, bringing her anger to the fore again. "You did this deliberately to separate me from Brill!"

Salinda sat very still and kept her voice low and even. "I assure you I did not."

Laidan's skin was reddening as she let her anger boil. "I don't believe you. He wanted to be with me."

"Perhaps. Yet if he was as serious as you say, he would have spoken up about it and asked for your hand in marriage. He is so moral about such things."

"That's about enough from you, Salinda." Laidan climbed to her feet and, grasping her robe in her fist, moved it out of her path. She was aiming for the door but stopped and turned before exiting. "You can have this cadre if you want it, and Garan will suffer for it, believe me. He'll find out that Thurdon was my real father. A blood relation. Garan was nothing to him."

With that she ducked out the door. Salinda climbed to her feet, breathing evenly. She saw Laidan head out of the node. She shook her head. "I hope I don't have to send Nils to find you." Salinda groaned to herself. *Nils will not take this well.* Salinda had her work cut out for her if she was going to remedy the girl's tendencies. Such a beautiful creature too. A pity for beauty to be a curse.

Chapter Sixteen

SAFETY'S SEDUCTION

Mandin sat in Toola's kitchen darning a rip in the seat of her trousers which she had snagged on a fallen branch while they had searched the swamps for signs of the rebels they'd been tracking. A cup of tea sat on a small table by her side. She looked up when a smiling Toola came in, her long dark hair braided and coiled around her head and secured with a jeweled comb. Her eyes tracked the other woman as she bent to coax more heat from the fire in the grate and stood up again to stir a large pot of stew simmering on the stove. The cooking meat smelled wonderful. So much better than dry bread, scrounged nuts and roots, and watered wine on the trail, thought Mandin as she lowered her gaze once again to her mending. Mandin felt cozy for the first time since the Inspector and his rebels had come to Vanden and destroyed her life. Taking a sip of tea, she sighed loudly and grinned at Toola.

Toola drew up a seat. "I have asked around about your daughter, Eneit. I'm so sorry there's nothing to report yet. You must trust me, Mandin. I will help you find her. I know the sort of places they will take her." Mandin sucked in a breath, eyes widening in alarm. Toola leaned over and patted her on the knee and made soothing noises. "Don't fret now. I'll send one of my men around to see what they can find out about new slave shipments."

Mandin nodded, too moved to speak about what she really felt. She was halfway between despair and gratitude and both seemed to stick like wet dough in her throat. It was strange, accepting hospitality from a madam. On the other hand, she found that she liked the woman, despite her profession. Perhaps this was only natural, given everything that had happened to her in the last few weeks. She was a rebel now and no longer a respectable village woman—that Mandin was dead and gone. Toola was watching her speculatively, and then Mandin remembered her manners.

"Thank you, Toola. I didn't think someone like you would have such a big heart."

"Like me?" Toola sat back, her expression suddenly serious, her voice taking on a hard edge. "I'm the kind of woman who is trying to survive. I've no husband. No circle of townswomen to comfort me. I live in a city—a hard city, full of wealth and poverty, crime and chaos."

Mandin stared at the floor, not sure how to deal with Toola's reaction. "I...I only meant...Oh, my mother would blush if she had known I would end up sitting here in your kitchen, in this kind of establishment. I am sorry. I didn't mean to cause offense."

Toola smiled again and her voice softened. "Sartell is not so against the profession as the provinces are. Some of our clients are very powerful. We need to keep them on our side so we stay legal and prosperous. Think of what would happen to all of us if we were outlawed. We would starve or be killed even though we had been serving the government, the nobility and the fat merchants over the years—the very people who control this city and our lives."

"Yes...I am from the provinces, and I'm sure a little backward in my thinking..."

Toola stood up and smoothed her elaborately arranged hair. "Where would men go to fulfill their desires if we were not here? Mmm? Do you think these needs would disappear if there were no whores?"

Mandin shook her head. "I see what you are saying...I don't mean to speak against what you do. It is just that I have been brought up to think differently. You know, to save yourself for one man. Be chaste. This is all so new."

Toola grabbed the pot off the stove and spooned some stew into a bowl. She blew on it before handing it to Mandin. "So if there were no places like mine, what would the men do? I say again, would they stop wanting sex?"

Mandin thought about her answer. She could see Toola's point.

What would the men do with their lusts if there were no women willing to accommodate them? Her mother had always said they would marry chaste women, but even in Vanden husbands strayed. Most village folk turned a blind eye and blamed the other woman, be she a whore or some lonely widow. "I don't know the answer, Toola. But I understand what you are saying. It is not a fair world, is it?"

Toola smiled and sat down opposite her. She leaned forward and patted Mandin on her bare knee before reaching for a bowl of stew. "No. Men are so brutal. Now, I know you will want to search for your little Eneit yourself so I will assign Linel to you. He will guide you through the city and keep you safe. That is the best way to find your little girl before some horrible man defiles her."

It was cruel to hear it said so matter-of-factly. Moved beyond words, Mandin hugged Toola spontaneously. The other woman spoke, her breath caressing the skin of Mandin's cheek. "Be careful, Mandin, and listen to Linel. I would hate to see you captured yourself and sold in some decrepit flesh pit."

Mandin released Toola and gazed at her in amazement. "Me? Fat old me when there are all these pretty young things around?" She laughed suddenly, amused by the face Toola pulled. Then as the madam moved away, she gave Mandin a healthy view of her breasts as her dress gaped open. Mandin blinked and glanced away. Probably Toola wasn't aware, but it would be impolite to point out her state of undress, and perhaps overly prudish, too, given their previous conversation and current location.

Mandin swallowed the last of the stew and sent her gaze around the room again. Breathing deeply, she realized that she felt safe here. Danton was close and would look out for her. If only her daughter had found such a safe haven. Then her thoughts turned ugly, making her squirm in her seat. There was nothing to be done about the rapes Eneit had probably endured at the hands of her captors. Mandin had been raped by those bastards too. She understood what it was. But what had it done to her daughter? Could she even look at a man again? When Mandin thought of her sweet girl in the same situation, she shuddered. All those men, partaking of her small, young body—how would her Eneit survive it? Would Eneit ever feel joy again? Had they maimed her or killed her while seeking their pleasure? Toola must have sensed where her thoughts were heading.

She stood up and held out her hand to Mandin. "Perhaps a trip to the baths is in order. I think the men have left it now. If you don't object, I'll join you."

Nodding her agreement, Mandin stood, retied the borrowed wrap around her waist and took the proffered hand. "Yes, a bath would be good after so long on the road. We don't have communal baths in Vanden."

"Don't let it worry you. You needn't be shy with me. We are both grown women, after all. If it worries you I can say that we won't be disturbed. Afterward I think a massage will help you to rest. I know the very oil to use to take away your cares."

"I'm sure I will be fine."

"No, I insist. In fact, I will massage you myself. No one else deserves my personal attention."

Mandin blushed and thanked Toola.

As they left the room, Toola gave orders for wine and goblets to be delivered to their private bath.

◙◙◙◙◙

Brill woke up curled into the body of Lexia, his hand still clinging to her neat, tight breast. What a night it had been. Lexia was so pliant, so willing and so sweet. She had sought guidance from him, consulted him on every little thing. He had felt like a king. It was the only word he could use to describe it. She made no demands. Her only aim appeared to be giving pleasure and making sure he was comfortable, satisfied and relaxed.

When he had clung to her and begged her to stay with him, she had smiled. Then he had taken her lovely body again and again, until there was nothing left in him. Thoughts of Laidan were fading fast, the need he had felt for her lessening with each of Lexia's caresses. The waning of his desire for Laidan surprised him. Hadn't he loved her? But Lexia sent all thoughts of her scurrying away, especially when she put her mouth on him. By the source! It was like dying and being born at the same time. Exquisite torture. Then total release. He hadn't realized sex could be so addictive and pleasurable. Memories of Laidan's pale flesh now warred with Lexia's spicy and dark complexion. As he gazed at her naked sleeping body, he wondered if he could taste her one more time before business intruded. Would Danton even speak to him again after his preachy sermon about fidelity and love? What a stubborn burden beast's ass he was. How could Danton stand him?

Already he was hard just looking at the girl. He wondered if she would mind if he . . .

☙☙☙☙

Danton had come to collect Brill before heading out to meet his men, but found the boy otherwise engaged. So he backed out of the room, thinking it wouldn't hurt to leave Brill to assuage his broken heart. He was sure Laidan would waste no time either, lusty creature that she was. After all, she was unlikely to see Brill again for many months—if ever. It was time for Brill to grow up and not be taken in by a pretty face and winning ways. Only experience was going to harden his heart. He was sure Lexia would serve the purpose. She might look all innocent but Danton suspected it was a precisely timed and well-presented act.

When Squab, who was waiting in the corridor, realized why Brill was not to accompany them, her expression turned to a sneer and her scar twisted her features, making her uglier.

"Forget your thoughts of condemnation. He has my approval and blessings. Let's go."

Danton had known Squab before she had acquired her disfigurement. He knew how she had earned it, too. No man had a chance with her. She could bite a man's privates off without regret. He had seen her do it. Then again, the man had done some pretty awful things to her. And that was her own father. No wonder she preferred women, and when she could get one she tended to look after them, too.

They headed back toward his room. "We'll take the tunnel. That way we can leave undetected."

Danton flicked open the door to the linen cupboard while Squab kept watch. When he had unlatched the back panel that disguised the exit, she bent down and asked, "Are you sure it is safe? I don't trust it."

Squatting beside her, he said, "It's better than being seen leaving here in broad daylight, and we can make sure that it still operates as it should." Still she hesitated. "Look, Brill can take care of himself, and I trust Toola to look after Mandin."

Squab gave him a queer look, then nodded. She got on all fours and pushed the lower panel. Danton heard a *pop* and then Squab's generous behind disappeared through the entrance. Giving the corridor a quick glance to check if they were being watched, he then crawled forward into the dark narrow chamber after her.

Once inside the tunnel, he turned around and refastened the latch. Squab had found a light and lit it. Once through to the passage proper, there was room enough to stand. Walking briskly, they followed the passageway. Danton reckoned that they would end up in the stable yard next to Woodley Tavern. Danton recalled that there had been a fork in the tunnel in previous years, but that wasn't there anymore. It only went to one place. He made a mental note to go back and check whether the other exit had been closed off or merely disguised. It was a disadvantage if there was only one tunnel exit and it was known to your pursuers. It was also a good way to betray someone, if you needed to.

They tentatively opened the exit, which imitated part of the fencing for the yard. It opened onto the stable yard. A few burden beasts growled and groaned as they ate their fodder. Carefully, they exited one at a time. Then when they reached the street, they took turns blending with the milling crowd. Danton had the uneasy sense he was being watched, but that impression warred with the surety that his disguise—no beard or eye patch, and a bandana to disguise his curly hair—would serve to camouflage him.

Squab walked on ahead, doing a good impression of a drunk. She fit right in as most of the people exiting the tavern were the worse for wear from drink, wending their way home to sleep it off. Some old man slapped her on the ass. He didn't catch what she said as what he heard came out as a growl. The man recoiled and staggered into the gutter.

Two streets down was the turnoff. Danton kept his distance, watching for when Squab would change direction. He followed her down a laneway, then into a roofed alley and then up another narrow street. From the corner he could see where she paused, apparently looking around at the traffic and the passers-by, before she slipped through the front door of a rundown inn. Danton waited, checked the street casually, turning slightly to see if anyone was behind him. The street was busy with people hurrying along, a few with handcarts laden with cloth, vegetables and urns, a few burden beasts leaving piles of dung in their wake as they moseyed past. Danton ducked down the street and slipped into Squab's residence.

Squab had one of his men, Flick, staying with her, pretending to be her husband. Both of them had it about that they were looking for work. This was good cover for the frequent meetings they had with Danton's dispersed men. Squab said she had sent Andy and Shifter off to be laborers at the mines along with another ten of Danton's men. Another group of his men spent most of their time unloading wagons at the docks. Another group of twelve, she had sent off to scout around for news. She had paired them up so that they could find work and shelter. They all knew where to find her on specified days.

In the foyer of the inn, Danton quickly sized it up: rooms upstairs and a bar down below. Squab hung back in the shadows, her body tense and ready. She eyed the doorway expectantly. Danton thought she was worried about being followed too. "Are you sure we should go up? Won't it look strange if Flick is posing as your husband?"

Squab edged closer, relaxing slightly when she took her gaze away from the threshold. "It should be all right. We told the innkeep we were expecting a colleague who could show us a place to gain employment. Flick also dropped a hint that you owe us money."

The innkeeper was in the bar polishing the countertop. Danton grinned. "Thanks. That figures. Flick was always up for a game. How will you get word to the others?"

Squab jerked her head up, indicating he look up. "We'll talk about it upstairs." Just then the floorboards squeaked as someone walked above. "Flick is pretty good with strategy—for a man, that is."

Danton frowned at her and shook his head. "Squab."

With a grin, Squab added, "Don't worry. I don't think of you as a man at all, boss."

Danton had to laugh at that. A backhanded compliment if he had ever heard one.

"I hadn't reckoned on Flick being so versatile, or that you could pass the skinny little runt off as your husband. He must be a good actor too."

Squab pulled a face at him and then gestured for him to go up the stairs ahead of her. They pounded up the risers, making it obvious that they had entered the building. Nothing excited the interest of landlords more than people quietly sneaking around. Being overly noisy caused others to pull away and avoid contact. Danton had seen it many times. The landlord didn't so much as look up from his polishing when they passed the bar to take the stairs, which was just how he wanted it.

Danton hugged Flick and slapped him on the back. Flick grinned in return, and Danton couldn't suppress a smile. He was glad to see that more than one of his men had made it through. After giving them a flask of watered dragon wine, they sat in a huddle to talk.

"Are you sure it is safe to talk here?" Danton asked, looking from one to the other. Now that he had time, he noticed that both of them were thinner. Less bulk suited Squab, but Flick had lost so much weight his chest appeared bowed.

"As long as we keep our voices low and even, we should be fine."

"So what was the hint you were giving me, Squab, about treachery? Were you thinking of Toola?"

"Yes."

Danton frowned and scratched under his chin. "What have you heard?"

Squab exchanged glances with Flick. They had obviously discussed the topic previously.

"It isn't what I have heard but what is not being said," Flick began.

Squab interrupted him. "Mention Toola and her establishment and all mouths close. No one even gossips about her. There is something about that that makes me nervous. She makes me nervous." Squab sat in a chair, her plump arms hugged tight to her chest. Flick shadowed her, his hands opening and closing in a nervous rhythm. Danton could see that they took the potential threat Toola represented quite seriously. It gave him pause. The bond between him and Toola was unshakable, he was sure. Yet, he had always trusted Squab's instincts. Had he made sure of Toola before stepping into her web of control? Their separation had lasted years. A number of governments had come and gone.

Danton sat back and considered them both. "That's natural, I suppose. She is well known here and a survivor of a few regimes. She must have connections with the government."

Squab sat forward suddenly. "Even to the point where people are afraid to speak about her?"

Danton shrugged. He needed more evidence that Toola was not to be trusted.

Squab picked up the flask of wine Danton had provided and examined it, turning it slowly as she sorted through her thoughts. "When I first arrived in Sartell and visited the brothel, she tried to lure me into her establishment...I refused her offer."

"Why?" Squab was not a woman to refuse a free meal and the opportunity to take a romp with a luscious girl. Or so he thought. He'd only seen her with the lost street kids that she took under her wing.

Squab put her hands back in her lap and looked him in the eye. "Because I had a gut feeling. I sensed that she was looking for a way to hook into me, a way to have power over me. And she had me followed."

That made Danton sit up. "Toola? I don't believe she meant to harm you. She likes to know things, everything."

Squab and Flick both nodded. "Believe it. We had to move after the first visit. I'm telling you it is no longer safe to confide in her. She should not be trusted."

Danton grinned. "I don't trust her, not completely, anyhow. I haven't told her anything that matters. If you hadn't come to see me, I would have sought you out."

Squab opened the wine and Flick placed three cups on the table. She poured a little into each cup. "That would have been hard if you were dead."

Danton took the wine and downed it. Then, staring at the empty cup, he said, "You're that suspicious of her?"

Squab nodded. "Danton, the city has changed. She has changed, if she was anything less than vicious before." She lifted a challenging eyebrow at him. "She may be your cousin, but you haven't seen her for years. Things change. Loyalties shift. It's every person for themselves these days."

Danton grinned savagely, remembering the childhood he and Toola had shared. Life was hard then; sometimes you did things to survive. He tried to imagine where her life had taken her after he'd left to search for something better, and recalled their brief meetings in the intervening years. "Maybe you're right," he said slowly. "Maybe she has changed. People have to do things to survive. Things they wouldn't normally do. Leave it to me, and I'll sort it out. So, are the others at the warehouse?"

Flick shook his head. "A meteor a few months ago took out the whole south side river frontage, destroying those warehouses. There is nothing but a crater there now. And a few weeks ago we had a daytime shower that left nice neat holes in the city. The north side is relatively intact. No real damage. There are a lot of frightened people, though. Quite a few doomsayers roam the streets, preaching that the end is nigh. Luckily our people weren't there when it happened."

Danton nodded. It didn't pay to add weight to the ramblings of madmen, particularly when they spoke the truth.

"Anything else?"

"There are a few new hot pools for bathing in near the crater," added Flick.

Danton nodded. Flick was always making jokes. It lifted the mood a little.

Squab continued on with her report, making sure to keep her voice low and even. "We found them somewhere else to meet. They gather at Stilton Haulage on code days one, three, five and seven, and two, four, six, and so on. It has worked so far."

"So how many do I have left?"

Squab straightened as if he had delivered a heavy blow. "All of them!"

"Good. I expected no less. If only I was as fortunate. I have to find Merl and the rest. If he failed to contact you then either there was trouble or he was able to track the wine to where they are hiding it and hasn't been able to get word to us yet."

Flick leaned in close, invading Danton's personal space. "But Merl would have sent you a message. Do you think your cousin has intercepted it?"

Danton pushed Flick back by the shoulders firmly. He knew Flick was a good friend of Merl's so he did not reprimand him. "It is possible, depending on who is in power and who Toola is in league with. That wine is hot property. The Inspector was in with a powerful group. It won't be easy getting information out of Toola if she doesn't want to give it. Let me think about it. I'm sure I'll come up with something. Meanwhile, keep your ears open for news of Merl. I sent Stinger and three others after the wine. They were to meet with Merl and keep going. If Merl was not where he was meant to be they may have come here. Do your best to find word of them too. I've lost too many men."

Flick stood when Danton got up. "And Earl and Riken?"

Danton shook his head. "Sorry, they didn't make it."

Flick's face froze. Those two had been his best friends. Danton let some of the hurt he'd been holding back come forward. Flick saw the grief and nodded before turning away. Squab eyed them both before leading Danton back downstairs and out into the busy street.

♋♋♋♋♋

Brill found himself wandering down the corridor to the kitchen in search of food. Danton had slipped out while he had slept, probably with Squab. As Brill didn't know where Danton had gone there was no point in seeking him out. More importantly, Brill needed to keep a low profile, so he stayed in the bathhouse. Although frustrated about being left behind, he was conscious that he may have been observed doing inappropriate things with Lexia. He had found the door ajar, as if someone had come in and then changed their mind. His cheeks heated at the thought.

On entering the kitchen he found Mandin looking relaxed with her hands around a warm cup of tea. The sun streamed in, pale pink through the window. Toola stood leaning against the wall, gazing at the back of Mandin's head, seemingly in deep thought. She looked up at his approach.

"You slept well?" Toola asked, her lips redder than usual in the harsh morning light.

Brill's face heated up and he gulped before speaking. "Yes. Thank you." A hot flush spread up his neck. Toola knew what he had done. Brill had to think of himself as an ordinary man in every way. Nothing special at all. No high moral ground. At least he was not like the Inspector or Ange or any of the government's cronies, but he had fallen short of his father's expectations. Worse, he'd fallen short of his own.

"Tea?" Toola asked, pulling out a stool for him to sit on. He nodded his thanks and said yes to the tea.

"And you two? How did you amuse yourselves last night?" he said, trying to divert the women's attention away from himself. To his surprise, Mandin looked down into her cup, avoiding his eye. That was not like her. A blush stole up her neck and her cheeks grew very red. Brill wondered if Mandin knew what he'd been doing too. His own face felt like a beacon.

135

Luckily Toola took up the conversational slack. "We had a very long bath together and a luxurious massage. Didn't we, dear?" Toola handed Brill the tea and then placed her hand on Mandin's shoulder. The Vanden woman's expression froze, her eyes meeting Brill's for a second before she again buried her face in her cup. Brill couldn't quite grasp what was going on, only that something was.

The hand stayed on Mandin's shoulder, caressing it lightly before Toola stepped away and went back to leaning on the door and looking out the window. "Danton left us earlier this morning."

"Yes, I saw he wasn't in his room." Brill took a sip of his tea.

Toola turned to face him again, her dark eyes searching his. "He had fun with those girls last night, didn't he? Such a lonely life he leads."

"Yes, I guess it is in that respect," Brill answered, not quite comfortable talking about Danton when he wasn't around, even if Toola was his cousin.

"I recall he was in love with a woman once." Toola pushed away from the wall and sat down gracefully in a spare chair by the table. Her gaze lingered on Mandin before being directed back at him.

"You must mean Salinda..."

Toola's eyes widened. "Salinda, the rebel baroness of Sartell?"

Brill nodded, though inside he cursed himself. What had he done? "Do you know her?" he asked carefully.

Just then Mandin coughed and dropped her mug on the floor. It landed with a thud then shattered, sending clay shards in all directions.

"Forgive me. How stupid," Mandin exclaimed as she dropped to her knees to pick up the pieces. Brill joined her, picking up the shards carefully and placing them in his palm. She shot him a warning look and shook her head slightly. Enough for him to realize that he had said more than he ought.

"Do not trouble yourselves. I will call a maid."

"It's no trouble," Mandin mumbled. Brill felt her gaze on him again and looked up from what he was doing. He smiled reassuringly, letting her know he'd gotten the message.

"I hope this mug wasn't a precious heirloom?" he quipped to Toola.

Toola had gone to fetch a broom and then joined in cleaning up.

When the broken mug was cleaned away Toola sighed as if fatigued. "How tiresome. We should have left it for the maid. Do be so kind as to fetch me some wine from the cellar, Mandin. I need a long, cool drink."

"Yes. My pleasure," Mandin replied. At the door she turned and shook her head ever so slightly before pulling it shut behind her.

"We were talking before of the baroness. I didn't know her personally, of course. Not quite my circle. I thought she was dead."

Brill realized that he couldn't lie effectively and had no choice but to speak the truth—though as little of it as possible.

"No, not dead. Well, not last time we saw her and that was quite a while ago now."

"And you say this is the woman that Danton loved?"

Brill shrugged. "Maybe once...long ago."

"He has been moving up in the world, hasn't he? My, my, he is a surprise."

Toola sat down in the chair again after putting the broom way. She leaned across the table, capturing Brill in her gaze. "I did hear that she was sent to prison. I recall something being mentioned. Is that where you met her?"

Brill realized the woman had him pinned. "Yes. A while ago now."

"And you escaped. I think Danton mentioned that."

Brill nodded and knew himself to be sinking ever deeper. Had Danton told her that? If it was a guess it was pretty close to the mark.

"Her mother took it very ill indeed, when she was sent away."

"Her mother? Isn't she dead?" Salinda would want news of her mother, of that he was sure. The poor woman thought she was dead.

Toola studied him, her finger stroking her chin as she rested her elbow on the table. "Dead? I don't think so."

"You know something of the mother, then? Is she alive and well?"

Toola's eyes sparkled. "That depends. My memory is not what it used to be. Perhaps if you do a little favor for me, I can ask around."

"Favor?" Brill was well and truly captured in the snare. Toola was so much better at this than he was, he thought mournfully.

"Yes. Mandin needs help finding her daughter. I was hoping that you would accompany them while she searched."

"Them?"

"Yes. I'm sending my best man to help her. Linel."

Relief swept through him. The favor was not the imposition he'd expected. "I'd be glad to help her." Brill's mind was working furiously. How was he going to ease himself out of this situation? Why hadn't he been ready when Danton had gone off with Squab? Even though the favor Toola asked was reasonable, he had a feeling that he had sunk himself in a muddy cesspit. It would not be the last favor.

"Perhaps while you are out you can keep your ears open for news of Renell, Salinda's mother. She's a servant now, I think, in one of the larger houses, close to the center of power."

Brill nodded. "Of course. Thank you." Then he breathed a sigh of relief when Mandin opened the door. "Oh, here is Mandin with the wine."

Toola barely spared her a glance. "Put it there on the bench, dear."

Toola eased out of her chair and pulled the bell cord. Mandin swept Brill with a glance before focusing her attention on Toola.

"Here's Linel. You best be heading off now. I'll tell Danton where you have gone when he gets back. Here's hoping you find what you are looking for, dear." Toola put her arms around Mandin and kissed her full and long on the lips.

"Dearest, take care," Toola said breathily as she released the Vanden woman.

Brill's mouth dropped open. His gaze flew to Linel, who remained expressionless in the doorway. Brill looked down at his boots, not knowing what else to do. He'd had no idea that Mandin preferred women. Hadn't she been married?

Toola released the Vanden woman and guided her out the door. Brill walked behind both Linel and Mandin until they exited the building.

Mandin whispered to him. "Things are not what they seem."

Chapter Seventeen

INTO THE CADRE

A few days back into the routine of life in Barrahiem and Salinda was uneasy. Nils was happy that she was back so it wasn't concern for him that was bothering her. It was the fact that she had to transfer the cadre from Laidan to Garan. Cadres were usually transferred at death but transferring them between live hosts was something else. When one bearer of the cadre died they entered into the cadre and passed to the living host. Usually the receiver had been trained to accept it. So while in principle the cadre could be transferred between live hosts she had no idea how to accomplish such a task. There was a risk that transferring it between two healthy and living individuals could cause damage to the cadre or the carrier. She just didn't know.

The cadre, however, was not being helpful. It knew of a transfer between two living carriers but the detail was buried a number of lives back. Salinda would have to reach through the layers of lives that formed the cadre to find the specific instructions and explore the particular circumstances of the earlier transfer before attempting one herself.

Salinda wasn't confident about reaching through layers of lives. She had never attempted it. Some solitude was needed for her to sort out her emotions and help her decide what needed to be done. Leaving dinner half-prepared, she left the Barr family node and made her way down to the city balconies. There the stillness wrapped around her and the sound of the dark waters of the lake lapping the distant shore soothed her.

She pushed away the daily chores and little things that occupied her mind. Then she recalled what Thurdon had said to her when she was helping Laidan settle the cadre. He had wanted Garan to have it. She should not feel guilty then about transferring it to him. Then she recollected the recent discussion she had had with Laidan. The girl didn't want the cadre and had rejected it. Finally she reflected on the manner in which the cadre had been passed to the girl in the first place. All of these things confirmed that she was taking the right action. Yet her emotions still nagged at her.

When she finally put things in perspective, she knew it was not how Laidan felt about the cadre that was important, but that Garan would be a better carrier. He already had a power of his own. There was great potential in the lad with both powers combined. Yes, she said to herself. It was the right thing to do. The *only* thing to do. Her indecision was swept away. The cadre glowed within her mind. It told her she had to seek the answer within. "Within?" she said aloud. "Dive through the layers. A place where you will not be disturbed. The layers are hard to navigate."

With one last mournful look out to the lake, she turned on her heel and headed back to the family node. It was time to talk to Nils, and to prepare. Once inside the node, she continued the preparations for the evening meal. Garan and Nils returned from their foray into the depths of Barrahiem. Garan was talkative and excited. Salinda was distracted and tried to ignore his chatter. Nils took over the food preparation without complaint and left Salinda to her own devices.

Sitting down on the sofa, she watched while Nils readied the meal, while he continued his conversation with Garan. Nils was quite animated, nodding to himself and confirming points that Garan made. Salinda found that she was surprised by Nils's energy. Obviously he had enjoyed himself. Salinda stood up and peered out the window. The lights were not on in the other abode. Laidan hadn't returned yet. Salinda chewed her lip, wondering whether she should go after her or send one of the others.

Distracted by her thoughts she didn't quite hear what Garan said. Her name was repeated. "I'm sorry. You said something?" she said, turning away from the window. Both Garan and Nils were staring at her. Garan sat on the sofa and leaned forward eagerly. "I said that when I touched the power cells, as Nils calls them, they re-energized. 'Tis like there is a crystal inside them. But ones so sensitive I do not have to hum to activate them."

Salinda blinked. Most of what Garan said was beyond her understanding. "You've been playing with Hiem technology? Both of you?"

She looked at them in turn.

"Yes," they answered in unison.

"I thought you were exploring the archives."

"That is so," Nils replied. "I went to the archives while Garan repaired lights."

Salinda was about to comment when Laidan showed her face at the door.

"I'm not hungry," she said without making eye contact. Then, backing out of the doorway, she added, "See you tomorrow," in a tone so sullen, Salinda bit her lip. Stepping back to the window Salinda watched as Laidan entered her abode. Satisfied that the girl was going to stay put, Salinda sat back down on the sofa that Garan had just vacated.

Garan had stepped carefully over to the window. He seemed too big and tall next to the small aperture. "Sleep well," he called after Laidan.

Salinda repressed the urge to tell him he was wasting his breath. Then she caught Nils staring at her and changed the direction of her thoughts. As they ate their meal Garan and Nils told her about the project to light the city once more.

"That's fascinating. Do you think it can be done?"

There was a light in Nils's eyes. "It is a worthy venture. There is nothing to be lost in the attempt."

Garan looked from Nils to her. "Recharging the power cells was easy enough. 'Tis a large city, but if we worked every day it would not take long. And the result would be fantastic."

"Indeed," added Nils, sipping his tea. Then Salinda saw the glow in him, the happiness that could not be disguised. She had not seen Nils this excited before. She longed to talk to him about it, even though she had her own news to share.

They talked until late and once she'd said good night to Garan and pushed him out of the door, she sighed. Nils had entered their bedroom while Salinda turned out the lights. "This means a lot to you, Nils, doesn't it?" she asked him as she slid off her robe. Muted light drifted in through the window. Shedding his own clothes he stood there, his white skin illuminated by the light of the shuwai. Salinda caught her breath. He was so beautiful at that moment. Poised, confident and happy. It brought tears to her eyes. "Tell me," she asked him as she slid into bed. He joined her there.

"The lights bring me hope that my kind will be remembered. I know it is a vain hope and a ridiculous emotion. But the city filled with light will make it seem less empty. We will light the sacred lamp when it is done and then I will make sure that its flame does not falter again."

Caressing his face with one hand and smoothing the hair out of his eyes with the other, Salinda leaned forward and brushed a kiss across his brow. "Your happiness is important to me, Nils."

Nils came to her then, making love to her more deeply and movingly than he had before. As she lay in his embrace afterward, she tried to think of how to break the news to him that she needed to go away for a while. He was silent as she spoke of her need to concentrate and reach into the cadre to find out how to transfer the cadre from Laidan to Garan. Then, taking his silence as a good sign, she asked him to keep an eye on her charges and to care for them while she was absent. This, too, he acknowledged with a nod and a stroke of her hair.

"Nils? Aren't you going to say anything? Are you awake?"

"Yes. I am awake."

"So, can I go?"

"You seek my permission? I did not realize. I will take charge of the children. It is an extra burden but the lighting project will keep them busy."

Salinda lay there listening to him breathing. Carefully she pulled back to stare at his face and saw that his eyes were open. He looked to be thinking, long and hard.

"What troubles you?"

"I am thinking of a place where you could go, a place of solitude and reverence, such is necessary for the kind of task you undertake.

When I was a child my mother took me to an island on the lake. It is not far from the city and not far from the shore. It is a special place for women, a place of stories and secrets."

"Oh. I had not noticed it before. It thought you did not travel on the lake. Are you sure that it is acceptable? Isn't the lake sacred?"

"To swim in it and at that particular spot where we first mated, yes, it is sacred." He alluded to her dip in the lake that had precipitated their joining. "When the city was alive and full of people there was trade between N'Barek and here. Some preferred to ferry across. I will take a look and see if any vessels remain. With Garan's help, I am sure we can get one functioning."

"Very well. I'll talk to Laidan in the morning and ready my supplies. I'm not sure how long it will take, only that I need no interruption. Please wait until I return before you mention what I intend to Garan."

"I will, but Laidan may not wait. She may tell him before I have the opportunity."

Salinda sighed. "Yes. You are right. Answer his questions as best you can. I'll do the rest when I return."

As she nestled down to sleep, Salinda moved Nils's hand to her abdomen, and they both felt the child kick as she drifted off to sleep.

☙☙☙☙☙

Salinda rowed out to the island. In the end no mechanism could be found to power the little punt that Nils had fashioned for her out of old materials. It didn't take her long and within the hour she was lifting out the supplies Nils had packed.

The island was a mound of barren stone covered with a layer of soft white sand. Instead of trees, which she imagined any normal island would have, it had stone columns carved in various designs, mostly free-form geometrical shapes. They were quite interesting to Salinda, because they differed from the designs in the city. She could see the similarity in style but there was a hand at work that created greater movement and flow, as if the wind were blowing through the carvings, altering their shape, contorting them. With a smile she thought that a wind would probably make a tune, like upright flutes. Some of the shapes curved around themselves, or bent and twisted, grasping at empty air.

Overhead hung the bare roof of the cavern, so high that she could not see it clearly. Sleeping without a house over her head would be no hardship. She was used to no roof, only sky. She wondered what the next days would bring. As she laid out a ground cloth and stacked her supplies within easy reach, she had to admit to some trepidation. This would be her first time plunging into the depths of the cadre. The cadre had told her a transfer between living hosts had been attempted once before, many, many lives ago. Yet, the cadre was a different object now, larger, more complex, layered with many more lives and experiences. There was also an element of risk for her. The experience could change her, and most likely would. It would yield information but she may also gain unwanted things—experiences, knowledge, power. Those could do strange things to an unprepared or weak mind.

Before starting she made herself a meal and ate slowly, while listening to the rhythm of the lake as the water lapped against the shore. The lake had a gentle ebb and flow that was barely noticeable up in the city. Here in the midst of it, the sounds, the gurgles and splashes, surrounded her, enveloped her. Without thinking about it, she had begun to calm and to settle and to empty her mind.

Closing her eyes, she let the lake sing her down into the depths of herself, down into the shining mass that was the cadre. Here it seemed a glowing ball. She reached out tentatively but there was resistance to her short probe. Her mind was not to join with the cadre until she passed it on in death. Now she wanted to enter the cadre, without dying first. She knew the cadre was formed of many minds, each layering upon the other as lifetimes passed by. She needed to reach the life of the person who transferred the cadre between living people because the specifics were not available in the outer layers of the cadre.

With hardened resolve, she dove in, piercing the outer layer as if diving through the surface tension of water. Coils of life began to snag at her sense of being. Bits of her were dragged away, sucked down into the depths. Images of strange people and other places began to dance in her mind. They phased in and out with voices calling, singing, begging, talking, screaming. Whispers loud, whispers soft crashed against her mind like the ocean against the shore. Overwhelmed by the press of the congealed mass of minds, she used one of the exercises Mez had taught her to consolidate her own presence, her own sense of self, and became a wedge that sliced through the layers of ten lifetimes. Even though she made progress, she could tell she was still wallowing in the shallows. She had not penetrated very far at all. The extent of the cadre worked against her. So many lives. So many years. So much knowledge.

However, she gained some insight into what had gone wrong with Thurdon's transfer. The carrier had to work their way into the cadre, invest themselves within it so it could be passed on. Thurdon had not had time to perform the ritual, to embed himself into the substance of the cadre. No wonder the old man was so individual and distinct when he was first transferred. The very process of the cadre's formation, though, was working against her. She was looking for a distinct individual mind among a blended many. If she thought of the cadre as a brain, then it was possible to find the personality she was looking for. She just needed to trigger a memory and follow the thread.

Salinda threw out a dart of thought: *transfer*.

One large tendril of light shot out. A rending pain in her own mind induced a scream that echoed off the lake around her.

Then she came to, face down in the sand on the shore where the lake lapped at her feet. She had moved from the center of the island to a place where she could have drowned. Day one had not been a success. After the slow crawl back to her campsite, every muscle in her body had been wrung out and bashed against the rocks like laundry. Ever so carefully, she pulled herself into a sitting position and sipped water from her supplies. There were two choices open to her: sleep or try again. A quick assessment of her physical pain and she realized that sleep was the only option for now. As she closed her eyes the kernel of light in her mind expanded.

☾☾☾☾☾

Nils stood in the passageway, pleased with how the lights were looking. Garan stood on his tiptoes while Laidan passed him repaired lamps. Garan turned around suddenly and dropped the lamp he was holding. "What was that noise?"

Laidan chewed her lip. "I didn't hear anything." Her gaze sought Nils, her expression questioning.

Nils had felt it, more than heard it. "Salinda?" He could feel the tug and twist on his bond. Salinda was suffering, but safe. He began to regret his acquiescence to her plan to venture off alone. Maybe she needed him to look after her. Yet he could not go against her trust now and go to her. Nor could he leave these two alone in the city.

Without warning, Garan was standing next to him. Nils stepped back and realized that the boy had walked up to him while Nils's mind had been on Salinda. "Why did she go away? Is she all right?"

Nils's gaze shifted to Laidan as she walked up behind Garan. The girl had accepted Salinda's absence without comment.

Nils angled his head to one side as he regarded Laidan. "Salinda is well," he said. "She will be back soon and will talk to you then."

Garan's expression was puzzled. He looked down at the ground and shuffled his feet.

Laidan flicked her hair over one shoulder and nudged Garan with her elbow to get his attention. "It's because of me. She wants to give you this." She pointed to her head.

Garan turned and gaped at her. After a moment he said, "The cadre? But..." Garan looked from Laidan to Nils, mouth opening and shutting.

Nils raised a hand for quiet. "It is for you to discuss with her on her return. Now we must work so that this section can be completed. Laidan, leave those lights there and come with me to fetch more. Garan can continue on without us."

Laidan returned to where she had been working and stacked the lights up in a neat pile. Garan would be able to access them with little difficulty. With a backward glance over her shoulder, she accompanied Nils to the manufacturing storeroom. Nils was pleased he had delayed the inevitable discussion between the two young ones.

As they walked, Nils reflected that Laidan had been well behaved and had taken the news that she was to be left in his care without comment or reproach. She appeared more at peace than before, a little more thoughtful in her actions, and her level of respectfulness had increased noticeably. Now and then, Nils caught her staring at Garan with a wrathful expression, but he sensed her anger was less directed now. Perhaps the thought that the cadre would soon be gone gave her comfort.

Nils was keen to witness this cadre and its transfer. It would make for very good reading in the archives. Would anyone believe such an account? Nils, the chronicler of dragons. Nils and his account of a magical, mystical cadre. With a slight twitch of his brow, he mentally added, Nils's record of a boy who could recharge power cells with a touch. Surely they would think the demise of his kind had disarranged his mind. He made a mental note to ensure he captured evidence. Who knew what type of person would inherit the vast store of knowledge in the archives? Would that it was his own kind, but that was a vain hope. They were dead and gone. Soon he would join them. Perhaps Garan's prediction was right and his child, his offspring, would inherit it all. Believing that would be giving in to hope. Nils was not quite ready for that yet. He doubted that any of them would survive.

Laidan began to chatter as they sorted through the shelves. Nils nodded absently, pretending to listen. He wished that Salinda would return soon. He feared that Salinda was suffering, physically as well as mentally.

⬱⬱⬱⬱⬱

Salinda prepared for the next dive into the cadre. She stacked her supplies around her to prevent her rolling away down the slope into the water. The kernel of light had been a thought and had provided a name, a way to map through the cadre. Lying down on the ground, she began the incantation that would settle her mind, help form herself into the wedge. Then she was in. This time she ignored the images, the incredible babble of voices and whispers that were hundreds of minds' memories and thoughts, and spoke the name: Keron.

It was like being sucked into a vortex. Down into the deeper layers of the cadre she dove. Lifetimes of experience flashed up into her mind. A city sprawling with people. She did not recognize it. Another continent perhaps? It was after Ruel had fallen, judging by the sky. Another image shot up at her. With it knowledge of the past. Important information. When the cadre was first formed there had been seven minds—seven minds that joined to form the core of the cadre. Who they were, why they joined together and how they had done it was still a mystery.

Keron, where are you?

The mind image of Keron took shape in her mind. Using that as an anchor, she dove into the sea of ideas and images, seeking within that personality's particular thoughts. She was near the end of her strength when she stumbled upon something. Keron was near the center of the cadre: its origin. She was not to go there; to do so would risk the unraveling of the cadre. It would not survive another division. Division? The cadre had been divided? Did that mean the other was once part of this one? Why had it been divided? Could they be rejoined, and if

147

so, how and when? That was it though. If the cadre had been divided then it had been transferred. She had to peek into that moment. The cadre fought her because it did not want to be divided again. To calm it she thought of Mez, remembering his gravelly voice as he talked about the sun, rain, dragon dung and the care of grapes. Mez was part of the cadre now. It would recognize the memory, recognize her. Trust her perhaps. Something clicked, the barrier dropped and she slid through. Once in the next layer, she did not expect the pain.

Her heels banged on the ground as she tried to win through the agony in her head. Here were minds, full and bright in their intensity, a group of old ones bound tight in a purpose. They did not wish her there. They did not wish their number divided: Merkon, Taha, Rinul and Benenge. They were the ones who had given their lives to form the cadre. The other three had been separated out, taken, ripped away in an hour of need. They stood together and tried to push her out and shouted at her in unison. *Be gone!*

In their minds Salinda glimpsed the great machine, saw them enter and disappear. They had given themselves for the future of Margra. Their faces showed their hope and fear. Her tears began to fall. What a sight, what feeling, what bravery! She could not match it. The essences of what they once were rounded on her and pushed harder. She saw in their minds Keron who had split them, heard his words, saw his method. Then they attacked. *You risk great harm being here.* They tore bits off her as she passed out of the core. She had not gently caressed the core as she had intended but had blundered in there to the raw center.

Her eyes had been open for quite a while before she was able to blink and clear her vision. To breathe was to long for death. Her body hurt like the slash of the Inspector's whip except it emanated from inside her. After a time she could see the blur of the cavern roof overhead. When the pain dropped a level she rested and let the experience of the last few days filter through her consciousness. Her view of the world was now altered. She had done what Mez had never done, what no one had done before, because the cadre was now something more than its originators had envisaged. She had swum the tide of mind and power and survived.

Chapter Eighteen

NAVIGATING THE PECKING ORDER

Gercomo eyed the dragons surrounding him as he lay half-buried in warm sand. None came near him. Hopefully that was because he was beneath their notice. His hunger had intensified. Sniffing the air and letting his dragon sense roam, he realized that the rest of the dragons were hungry too. While he looked on, four of the herd headed out to search for food. Their wing beats lifted up dust and sand as they took off over the plain.

A short while later another three returned, their claws scraping against the rocks as they made their way back to report. A ripple of frustration flowed over him, emanating from the herd. All of them were very hungry indeed. Gercomo wondered if they had always had an issue with the scarcity of food. The thought of those eggs came to mind. If only he could find the opportunity. The returned dragons went off to rest among the boulders and in between the clefts surrounding the pit. More dragons took off in search of food. Gercomo closed his eyes, letting the warmth of the earth cover him. *Soon,* he thought, *soon.*

There was no sign of the other dragons returning. Those that remained were dulled by hunger and sleep. He found he could understand their feelings and feel their presence more keenly the longer he remained with them. It was the opportunity he had been waiting for. After sniffing the air and reaching out with his dragon sense, keeping his own thoughts guarded, he stood up, shaking the sand from his back and curling his claws to smooth out the cricks. Then, as casually as he could, he wandered to the wall of the pit and circled it, assessing the easiest path he could see. All was quiet and still. None of the dragons had taken note of his movement. Carefully and quietly he scrambled over boulders that provided a barrier to the hatchery. His size gave him an advantage in the closed space. Once in the hatchery proper, he swiveled around, inhaling deeply to catch a particular female's scent. It took a few sniffs to pinpoint the spot.

Reaching out again, he sensed that the other dragons were still sleeping. In the distance, though, one strong presence was drawing closer. He had to hurry.

Placing himself carefully, he lowered his head and received a full bouquet of her scent. The life force in the eggs had increased; they'd had time to mature. A nudge with his snout and the eggs were bared to daylight. In one gulp they were down his throat. They tasted good— young, small life forces. Enough to keep him sated. He covered the nest hastily, then leaped over the boulder and back to his resting place.

The brooding alpha male approached. Slinking over to his nesting spot, Gercomo re-covered his hide in sand and feigned sleep. The bull roared a command. Shaking his hide free of dirt and pebbles, Gercomo walked forward and lowered his snout. The vibrations of the bull's footsteps tickled Gercomo's snout, but he kept his head down and his mind blank.

Gercomo abased himself. The bull sniffed the air around him. Then after a few moments turned away. Gercomo lifted his snout, cautiously assessing the situation. The bull's head turned toward him, nostrils leaking steam. Then he continued to his own roost. Gercomo cocked an eye open, watching the bull scramble up the side of the largest mound of rock and settle himself down. Gercomo felt a grin inside of him. He was beginning to get ideas, beginning to see opportunities that could be exploited. *No point in rushing*, he thought. *May as well take the time to think things through.* Dying needlessly was not part of his long-term plan. For now his hunger was sated and he had taken some small token revenge at the same time. He returned to his resting place within the herd and nestled into place.

ᝏᝏᝏᝏ

The days passed slowly for Gercomo but at least he was free of the pit and no longer subject to random bullying. So far the eggs he had gobbled greedily had not been missed. The herd continued to avoid him, as though he was a pile of dung accidentally placed in the middle of the herd instead of in the crevices usually frequented for waste disposal.

Gercomo decided it was time to fly. It was time to test the boundaries of his expanded prison. If he did not find food for himself soon, he would starve. What food was brought back to the herd was shared only between the herd, but not him. In the last week only part of a burden beast had been brought back. Not even the bones had been left behind. It had come to the point where survival meant taking risks.

Gercomo shook the sand free from his hide. He pissed on the rock, marking his roost, and then ambled down the path the dragons took when they were departing. A few heads lifted as he passed. The bull stirred, his brooding presence centered on him. Gercomo let the thought of food fill his mind. He pictured a burden beast, fat and succulent. An image of the woman he had eaten broke through. Yes, he had been thinking of finding some humans to eat. The bull growled low and leaped from his roost. The ground shook with the impact and Gercomo lowered himself to the ground, squashing himself as flat as possible. The heavy steps thumped the ground. Gercomo's fear rose. Had he been too hasty? No, he must eat to live.

The bull pushed him with his snout. Gercomo panicked and let all kinds of thoughts into his head. *No, no…don't*, he thought. *I'll bring you food. Lots of food*. The bull stopped his attack. Gercomo lifted his head and met that gaze. Was he imagining it or did the bull like the idea of food being brought back? Gercomo lowered his head and then slowly turned to continue on his way out of the herd. A grunt from the bull made him pause. He angled his head around and saw that two other bulls were following him. So they were going to let him fly, but he was to be accompanied. No chance of escape. Also he would have to make good on his promise about the food. Interesting predicament to be in. Gercomo did not know where he was in relation to any towns or even a stray burden beast. He would have to trust to luck.

Yet his mood was cheery as he began his run, flapping his wings, leaping up to catch a thermal. He had had a victory of sorts. Communication was the key. Now that he had that, he could refine his plans, work them around, twist them. He had to prove that his size did not reflect his personal power or his intellect. He had to best the bull.

Chapter Nineteen

A SLAVE TRAP

The streets of Sartell were confusing and overwhelming. Mandin had never traveled to a city before, and now that so much had happened to her, she wished she had never set foot in the place. Sometime during the previous night, she had slipped from being comforted to being preyed upon. There was no other way to describe it. At first she had not known how to fend off Toola, as she was so friendly, so subtle in her intrigues. Lulled with a warm bath and heady dragon wine, Mandin had fallen into a trap. How could Danton trust this woman? Did he know what lengths she would go to to get what she wanted?

First, she had used the lure of finding Mandin's daughter, Eneit, to cast a subtle web around her. Then Toola had talked about her vast contacts, further drawing Mandin in and making her drop her guard. Then with the bath and the massage, she'd claimed Mandin's body an inch at a time. A casual touch—a strange seduction. She was sunk in it before she knew what was going on. Her face heated at the memory. Was it true that she had participated unknowingly, unwittingly? She had so many doubts about herself now. It wasn't as if she was ignorant about women making love to one another. After all, she had heard of these things before, whispered in the markets, hinted at around the fireplace. Vanden did not have the patience for such waste of passion. It was man and woman, however disharmonious, because marriage was for procreation, for in children there was survival.

The worst thing, which burned Mandin with shame, was that

Toola had done things to her, created such sensations in her body, that Mandin had found herself somewhere she had never been before. Orgasm. Just like that. A rumored by-product of the marriage bed, though one she had never experienced before. Then in the afterglow the woman had meted out instructions and Mandin, drunk on wine and sex, had complied. Foolishly. Even now she could not recall the point where she could have left the bath and walked away. Now she experienced all manner of feelings of shame and obligation. What was worse, she knew with certainty that the situation would end badly. As bad as the day Lenk had welcomed Gercomo to Vanden, as bad as the day the prince and princess were found poisoned and as stiff as boards.

Her burning shame was going to be a constant reminder. Brill knew. How could he not know after the way Toola had kissed her when they left the brothel this morning? How was she going to get out of this predicament? How was she going to do it without damaging the rebel cause and her own search?

The stink of the city intruded upon her senses and the press of people drew her back to the moment. She'd been following along blindly as they wove through the crowds going about their business. Just the number of people she could see near overwhelmed her. There were more people in the streets than in all of Vanden. Linel accompanied them and he was frightening to behold. His face was a mass of scars and he had one burned, shriveled arm. Mandin couldn't quite figure out if his disfigurement was a result of being a slave or whether it had come about by other means—like punishment meted out by his boss. He certainly behaved in a slavish way toward Toola. It was the way he watched her more than anything else that gave it away. There was a hound-like devotion in his eyes, the way his whole head as well as his eyes tracked her. Did the woman sleep with him? Beat him? Mandin's own experience limited her contemplation of Toola's array of depravities.

The man limped, as if his right foot was shorter than the left. Toola had said that the bottom of his foot had been sliced off years before, so that might account for it. Mandin shuddered. It was natural for her to recoil from it. Disfigurement of any kind usually meant ostracism. Birth defects were eliminated completely. She had lost a child once, a boy born with a harelip. The village elders had taken it and exposed it or drowned it. She never knew. Even then Mandin had considered herself lucky. All of her sister's children had been destroyed. All of them had had some kind of defect, from a turned-in foot to curly ears. That was why Mandin was alone in the world now. Merta couldn't take it and had thrown herself in the river during a storm. Her bloated body had turned up a week later farther down the bank. Her husband had married again; some young thing that Lenk had imported. Well used, too, beforehand, if the stories about Lenk were true. Her brother-in-law had always been atop the poor girl. Childbirth had carried her away after the third birthing. Mandin had always hated the man. Now he was ash on the mountaintop, crushed between Gercomo and the might of the observatory. She was not sorry about that.

Since leaving the brothel, Mandin had had no chance to talk to Brill without Toola's man overhearing. Linel stopped at the head of a laneway and pointed with his arm to something down the lane. The young lad turned where directed and Mandin kept up the rear. How easy it would be to get lost, she thought. As she turned into the lane, she was overcome by the stench and the shadows. *But it is sunny*, she thought to herself, and then looked up. Piled high along the sides of the buildings were cages made of old metal and salvaged wood. In them were people—slaves. Some rested against the bars, pushing their faces out as if to breathe the clean, free air. Everywhere was the smell of shit and sweat. Mandin lifted the edge of her tunic shirt to cover her mouth. Brill's face was a study of horror. She shook her head at him, warning him to say nothing. Her gaze flicked over to Linel and, lowering the cloth covering her nose and mouth, she smiled at him. "A slave market?" Her enthusiasm was feigned. Her daughter could not be in a place like this—must not be in a place like this. How could anyone exist here?

As they walked down the lane, she saw that there were many slavers. Some were small-scale operators with only one or two slaves. Linel walked right past them, obviously aiming for one particular slaver. On the left-hand side, three-quarters of the way down the wall, the cages were stacked ten high. She saw a gantry used to lower the cages for potential buyers' inspection.

Linel signaled to the owner of this particular stall. The slaver's clothing was as ragged and as filthy as his merchandise. The sour smell of unwashed bodies and urine wafted over her as he leaned in close to inspect his prospective customers. "Toola's man," he said, squinting at them. "What can I do for her?—your mistress."

Linel spoke slowly, his voice gravelly. "These people are searching for a girl..."

At this the man eyed them both more closely. The stink from his rotting teeth nearly bowled Mandin over. "If they have money, I've got girls." He grinned and it wasn't pretty. "Greetings friends of Toola. Bisma is the name. What is your desire?

Brill barged in, his elbow hitting Mandin in the ribs. She glared at him but remained silent. "We are looking for a particular girl. She was brought in with some others from the countryside by a group of men. From upriver."

The man rubbed his chin as if considering. Then he caught Linel's eye and his eyes widened. "Can't say I've heard of such a shipment. Get stock in all the time."

Mandin thought the man was seeking a bribe. Brill thought the same by the looks of things. He dug into his purse and drew out a coin.

The slaver studied the coin after it was placed in his hand. "Most of the slaves we get are from upriver. More are coming in every day." He looked at Brill and then met Mandin's eye, then his gaze slid to Linel's. Mandin caught the man's shudder. Something was going on that she didn't understand. The slaver acted as if he was afraid. "What we get in this market is low quality. Dust mad, most of them, so the price is dropping considerably."

"But these are all girls. All good quality," Brill said.

The slaver stretched his neck and rubbed it. Beneath partially lowered eyelids he watched Linel. "All the good stock has been going elsewhere. I don't know where. Can't interest you in what's left of my prime stock?"

The slaver knew something, she was sure. But for some reason he was holding back. She needed to talk to Brill but not with Toola's man present. Mandin lifted her chin, once again taking over the direction of the conversation. Brill chewed on his bottom lip. "We have time. When did they come in?" Mandin hoped that a mistake might be made; one of the girls, if not her Eneit, might be among them despite the slaver saying otherwise.

"I get some fresh every day. Any particular size or shape you're after?"

"No. Just show me what you have. The one I'm after might be among them," she said, hoping to give a worldly impression. She dared not look at Linel. What tale would he take to Toola?

The slaver screamed out orders and cages began to move along the gantry. Looking up, Mandin saw a cage coming from a complex behind the stall front. *So*, she thought, *he has other slaves that he keeps out of sight*. Hope blossomed in her chest.

When the cage rested on the ground, Brill recoiled. He said nothing but his face paled and the hand he held over his mouth shook. Inside the cage were two girls and a boy. They looked about eight or nine years old. None were from the Vanden lot. Smaller, darker and hollow-eyed, they gaped at her as if they hadn't seen a woman before. One grunted and pointed to the slaver. Then the three of them grunted and chirped. It appeared to be their language. Source! They were taking the Lesserens' children and making them slaves. Even Mandin had heard of the villages of half-men, living in the wilderness and interbreeding so much that they had become what was known as lesser-men— Lesserens.

"What kind of filth are you pushing here?" she said. "Do you think I'm some country hick that don't know the difference between real humans and animals?"

She turned on her heel to walk away. Disgusted, ashamed and mostly filled with dread. Her daughter wasn't there.

The slaver waved his arms as he followed her and the offending slaves were lifted away. Brill jogged at her side. Linel kept pace with her easily enough, his dog-like expression never wavering. An odd thought occurred to her: that he could be memorizing everything she said and did. What did that mean for her search?

"Naw, naw, don't get riled. I'm telling ya that there's not much around. Come around again, later or tomorrow, and I'll see if'n I have better."

Mandin slowed and glanced over her shoulder. "We'll see, though I'm not impressed so far with your wares. I can't see you stocking anything human, let alone high quality."

The slaver bowed low to her. "Surely I am not at my best, mistress." Brill asked Linel a question about the other stalls, and Toola's man turned away from her conversation with the slaver. To her surprise, the slaver winked. "Come alone," he whispered and jabbed a finger in Linel's direction. Linel swung around abruptly and the slaver bowed low and then scurried back to his stall, shouting at his workers to lift this and move that. Mandin faced forward. "Shall we go?" Linel studied her and then his eyes slid in the direction of the slaver. That look gave Mandin a shiver up her spine. Had he spotted that brief interchange? For the first time in weeks, Mandin tasted danger on the back of her tongue. She didn't like the flavor of it at all. Yet, she needed to distract this man, needed to keep Toola out of her business.

"Linel, that is the most disgusting man I have ever met. Surely you can do better than that. My daughter would not be in a place like this. Isn't there a better market?"

Linel said nothing. He stepped in front of her, and when they returned to the intersection, he cleared a path for them. Brill looked done in, as if he had never seen real human misery and suffering before. Well, they did say he was a prince of some kind. He was a bit uppity, or had been at first. It made her wonder why he had become a rebel. What joy could there be for the likes of him? Lenk and his brother had been scum, but at least they had kept order. The prince had been fair in his way. High taxes, but at least he didn't paw too many of the young children. Unlike his brother, who had hunted a broad range of prey.

Linel did take them to an uptown market. It was cleaner, but the misery was the same. None of the slavers had anything to say. None acted as strangely as the one that winked at Mandin. Most acted if they couldn't be bothered even thinking about Mandin's request. All showed deference to Linel, knew him by name and sent greetings or promises of gifts to Toola. Mandin now suspected that Toola had a lot of influence in Sartell. Not all of it good. She may be new to a big city, but she detected a small town closed-mouthedness about the slavers' behavior and their reaction to Linel. Like he was the village bully and Toola was his mother who owned everyone and everything. She shook her head at the thought. Cities should have been different to towns. By the afternoon, Brill had recovered his spirits, although his shoulders slumped and his smile never reached his eyes. She supposed he'd seen too much misery, just as Mandin had. "How do they find so many people to sell?" he asked Linel as they left the market to head back to the brothel.

"Find them—unprotected."

Mandin shuddered once again. The dry way Linel spoke scared her. If Danton or Brill abandoned her, she would be unprotected, a potential human to be captured, harvested and then sold like meat. That is what Toola had hinted at. Was it true, then? Did she need that awful woman's protection? She shuddered. What sort of government was in power here? With all its problems, at least Vanden had had very little slavery. Only the prince's mansion could afford any.

As they pushed their way through the crowds, avoiding the pickpockets and the beggars and the rough-looking men, who could be rebels or town police, Mandin began to lose hope. How was she ever going to escape that woman's clutches? How was she even going to get Brill alone to warn him and tell him of her suspicion that the first slaver knew more than he was saying? She would need his help to find the market again. Then she could enlist Danton's help. If they found Eneit, they would find a path to the men who had taken her. That would lead him to the wine. The dragon wine was the most important thing to the rebel leader. That is why they followed the same path. For now at least.

Finding Eneit should have led them to the wine. But now that connection was growing thin. It was likely that Eneit and the wine had gone separate ways. The longer it took the more tenuous the connection and colder the trail. The time for her and the rebels to part ways loomed large. It made her heart race. Her thoughts were running rife and her choices were soon to be limited. She had to save her daughter and at the same time she wanted to help Danton find the wine.

By the time they slipped through the entrance to the bathhouse she had convinced herself that Toola had every room covered with spies, or at least a spyhole. It must be so, because that woman knew everything that went on. To speak to Danton where no one else could hear was going to take some ingenious thinking.

Chapter Twenty

INFORMATION BITES

Danton was in the bath relaxing alone when Mandin and Brill returned from their outing. Toola had made herself scarce so Danton was unable to pump her for information and test for himself whether Squab's conviction that something sinister was going on was true. He began to think that Toola was avoiding him and then laughed off his paranoia. She was his cousin. She was blood. They had helped each other too often to stoop to betrayal. He was wary of revealing too much to her but he was not convinced that she was guilty of formulating some deeper plan against him.

When Mandin stopped by the bath, a deep vee of concern between her brows, and then knelt down beside him, he grew concerned. Outwardly, she looked well. Since she had left Vanden, she'd lost weight and was fitter and healthier. Brill hovered in the background, looking pale. Obviously something had happened.

Mandin's gaze met his. She leaned forward, giving him a glimpse of the tops of her breasts. "Mandin?" he said, leaning away from her.

In a startling move, she ran her fingers through his hair. Danton's body tensed. Something was definitely wrong. He relaxed as Mandin leaned in close. "What is it?" he said under his breath. "Danton, you cheeky man. Oh stop," she said out loud. The sound rippled off the bathwater and echoed around the room.

Brushing her cheek against his, she whispered right into his ear. "Invite me to your room tonight. We have to talk."

He froze for a moment, then reached up a wet hand to stroke her cheek. "You're looking good, Mandy," he said, not quite prepared for sweet talk. *Lame,* he thought. *So lame.* "No luck in your search? I'll make it up to you later." He cringed inwardly, but what was he supposed to do? He had no desire for Mandin, nor she for him for that matter. Things must be bad. As Mandin walked away, exaggerating the swagger of her behind, Danton sunk into the water. Very bad. He wondered what had happened. But if Mandin was acting cautious in the brothel that meant she was suspicious of Toola too. He swallowed hard, not liking that this added further justification to Squab's distrust. The possibility that Toola would betray him made him feel vulnerable as well as stupid. He came up for air to find Brill standing above him.

"I was looking for you earlier," Danton said, wiping water from his face and then shaking it out of his ears. "Why did you go with Mandin when we had other business to attend to?" he asked Brill.

Brill tilted his head, then looked around. The brothel attendants went about their business, stacking towels, folding robes. Others brought water and filled long-neck jugs or wine to fill decanters. Delicate hands arranged fruit on platters. They were not alone. Danton's heart leaped. "I'm sorry I wasn't around. Toola asked me to go as a favor and as it was Mandin I thought it would be all right."

Danton's eyebrows rose. "A favor? Interesting."

Brill knelt down, not as close as Mandin had. "We need to talk," he said in a soft voice.

Danton sat up higher in the water. "Next time check with me before you go running off to do errands for others. You work for me."

Brill stared, but relaxed when he saw Danton's wink. "Yes, sir," he replied in a clipped tone, one that echoed. "Understood."

Danton nodded, the sense of gloom gathering, making him clench his teeth. He scratched under his chin to give the impression that he wasn't concerned or interested.

"Pass me a towel would you?"

Brill went to a pile and retrieved one to pass it over. Danton leaned in casually and in a quiet voice he added, "Be ready for anything. Be ready early. Use caution."

Brill eyed him for a moment longer, then nodded. "See you at dinner then." Brill walked off. The lad looked like his world had fallen down. Danton felt a slight twinge of guilt. He had meant to educate the lad, not undermine his whole physical and moral foundation. Danton delayed as long as he could in the bathhouse. He ignored the other patrons and the girls. He needed to think. In his mind he mapped the physical layout of the bathhouse and brothel. Then he began to analyze the set-up and the key places where spies could hide, where conversations could be overheard. He didn't like what he was coming up with. His room appeared particularly vulnerable. He couldn't so much as fart without someone knowing. If what he now suspected was true, the fake liaison suggested by Mandin would have to be convincing given the level of scrutiny.

Later, as Toola hosted a meal for them, Danton saw that she did her best to impress them. Her girls would not start work until after the meal so she arrayed her elite ones in virtually nothing and set them to serve the food. Brill didn't seem to know where to focus his gaze. A well-built male from the men's club across the way, wearing only a fine ribbon wrapped around his penis, was also serving food. Mandin appeared quite fascinated with him. Danton would have fun later asking her what interested her more: the size, or the color of the wrapping?

Danton had to do his best to think up a plausible lead-up to the introduction of Mandin into his love life. He knew Toola was no fool. With all these beautiful whores around, his cousin had left him very little room to maneuver. He had sampled a couple of them already. How was he to explain that? His only hope was that Brill went along with it, since he'd had no chance to warn the lad. Danton knew he was taking an awful risk. If Mandin had chosen Brill as her quarry, they could have put about that the lad had a mother complex. That thought made him grin evilly.

"What makes you smile so, Danny?" Toola asked as she shook her hair out. It fell long and dark down her back. Danton noticed that her smile didn't extend to her eyes, which were tracking everything in the room.

"I was thinking of Mandy actually."

Toola's eyebrow arched at that, then her lips narrowed. "Really? I thought you did not fraternize with your followers."

Mandin's gaze was on him. He met her eyes and she swallowed, bright spots of color in her cheeks. "Don't worry, pet," he said to Mandin with a smile. "Toola won't mind that we have a thing going. She won't tell your village friends about us."

"Oh delicious, Mandy. I may call you Mandy too, mayn't I?" Toola leaned forward in her seat, giving Mandin a good view of her breasts. "That sounds ever so racy. Do you mean to tell me all that guff about fighting rebels and searching for your daughter was a lie? How deceitful."

Mandin was in full blush. Danton happened to glance at Brill and saw that the lad was watchful but quiet. Good. Brill was keeping up the charade. Danton's balls were tight. This could go so wrong. So much relied on Mandin's ability to find some coquet in her plain, straight-speaking, unromantic body.

"No. It was all true," Mandin replied. "I just left out some of the detail. Danton and I, well, that just happened, you know..." She shrugged and then wrinkled her brow. "About a week before we hit Sartell. We had to keep it quiet, though, because we thought Brill wouldn't understand." Mandin turned to Brill. "I'm sorry, Brill."

"I see." Toola chuckled. "And you played such an innocent with me, letting me taste you, and all the time you were a player."

Mandin coughed and picked up her spoon, and began fiddling with it. Danton raised an eyebrow. "Have you been unfaithful to me, you little wench?" Danton was open-minded and while he knew about Toola's tastes he was surprised by Mandin. Her being a country town woman and all. "I suppose I deserved it, playing with those whores and leaving you abandoned. Forgive me?"

While watching the scared expression on Mandin's face, he knew. He knew that Squab had been right. Squab liked women. But Mandin wasn't like that. She had been a wife and a mother before all this came about. So Toola had seduced her. That made things both easier and more complicated. Toola had the measure of this Vanden woman. Play-acting was going to be difficult. Things could go terribly wrong if they didn't start moving the way he wanted them to soon. Mandin was afraid. Toola had her pegged.

"Well Mandy? What do you say? Spend the night with me?" Danton put on his best soft voice. He couldn't remember ever asking a woman to sleep with him before and wasn't sure he was doing it right.

The two spots of color on Mandin's cheeks glowed a vibrant red. "Yes," she said in an almost whisper, nodding a bit too vigorously.

Toola turned to her. "What, giving in without a fight? I'm ashamed of you, Mandin. You should have held out for at least a minute." Toola eased herself back into her low chair and watched, twisting her dark hair slowly in her fingers.

Danton could feel her eyes on him. With each moment he grew more and more certain that Squab had been on the money.

Mandin launched herself out of her seat, balling her fists in front of her ample stomach. "I know you didn't promise me nothin', but don't treat me like I'm one of these whores. Show me some respect in future."

Danton flapped his hand dismissively. "Women," he huffed.

Mandin let out a snarl. She was warming to this. About time too.

"How dare you try to put me down. Why you're...you're just a dragon's smelly ass."

Danton had to turn surprise into mock anger. Where had she picked up that expression? He leaned back and gave her a come-hither gesture, curling his index finger. Mandin's face and neck were streaked with red as her heaving breasts strained against her shirt. He was about to issue a command when he was interrupted.

Brill rocketed out of his seat and pointed accusingly at Mandin. "Mandin! All the time I thought you were faithful to the cause, but you were just lusting after Danton, slinking off with him on supposed reconnoiters." He swung around, winked and waved a fist at Danton. Good, the lad was quick on the uptake. "You sent me off to do all the hard work and all the time you were sticking your rod in that." Brill's cheeks grew red. It was hard for him to speak in such low terms but Danton was pleased that he tried at least.

Danton was on his feet in a second, fist already smacking against Brill's chin.

"I've had enough of your pious ravings," Danton said to Brill as he fell back. "Mind your own business and do as you're told."

Danton left Brill where he had sprawled in among the cushions and an upturned chair, grabbed Mandin by the arm and wrenched her toward him. "Come on, let's get out of here."

Dragging Mandin out after him, he heard Toola's quiet laughter. The only thing that bugged him was that he didn't know if she had bought it or not. He would have to get it out of Brill later. Right now, he and Mandin had to make a convincing impression or there was going to be trouble. If his hunch was right, there were spies everywhere, so a tame, pretend romp in the sack wasn't going to cut it. Was Mandin going to get more than she had asked for? Danton didn't like the feeling of dread roiling in his gut. One half of him didn't want to believe that Toola meant him harm. He rationalized that she was just playing one of her games. Yet, he had to trust Mandin and listen to her opinions too.

At the entrance to his room, he said in a loud voice, "Just come to bed, Mandy. I said I was sorry about the whores."

Once inside the room, Danton did a quick check of the walls and the curtains that hung on three-quarters of the walls to disguise the fact that there weren't any windows. While he looked he said to Mandin urgently, "Take off your clothes fast and get under the covers."

A quick nod and she began to strip. Danton found two spyholes while she disrobed. Looking up, he thought there might be more in the ceiling. "By the Wing, I should have known," he whispered to himself. What could Toola gain from spying on him? He thought of what Brill had said about Toola asking for a favor. Leverage? Information?

Stripping off his own clothes, he slid into bed next to Mandin. He urged her head onto his arm as he lay sideways next to her. "Good," he whispered to her. "Hopefully Toola needed a few minutes to set up her spies. Run your hands down my back and tell me as softly as you can what happened today. Try not to be distracted by what I do, all right?"

"Toola knows about Salinda. Brill let it slip by accident. Ooh." She moaned accidentally as Danton kneaded her butt.

"And she seduced you last night?"

Mandin nodded and nuzzled her lips against his neck. "I am so ashamed," she said out loud.

Danton said for the benefit of Toola's spies, "Don't do it again. I won't tolerate you going off with others. Got it?"

"Yes." She moaned again loudly, although Danton had done nothing. She was getting the idea. He slipped his leg between hers and made rocking motions. Her eyes flicked up to his. He could see them glisten in the gloom.

"Trust me," he whispered.

She nuzzled him again and scraped her fingernails down his back. "I do. I do," she said with a delicious moan in her voice. Danton found himself beginning to get turned on. This would not do. He tried listening for the sound of spies, hoping that would take his mind off his arousal.

"We went to the slave market today," Mandin continued in a whisper as she wedged herself half under him, moving her hands to his chest and throwing her head back. "She sent her man with us. I thought one particular slaver knew something but couldn't say. He winked at me."

Danton grinned and bent his head to kiss her neck. "Are you sure you didn't tempt him?"

"Be serious," she hissed. "Oh!" she groaned out loud. Danton held himself still.

"Sorry," he said. The pretend sex movements were becoming more uncomfortable for obvious reasons. He found this moment particularly embarrassing. He'd always kept a professional distance with his band, and now he was faced with revealing a side of himself he kept hidden most of the time.

"Mandy?" he whispered in her ear.

"Yes, Danton?" She shifted further beneath him, and they connected under the sheets.

"I'm sorry. I can't help myself."

She reached down and pressed him to her. "I understand. I'm finding it quiet enjoyable myself."

Danton found not pretending a lot easier and forgot about spies for a while.

ᔕᔕᔕᔕᔕ

"Enter," Toola said at the sound of the knock. Linel stepped back into the corner, his most comfortable spot. She could resume talking to him later. Despite being a near idiot, Linel had some queer abilities. He could recount scenes and discussions accurately and in minute details. He'd been regaling her with the scene from the slave market. For the present she was keen to hear what the spy reported from Danton's rooms. Lexia stepped through the door, eyes on the floor in front of her.

"Well? What do you have to report?" Toola eased back into her seat, enjoying the girl's discomfort. The girl did not look up. "Come on, look at me! Am I too ugly to look upon?"

Lexia's head shot up. "No, ma'am, not at all. It's just that I…"

Toola sat forward. "What?"

"When I took up my position they were already under the bedcovers. They whispered to each other while touching."

"Were they naked?"

"Yes, I'm certain because I saw…"

"You're sure?" Toola's hold on her disbelief slipped.

"At first their coupling did not appear interesting."

Toola smiled as her grasp on what she saw as the real truth tightened. "I knew it, they were putting it on."

Lexia shook her head. "No, ma'am. Later they stopped whispering and then it became more interesting."

"Interesting? How?" Toola snarled.

The girl took a half-step back as Toola leaned forward and stared at her.

"Well, vigorous. Not imaginative, as you teach us, but they were certainly joining together from what I saw."

Toola's eyes narrowed and she drew her breath in through clenched teeth. She was thrown. Danton fuck that country tart? She shook her head and at the same time realized that she had to believe it. That made all their behavior unpredictable and puzzling. Toola liked puzzles normally but important things rested on her knowing everything, predicting everything. Danton was slipping out of her grasp like a greasy sewer eel. Unless it was a well-acted pretense—that she could believe. But that would mean Danton and Mandin suspected her. She was slipping up if that were the case.

"When they finished with this coupling did they speak further?"

"No, ma'am, the man went straight to sleep. I'm not sure about the woman. She lay very still underneath him."

"Grrr. This is ridiculous." Toola launched out of her seat. She eyed the young girl, Lexia.

"Strip!" Toola yelled.

"Ma'am?" Toola liked the sound of fear in Lexia's voice.

"You heard me—strip." Toola almost growled out the command.

Lexia lifted her frightened eyes to Toola. The trepidation in them made Toola smile. Lexia parted her robe and let it fall to the floor. All that remained was the light chain around her waist, artfully placed there by Toola herself to offset the slight flaw in the girl's figure. "Mmmmm," she said as the possibilities shifted and rearranged as she altered the variables. Lexia had some importance in her current plans. Not too much damage, then.

"Ma'am? What did I do?"

Toola kept her expression still.

The girl reacted by falling to her knees and touching Toola's feet. "I am sorry, whatever it is. Please, I'll make it up to you."

Toola shook her off. "Brill refused you tonight; therefore you are defective or inept. If you couldn't entice that naive lout, how could you please a proper client, one who knows what he wants, one who pays?"

The girl looked down and her hair fell forward to blanket half her face. "I did everything you told me to, honestly. I was sure he enjoyed it. He even took me while I was sleeping."

Toola turned away. Her eyes scanned the room as she planned the punishment.

"Nevertheless, he was displeased with you. He sent you away tonight, didn't he? I should paint you so he could better aim his dart."

"Oh no, ma'am. He seemed upset this evening."

"Upset?"

"Yes. He would not let me touch him. There were tears in his eyes when he turned me away. It was like he wanted me but for some reason denied me."

Toola stared at the girl. "Are you saying he doesn't like women?"

The girl nodded vigorously. "Yes."

Toola thought through the possibilities. Was the boy enamored of her cousin? Was that why he was so difficult to please? Brill had been difficult to tempt. She replayed the conversation by the pool, Danton teasing the boy to make him choose a woman. Then again, Brill's father had been a world-famous prude. It could be the boy was clinging to ideals. Ideals that now lay in tatters.

"Linel?"

Her man limped from the corner, the eagerness in his eyes making her shiver. "Yes, mistress?"

"Beat her but don't damage her."

Lexia threw herself flat on the floor and begged for mercy in a high-pitched voice. Toola grinned, enjoying the girl's distress, and then licked her lips as she took her seat ready for the show.

☉☉☉☉

It was in the early hours that Danton woke, half-lying on top of Mandin. He stayed still so as to not disturb Mandin and bring about an awkward situation, then he thought about how to move without waking her up. Memories of the previous evening converged. He repressed the urge to groan as he rubbed sleep from his face. It was near morning and it was time to move. The conflicted feelings and guilt about what had happened between them had to be pushed to one side. There were more important things than modesty and recriminations. Mandin was desperate to save her child. She'd do anything to get her back, even sleep with an old reprobate like him, and he should have done more to care for and protect her. Yet, in between their fake and real lovemaking, they had managed to come up with a plan. Danton was to be the wing dust in Toola's dinner. Hopefully that would work.

He looked at Mandin in the half-light, wondering how to proceed. There was going to be awkwardness, the not knowing what to say, the "that wasn't bad but do you mind if we don't do that again" discussion.

Mandin shoved at his shoulder. "Get off me. You're heavy."

So much for awkward moments. With a chuckle, Danton rolled off her and went to dress. Once decent, he mercilessly pulled the covers off her. He put on the light and couldn't help noticing that she was a well-used woman, attractive in her youth, before the children and the struggle to survive had left its mark on her. She did have a nice, big behind, though.

"What are you looking at?" said the voice from the bed.

Danton grinned as he tied his trousers. "Too much and not enough. Get up, time to move. I'll fetch Brill and meet you out front."

Danton flung the door open, hoping to catch someone listening. He saw the cupboard where the secret passage was and bent to check it.

He rattled the door and found that it still opened at a push as it should. That gave him some small relief. Perhaps Toola didn't mean to betray him at all. Perhaps she couldn't resist her usual tricks in trafficking information. It was what kept her alive, after all.

Brill was sitting on the step up to his room waiting, staring into space and rubbing his jaw. "Danton!"

"Yes, it is me. Sorry about the…" Danton mimicked a punch. Brill had a light blue bruise forming where Danton's fist had impacted.

Brill grinned and then winced. "Sure you are. What's happening?"

"I'll be going with you to the slave market to look for Eneit this morning. I might be able to help and also sniff out if there is any trace of the wine shipment. It worries me that there hasn't been a whisper of the shipment. Surely Sartell is the best market for it."

"Good. Wait till you see it. Although, you cannot believe the conditions the slaves are kept in within the city, and there are so many of them. Some are not even human."

Danton scratched his chin and frowned. "Why do you think I'm in this game? Had you never seen Sartell's slave markets before?"

Brill shook his head. "No, never. But Linel says things are worsening daily." Then Brill scratched the side of his head. "We didn't see wine for sale in any of the markets we passed through, although they seemed mostly markets for flesh rather than food. If the wine isn't here where could it be?"

"That's what I want to find out." Danton slapped him on the shoulder. "Get ready and meet us outside."

"Sure thing. What are you doing?"

"I'm going to say goodbye to Toola. Meet you out front."

Danton left Brill to make his way to the front of the house. Toola was dressed and sipping tea at a small table in her kitchen.

Her dark eyes glittered mischievously. "Morning, Danny. Sleep well?"

"Didn't sleep much," he countered. "But I never intended to."

Toola poured water into her teapot. "Ooh, you are too sly. Too long in the desert, I think—scraping the barrel with that one." Her gaze never left his face.

Danton grinned and lifted a shoulder. "Yes, maybe. But you found her to your taste, did you not?"

Toola poured herself a fresh cup. "Offended?"

"No, but remember she is mine. You have plenty of playthings in your employ. If you want to satisfy your unnatural tastes then do so with them."

Toola took her tea and placed it on the table. Slowly she pulled back the chair and arranged the cushion. In doing that she made sure Danton got a healthy view of her cleavage. Danton could see the red-stained nipples through the cloth of her blouse. "My tastes aren't unnatural," she said. "Nothing in this world is unnatural. If it were possible we would fuck dragons."

Danton surreptitiously scanned the room, taking in the fact that Linel was absent. He laughed at her words. "You think so? You obviously haven't seen a dragon up close lately. Anyway, I'm off to help Mandy with the search for her girl. You don't have to send Linel with them. I think I can find my way around."

Toola's dark eyes rested on him. "I wouldn't dream of leaving you unprotected. Linel is very useful as well as knowledgeable." There was a tone in her voice he had not heard before, a serious, dark tone that held more than a hint of warning.

Danton nodded. She had him cornered. If he called it, things could go belly up, and now was not a good time. He had to find his missing men. "Fine. If you send him I can use him."

Danton turned away to leave. When he put his hand on the door, she spoke. "I'm coming with you, too." She upended the cup of tea into her mouth and swallowed. "I have some business in the city to attend to. That won't interfere with your plans, will it?"

Danton smiled. "Not at all. It's been a long time since we went shopping together, cousin."

Chapter Twenty-one

EXPLORATIONS

Laidan brought another pile of lamp pieces to where Nils and Garan were working along the boulevard and placed them carefully in a neat stack. Salinda had been gone for five days, and Laidan found that her anger at the woman was wearing down. Salinda was not there to judge her and Garan had been particularly careful with her, not talking to her unnecessarily and keeping his distance. As she stood back, checking that the stack was secure, she saw Garan's curly, dark head leaning down over the light he was working on.

Nils stood on the boulevard looking out over the lake, a faraway look in his creepy silver eyes. He was doing that more and more. She'd noticed that he hadn't slept the night before but had spent it sitting up and staring in the living area of the abode he shared with Salinda.

Laidan had taken note because she had woken up several times herself and had taken a walk around the node. Nightmares had plagued her, and she had woken to get water several times. The cadre was restless inside her. So much so that she couldn't wait to be rid of it. Nothing but trouble had come of it. Her life had been turned upside down by it. If she didn't get rid of it, it would destroy her happiness entirely.

Kneeling down, she placed components in front of Garan while he assembled another light. He smiled at her and grabbed the first thing she put down. He looked at it and put it to one side and reached for another piece. The work lifted his mood, made him happy even.

"I must go," Nils said suddenly, looming over them.

Garan frowned and stood up. "Is it Salinda? Is there something wrong?"

"I cannot tell. I sense nothing where there should be something. Therefore I must go to her. I am not sure how long I will be. Will you look after Laidan and yourself?"

Garan nodded. "Yes, of course. We will be fine." Garan cast her a lopsided smile and asked, "Laidan?"

Laidan looked from one to the other. It made no difference to her. She was a prisoner in this city. She shrugged. "Yes. No problem. I can cook something for dinner."

Garan's smile contracted. "That will not be necessary. I think we have plenty of food left over."

Laidan narrowed her gaze and then smacked his shoulder. "Beast. What if that food runs out? What will you do then? You'll be sorry you made snide remarks about my cooking."

Rubbing his arm and pulling a face, Garan said goodbye to Nils. As they both watched him depart, Garan said, "I hope she is all right."

Laidan shrugged again. "Me too," she said half-heartedly.

"While we are alone, I wanted to say that I am so sorry about Salinda's plans for the cadre. You must feel terrible about Salinda wanting to take it and give it to me."

Her eyes widened. "You have nothing to be sorry for. At first I was angry she was giving it to you, because I was angry with you, period. But I don't want it. Truly."

"Nevertheless, think of what you could have done. You could have learned so much from Salinda and been a great woman."

"You mean like Salinda?" Laidan screwed up her face. "You think I should be like her? Why?"

Garan raised his hands in a calming gesture. "I'm not saying you should be like her." Laidan relaxed her face and composed it into a neutral expression. Garan bit his bottom lip and continued. "She has such nice characteristics though. She is solid, calm and very self-contained. She has seen a lot, so you know when she talks it is with authority."

On hearing Garan's appraisal of the older woman, Laidan pushed out a lip in a pout. Picking up a hank of hair, she chewed on it for a few moments. Then she said, "She's not pretty."

"No, not pretty so much." Garan relaxed and looked out across the lake as Nils had done. "She has something about her though, a calm beauty. I think it is her eyes."

"Her eyes? But they are dark and slanty, nothing unusual in them. Every second person you meet looks like that." Laidan was angry. Why wasn't he praising her eyes, her blue eyes, which were special?

"Not the color or the shape," Garan continued, his eyes taking on a distant focus. "'Tis the look in them: there is always a faraway quality in them as if she is seeing into the future, seeing beyond the moment." Shaking himself, his eyes shifted to meet hers. "Her eyes are not as beautiful as yours, of course."

Garan smiled at her and Laidan responded in kind. Despite all the horrible things she had said and done to him, he could still care about her, could still be nice. She held out her hand and he took it and kissed it. Such a romantic thing for him to do. Laidan's mood lifted and a smile spread across her face. "Thank you, Garan." With her other hand she caressed his face, touching with her fingertips the rough where his beard was growing in since the morning shave. The way Garan looked at her thrilled her. She had power once again.

"Best get back to work," he said, dropping her hand and kneeling down again.

Laidan sniffed and stifled her feelings of rejection. There was no need to be upset with Garan. They were alone now. She had time to bring him around to her way of thinking.

❦❦❦❦❦

Garan squeezed through Laidan's door and found a meal already laid out for them. He had not been in her abode before and saw that it was much the same as his. Laidan had not put any personal items around to make it more homely. Then again, she probably did not have much in the way of possessions as she had traveled with Thurdon all her life. What would the old man have said about her now? Would he approve of Garan taking the cadre from her? Would he approve of Garan loving her but not being able to have her? It seemed so long ago now that the Master Elder had told him those dreadful words. He may not be able to be with her as a husband but he was sure glad she was friendly toward him again.

Laidan came into the room, face radiating with a smile. "Please come in, Garan. Don't stand there like I'll bite you."

Garan bowed his head and looked at the floor. Could she see his hopeless devotion? He had to do his best to keep his distance from her. He sat down on one side of the low table and his gaze roved over the food. Laidan had been to the gardens as well as reheating the soup Nils had prepared the night before.

Laidan arranged herself on the sofa across from him and smiled slightly. "Eat. You've been working hard. No point in waiting for good manners. The sooner you have taken the edge off your hunger, the sooner we can relax."

"Relax?"

"You know, sit back, talk...that sort of thing."

Garan nodded and began to eat. This was a strange mood. Being civil to him was a gift Laidan rarely bestowed, but actually talking to him like a person, someone she wanted to be with, was surprising indeed. It should have made him cynical; instead he was nervous. Laidan poured him tea and offered him lots of dishes to try. The change in her attitude definitely made him uneasy the longer it continued. Friendliness was the absence of anger and some acknowledgment of his presence. This was more. This was "look at me, be with me, love me" treatment. In the absence of Nils and Salinda, Garan's anxiety juddered his heart uncomfortably. At the same time he was titillated by where this would go. Would she throw him out on a whim? Would she laugh at him? Or would she tenderly press her lips to his? Garan let out a sigh. *Do not go down that path.*

When he had eaten his fill, Laidan rose and cleaned away the plates. He heard her singing in the kitchen. She came back out and this time she sat next to him, shooing him over so there was room for her on the sofa. His eyebrows rose in query and all he got in return was a smile.

"Do you really think my eyes are pretty?" she asked suddenly.

Garan's eyes widened. "Of course, so does everyone who meets you."

"But do you like them?" She leaned in closer.

Garan held her gaze, conscious that her mouth was so close to his. "Of course, I said so. I do not lie."

She held her head steady, eyes unblinking, and then she leaned in close and pressed her warm lips to his surprised ones. She reached her hand to the back of his head and held him there while she kissed him deeply. Garan, unresisting at first, was a bit shocked, then he tried to pull back, thinking about guilt and consequences and the breach of trust. Salinda would not like him dallying with Laidan, no matter how much he swore he loved the girl. Garan removed her hand and broke the kiss as gently as he could.

Laidan sat back when he broke contact, a questioning expression on her face. "Garan?"

"Yes?" he said in a whisper. It was hard to keep his mind focused. His heart thudded as though he had run a sprint way past his endurance. All the blood in his body had relocated to his groin, and he shifted to make himself more comfortable. His mind was lulled as if by a spell.

"You don't want to kiss me!" she accused.

Garan backpedaled mentally. "That is not quite true, Laidan..."

She thumped him on the shoulder. "You don't like me? I thought you did." Her forehead creased and her lips began to pout.

Garan felt so small, knowing what this rejection would cost him. "I do...I do like you, but I do not think this is a good idea. Being alone together, kissing, touching...'Tis not right." Garan sounded doubtful even to his own ears. Having her this close and willing was tempting, a heady circumstance that was part of his deepest, saddest longings.

Again, she leaned in close to him and rested her head on his chest. "You didn't always think so. Confess it. You want me."

Garan's thumping heart increased to an uncomfortable jerky rhythm. Laidan could probably feel it through his clothes. Why did she choose to tempt him now when he was honor bound to care for her? Short of running out of the abode, he was not sure what to do. He could not make love to her. Instinctively, he knew there was something wrong with Laidan, but he did not know what it could be. They had not talked as friends for so long. Estrangement had been difficult. But intimacy was even more fraught. How could her hate for him have dissipated so quickly? Had it been all pretense after all? Why had she become so forward? "I...er." He could not form the words.

Gazing up at him from his chest, she reached up, caressed his hair, and drew his mouth closer. There she proceeded to kiss him, thoroughly and deeply. The heat in the kiss floored Garan. It was beyond anything they had shared before, full of confidence and seduction. Her tongue intruded into his mouth, teasing his own. The need seemed to burn within her as her body pressed close to his, her hands explored his. Her sneaking fingers probed beyond the fastenings of his clothes to stroke his heated skin. It both thrilled and frightened him. This was not the same as the questing kiss they had shared when they were hiding from the rebels, a kiss that had been laced with dragon wine. Right now, Laidan was sober, unafraid and very sure of herself. She released his mouth, and before he could speak again, she captured it once again. This time her kiss stirred more than Garan's heartbeat; his whole body was on fire with desire. This was an assured kiss, one meant to stir the passions, an experienced kiss. He was caught between pushing her away and falling under her spell. When Laidan's hand slid along his thigh to stroke him between his legs, he jerked away and tumbled to the floor.

"Laidan!" He gasped there, sucking in breath while he knelt on all fours.

Laidan sprawled herself on the sofa, parting her legs suggestively while regarding him with a heavy-eyed look. Her lips were red from the kiss and slightly puffy. Her fingers gathered up her robe, drawing it up past her knees and higher still. Garan was not sure what he was seeing. Her body undulated on the sofa. "Don't be shy, Garan. I know you want to. You want my body."

Garan crawled to his feet, using the table as a prop. Dazedly he shook his head. Never had temptation ridden him so high. His throat was tight when he said, "I am sorry. I cannot do this. 'Tis not right." He could barely look in her direction. To do so would sink him. Closing his eyes, he tried to push the lust he was experiencing down inside so he had the strength to leave and not sink himself in her willing flesh. Laidan was too innocent to know what she was doing, what she was offering him.

With great effort, Garan strode to the door and squeezed himself through the small aperture and then crossed to his own abode. Laidan had stirred him up good and proper. She had brought him from the edge of despair to the pinnacle of desire. Now he was staring down a precipice and he was not sure he could stop himself falling in. Should he turn about? Go back to her and lose himself? He knew he could not.

There were things to be done. If he could be sure Laidan loved him and shared the desire to stay at the observatory to work to save Margra, then maybe he could contemplate marriage to her. But he didn't think that was what she was offering him. It was quick. It was easy. It was not good enough.

He prepared for bed, the smell of her on his clothes. Not going over there to be with her was one of the hardest things he had ever done. Thoughts of where that kiss could have led played havoc with his calm. But he could not shake off the thought that all this was transient, a game to her. To this he could add other reasons. Salinda's trust in him. The Master Elder's words. Thurdon's wishes and the respect of his fellow Skywatchers. That was more important than sating a need. In time, he hoped Laidan would understand and respect him for his choice. That thought made him chuckle. Not likely; he would be lucky if she ever spoke to him again. He picked up the bowl of cold water he was washing up in and tipped it over his head. Tears threatened. He loved her. By the source, he loved her. She had offered him his heart's desire and he had turned her down.

♋♋♋♋♋

Nils dived into the lake, leaving his robe in a pile on the shore. There were no other boats so swimming was the only way to reach the island and Salinda. Nils had a growing uneasiness about her condition. Although he had agreed to leave her alone, he found he could not. Not after so much time had passed.

Once in the water, the change took place, its inherent power altering his shape. He reveled in the lake, in the way the gentle power of it tingled his skin. The transition to gill breathing was smooth and his form melded easily with the water, allowing him to arrow through the dark current with ease. Alone with his thoughts he wondered what it would have been like in the lake, to swim with the others of his kind at the time of mating. He imagined himself in one of the communal bonding ceremonies where the water was alive with mating Hiem. It was a sight he would never see. Another ritual lost to time and despair. The dark envelope of the lake did little to ease this heartache. The lake was the core of his people's lives. Loneliness and longing found him again.

The shore neared and Nils took a slow float up to the beach, allowing his body to revert back to air breathing. There was a moment of discomfort, as though he was choking on water as he heaved it out of his lungs, and then it was over.

Looking at his surroundings he recalled that he had not been to the island since he was a small boy. Ahead were the Tinakua, the sculptures crafted by the females of his kind. The tall carvings were women's stories, their lives and their dreams, etched and woven in stone, to be retold through touch. Naked, he strode among them, reaching out to feel a curve of love, a harsh corner of pain and the flush and flow of childbirth. He passed another in his search for Salinda and ran a fingertip along the name etched at the base. There was such music to this female's story, the curls and twirls of her young life, rippling underneath his fingertips to end abruptly—a postscript from her mother informing the reader of the termination of her life. It was hard, sharp, grief-filled and bitter.

He walked on and found Salinda on her back, half-buried in white sand, skin alive with power. Flame rippled across her unconscious form, burnishing her skin to bronze. As he approached, the power brushed against his skin and he stilled. He cast his gaze about, assessing her supplies. She had eaten a little and drunk a bit more. However, she looked ill underneath the power. She had dark rings around her eyes, her cheeks were slightly concave and her lips dry.

He sat on her ground sheet and waited for a while, hoping that she would wake and allow him to approach. For hours he sat and watched and nothing happened. Eventually, he crept forward and called out to her, "Salinda! You must wake."

There was nothing, no reaction. Nils stood up. She was living and breathing and that had to be enough for now. He would remain nearby in case she needed him. In the interim, he would explore the women's stories while he waited. Soon she would wake, and if she did not and she seemed in danger he would wake her, even if there was a risk to himself. Her death would be the death of him anyway, as there were none of his kind to sustain him through the loss of a mate, no kin to provide support for his absent bond.

As his gaze tracked the various towering sculptures that surrounded Salinda he began to think of the two women whose lives he had destroyed with his actions: Acendrian and Luca. Would they have written their stories here? Stories of love and birth and death? He wondered what had happened to them.

He leaned against the first pole he came across, for this story needed a body pressed against it to be understood, hands caressing to tease out the story so ingeniously embedded within the stone. Such passion, thought Nils, as he re-lived the moment of the woman's realization of her secret love. With his toes he felt how she'd nourished it and yet was chaste—a bittersweet tale. Nils found he was rather exhausted after experiencing that tale when it was done.

Then came the memory, a child's memory, from the past. He remembered running here while his mother made her story. He forgot about finding his lost loves' stories and tracked through the sand searching for his mother's. It was there on the outer rim and alone it brooded upon the lake. He did not recall it being placed so—perhaps it was moved after her son had shamed her. Her story was not much taller than Nils. He trembled before it. A woman's tale was to be shared among the women of the clan, daughters and granddaughters. Only in special circumstances could a man be invited to read them. As he was the last of his kind, he was the only one left who could read them. It was said that a woman's true heart was written there, the voice that never spoke in life. A voice that was hidden from the males of their kind.

Hesitantly, he reached out, a fingertip tracing her name: Isagar of Barr. There was strength in how she etched the name, as if she was proud to say it. *Let anyone dare to stop me*, it seemed to say. With his cheek pressed to the beginning of the tale, he experienced the softness of her youth, the warm embrace of her parents. Then with both hands he caressed the story of her bonding and the birth of her sons. Here were happy swirls and warm, contented hollows. Then a sharp, sloping zigzag cut off abruptly: the imprisonment of her son. Him. Nils of Barr. His fingers trailed on with the rest of her thoughts, her love, her devotion and the broken-hearted sorrow. And before the end of her story, it told of long days and nights watching over Nils in his prison of sleep.

Then a message plainly written: *If you see this, my son, know that I understand and forgive*. Nils staggered back, wrenching himself from her story as if he had been wrenched from her embrace. "Mother?" She had loved him and forgiven him and had thought enough to put it in her story. Nils wept, hugging the pillar of Isagar of Barr. He did not know whether the story gave him happiness or pain, both were so intertwined within his soul. He stayed as long as he could, until the twisting of the bond with Salinda urged him back to her side.

As he watched Salinda trapped within her cocoon of power, he tried to think of a way to reach her. There were two possibilities— calling to her or reaching out to her through their bond. His emotions were already too raw. Could he now push the boundaries further and use their bond? Intellectually he knew about bonds; all his kind were taught about them. Because he was bonded to a Sundweller, one with perhaps a trace of Hiem, he had not thought about its uses. So far it had given him pain along with the comfort of knowing he was connected to another living being. Calling out to Salinda had had no effect. Tentatively, he crept along the bond, pushing his awareness out to the warm presence that was Salinda. She was like a pulsing ember. He had held back from her previously, but now he would be required to twine with her, deepen the bond, to trust her with his heart. His breath came in rapid pants, more from fear than any real exertion. If he did this, would she then be able to feel him? He had to take the risk that she would treasure this new intimacy rather than be afraid of it.

The glow of her essence increased as he lingered there next to it, as if she sensed his presence. Filaments began to expand and separate, and so, like touching hands, he reached out to her. Air rushed out of his lungs as their bond became taut. Salinda sat up at the same time, the flames floating away from her skin to dissipate in the air around her. He rushed to her as she fell back, caught her and then laid her gently on the sand. It had worked. He fed her water, and she drank feebly, water leaking down her chin, too weak to take enough in.

Smoothing the hair away from her face, he watched over her. Then when she had taken more water and a little food, he bathed her while she rested. Nils could feel her breathing now, through the bond, and a little beyond that he detected the pulse of the new life within her— their child. He said a welcome chant to the child, although he still regretted the conception. What kind of life would this child have? *A Hiem alone is no Hiem at all.* And the child was to be half-Hiem, and what kind of life was that, stuck between, never being a true Hiem or true human?

Nils fell asleep beside Salinda, nestled in the cool sand of the island. His hand rested on her abdomen, feeling the occasional kick of new life. Among the torment of his soul, the restless pain of grief, there glowed a bond that anchored him, no—bound him to this time, bound him to this life. Something there spoke of hope, of a future, if only he would reach out and take it.

When he woke next, Salinda was awake. She sat up carefully, as if her muscles pained her. She said nothing while he handed her small portions of food. After swallowing the last of it, she spoke. "Nils." Her eyes glowed with a golden hue.

"Yes?"

Her eyes were wide and fixed on him. "I am different—changed. Yet you have done something to me too. It is hard to differentiate between the cadre and you now."

Nils moved closer and ran his fingers through her hair so that it no longer stood up. "I could not wake you so I had to use our bond. I strengthened it and used it to jerk you awake."

Salinda nodded and touched his hand. "Oh? Is that why you are naked?"

Nils looked down and tilted his head to the side. "My clothes are on the shore as I had to swim across. You were in trouble so I forgot to bring something in my haste. Forgive me, my nakedness has offended you."

Salinda reached out and traced her hand down his arm. "No. I like looking at you. Your skin is so white and smooth. With your long hair free like that, you look beautiful to me."

Nils drew her to him, reveling in the feel of their bond. He had not realized that it would enhance their physical closeness as well. Their lovemaking was slow and gentle. Salinda's experience was still upon her, yet she responded as if they had spent a lifetime longing for a union.

When he asked her about the power he had seen, she explained it away as part of the knowledge she had obtained from the cadre. She had more to tell him but she needed to absorb it, understand it, before she could explain herself.

"And the child. Was it harmed?"

Her hand drifted to the mound where the unborn child grew. Her eyes glowed brighter for a moment. "No. He seems well. Although I cannot say if the child has been altered, as I have."

"Your eyes? They glow."

Her hand reached up to touch her temple. "It will fade in time, I suspect. But if there are other changes... I cannot describe them."

"Then we must return to the city. The children are on their own."

Salinda's gaze met his and she nodded slowly as if waking from a long sleep.

"Yes. But they are not children, Nils. You must stop calling them that because you will be deceived. They are adults in mind as well as body."

Chapter Twenty-two

A HINT OF PASSING

Mandin, with Danton and Brill by her side, followed close on Linel's heels as he led them back to Slaver's Lane. Once again the putrid smell hit her, almost making her gag. Danton controlled his reaction well. Brill's complexion grayed and with hand over his nose he breathed through his mouth. *By the source, please don't get sick*, she thought at the young man, knowing that she would not be able to control her reaction if he did. Focusing on the thought of finding her daughter, she was able to sublimate the smells and the misery.

They were alone, except for Linel. Although Toola had accompanied them, she had said goodbye in the main street and had headed off in another direction. Danton appeared puzzled by this behavior, if Mandin's observations were correct. Toola was certainly keeping them on their toes by doing the unexpected. Mandin had been convinced that they were close to uncovering the truth and Toola was bent on preventing them. What interest did Toola have in Eneit? Or was it something more? The dragon wine perhaps? Linel watched them closely, noting every gesture and every word. Despite his simple appearance, he missed nothing, she was sure.

Danton grasped her hand and squeezed it when they entered the shadows of Slaver's Lane. If he was trying to act like a concerned lover, he was doing a good job of it. The slaver who had winked at her the day before was situated at the end of the lane. She could see him directing cages to be moved and unloaded. He must have caught sight of them because he paused in what he was doing and then turned toward them. She saw his gaze travel over her rebel companions and then linger on Linel. Mandin gave Danton the previously agreed signal.

"Wing dust!" Danton exploded. "Which way did Toola go, Linel? I have to give her a message."

Linel slowed, his eyes squinting through the scars cutting through his face. "You can give her a message later. We talk to the slaver now."

Danton shrugged. "The slaver is important to Mandin, not to me. My business with Toola is more important. She'll be angry if I don't tell her what I know now. Tell me where she went and I'll go and find her."

Linel shook his head. The slaver approached them but stood silently, listening to the exchange. Danton shrugged. "Fine then. I'll go. I'm sure I saw which direction she was heading. If I get lost you can explain why to my cousin later."

Linel had begun to sweat. "It is best you stay together. Easier to protect."

Danton pointed to his chest for emphasis. "I've been protecting myself all my life. Toola knows that. It's these young, naive ones she wants to protect. I have something to say to her and you aren't about to stop me."

Danton made to move away. Linel looked at the slaver and then at Mandin. "We'll be right here, Linel," she said with a smile. "Toola can't be far away. We parted not five minutes ago. In that crowd she couldn't have got far."

Linel nodded and hurried after Danton, who had already merged with the crowd milling in the narrow laneway.

As soon as Linel was out of earshot, Mandin drew close to the . slaver. "I believe you know something about my daughter."

The slaver looked around, his eyes watching the departing figures of Linel and Danton. "Why would you say that?"

Brill edged in closer to her, lending his support. "Look, he's gone now. You can speak freely."

The slaver spat on the ground, barely missing Brill's boot. "Maybe. But how can I trust you? She has friends in high places. I go against her and I'm a dead man."

Mandin bit her lip and put her hands on her hips. Trying to keep the exasperation out of her voice she said, "Look, my daughter was stolen by a bunch of rebels. They killed my husband and she's all I've got left in the world. I'd die to save her. I don't know how else I can make it worth your while to help me. I can get the money to pay you. I won't tell anyone what you tell me. Please."

The slaver eyed her, sweat leaking down from behind his ears. He nodded once, as if measuring her truthfulness. "I risk my life speaking to you. Toola is a powerful woman, with connections to the people who run this city."

Mandin nodded. "She's a real bitch."

He nodded and opened his hands. "What can you tell me about your daughter?" he asked.

Mandin relaxed a little. So much hope was bound up in this man knowing something. "We think there may be seven or eight girls altogether, with ages ranging from about nine to thirteen. They were all untainted by birth defects and healthy when they were taken."

"Virgins?" he asked.

Mandin swallowed and found the next words hard to form. "When they were taken, yes."

"Then they would be selling in premium markets. In secret, you see. Not here where the general sales are. Can you tell me anything else?"

"We have two names—Torrens and Beck. They may not be using the same names in Sartell, though. Have you heard anything?"

The slaver's gaze raked the milling crowd. Without making eye contact with her he said, "I might have. I need to do some checking. It will cost you."

"How much?"

The slaver turned away again and gave hand signals to his men. Cages began to change position. A bucket of water was tossed over some occupants, who screamed hysterically. Mandin shuddered. This man was a lowlife and yet she had no choice but to bargain with him. "Come back here tomorrow, same time, without the escort. You don't know how much power that woman has. If she knew I was making inquiries on your behalf she'd have me erased faster than you can fart."

Brill piped up. "If you tell us your contacts we can pursue them ourselves. We need not put you in any more danger."

"Yes, Brill is right," said Mandin urgently. "I need to know now."

⅏⅏⅏⅏

While Linel watched over Danton and his friends, Toola sat in the Commissioner of Police's office, slowly sipping the generous portion of dragon wine her host had provided. It was a very good vintage. Toola made a mental note to appropriate some before she left. Dragon wine had been scarce in Sartell for some time. She had to supplement her own with a cheap substitute. "This wine is good. New shipment?"

Narin blanched. "Not new, no. I found it in a basement. It's been around for ages."

"Lucky find." Toola narrowed her eyelids. Narin was lying. The stupid fool was so transparent. How he'd come to be the Commissioner of Police was beyond her reckoning. "And my news?"

"This is important information you have, Toola." Narin was fifty and his belly fat spilled over the sides of his chair. He was Toola's creature, although he would never admit such a thing. The trick was that Toola made him think the situation was the other way around. That he owned her. Her smile could not be suppressed.

She sat on the only other seat in the room, a wide, wooden bench with curled arms, and kicked off her shoes and tucked her feet underneath her body. Relaxing against her cushion, she enjoyed the fact that her informality annoyed Narin. He wore a uniform and kept his office sparsely furnished. This was to make visitors feel in his power, ill at ease. Toola had brought the cushion with her and made appearing relaxed in his presence an art. He was easier to manage when he was disconcerted. "Don't I always provide you with the best quality information? I have been useful to you in the past, have I not?"

Narin crossed his arms over his wide chest and glowered at her. "Yes, yes, of course you have. You know I am grateful."

Toola smiled gently, using her tongue to moisten her lips. "Then it is not unreasonable to ask for your help in this?"

Narin stood up and walked to the window. The blind was down. He lifted the side and peered through the gap and then turned back to her. "If it can be done it will be. I'll send my best men to find this girl...this Eneit."

Toola's heart skipped a beat. She would get this Eneit and more besides. There hadn't been a decent shipment of serviceable girls in

188

months. Eneit would be valuable just in being owned. Then there was the added incentive to exact revenge on Mandin. The fool woman who had thrown her hospitality in her face and turned her cousin against her. There was also more to this story. By rights Eneit should have been sold on the open market. That she wasn't suggested that there was something else going on. Toola rubbed her chin as she pondered it. Some prominent families had disappeared. Not killed. Just gone. Then there was the shortage of wine and the low quality of the food recently. Eneit was the thread that would unravel this mystery.

Toola had lived in Sartell all her life. She understood its rhythms and flows like she did her own body. Something was decidedly off.

"By the way, how is my girl?" he asked.

After taking a long drink of the wine, she sat back and sighed. "Oh, Lexia is doing well. She enjoys being one of my girls. Loves me like a mother. Last night I gave her my special attention and she enjoyed herself immeasurably."

Narin stood still, his eyes tracking over Toola's body. She had dressed for the occasion, wrapping herself in dark red fabric with a hint of gold thread. It hugged her body. As she had arranged herself on the chair, the split in her skirt was open up to her crotch. His gaze was riveted. "And will she be at this little party you are giving later in the week?"

"Why, yes. She may be a little out of sorts, but you know she loves seeing her daddy—nearly as much as you love seeing her." Toola's eyebrows were arched as she put the empty cup down and stood up. Walking slowly up to him, she rubbed her body against his. She loved playing Narin. Ever since she had convinced him to sell his third daughter, Lexia, to her, he had been hers. He had been rather desperate for money at the time. To live and keep his position through a change of government had required healthy bribes and information. Toola had both, and an eye for a long-term connection.

Her hand caressed his erection. Narin's neck turned red and his bald pate had sweat gathering in the middle of it. She could take him all the way but chose not to. She stepped away from him.

His breath came in short, sharp pants. Toola expected he was thinking of Lexia—the incestuous bastard!

Now that he was distracted, she could get a little something for her time. "That wine was awfully good. I could use some at the party. Care to spare me some?"

He nodded. "Speak to Troven on the way out. He'll see that a case is delivered."

Toola kissed him on the cheek, dropping her hand to his crotch again to feather his erection with her red-painted nails. "You are such a darling. I'll make sure you have a special treat when you come over. I bought Lexia a new pink dress with little bows on it. She looks all of twelve years old."

His eyes watered with lust as he smiled at her. Then he frowned as his guilt came crashing through his sexual heat. That was how she had finally nabbed him: by knowing his desire and his fears. "Your secret is safe with me." She kissed his bald pate and prepared to leave. All the while she was thinking that he must have had a shipment of wine recently. That meant he was involved in something—something big. She wondered in which way he was connected and to whom. She would get it out of him eventually. Let him deliver her the girl first. "I'll see you in two days then?"

"Yes, certainly. I should have some news for you then." Narin went back to his desk and sat down. Toola closed the door behind her, a smile playing on her lips. Next she hurried back to Slaver's Lane to meet up with the others.

৩৩৩৩

Mandin saw the slaver's eyes widen as he looked behind her. "You bring great danger," he whispered. "See, she comes."

Mandin turned around and saw Toola approaching through the crowd. It was quite strange to watch. She didn't have to push her way through the crowd; people parted instinctively. Slavers stopped what they were doing and nodded a greeting to her. Mandin, Brill and the slaver watched as she took the last steps up to them. "Bisma, I haven't seen you in a while." She looked at the cages and the slaves within, screwing up her nose and sniffing over-loudly. "I must say the quality of your stock is going down." Then she walked up to Mandin and slid her arm through Mandin's crooked elbow. "I don't think you'll find your daughter here, Mandy. By the looks of it he only has idiots and half-humans, fit for perverts or for cleaning the sewers. Your daughter sounds like she is too high quality for the likes of him. Don't linger here any longer. There is a great restaurant in this part of town. I would so like to take you there."

Bisma bowed to Toola. "You are always welcome, Madame Toola. And you speak the truth. Good stock is hard to find these days. Someone is buying up large quantities of the best stock, which leaves only the dregs for the rest of us."

Toola glared at Bisma and then waved her hand dismissively. The slaver bowed low and then turned away without a second glance at Mandin. *So close*, Mandin thought, *and now we have to come back again*. Mandin chewed her lip, not willing to compromise Bisma by continuing to question him when he was obviously afraid of her benefactress.

Toola paused, her gaze sliding from left to right. "Where are Danton and Linel?"

Brill walked on the other side of Toola. "You must have missed them. They went looking for you."

"For me?" She placed a hand on her heart and smiled. "How odd!" Toola's smile did not reach her eyes. "Linel knows better than to come sneaking around after me. His duty is to protect you."

Mandin nodded to herself, satisfied that she and Danton had put a large quantity of dust in Toola's dinner. Unfortunately, it had not given them everything they needed. They would have to repeat the performance tomorrow and that was going to be very difficult, if she knew Toola at all.

♋♋♋♋

The next morning they were all up at dawn. Brill was subdued and had dark circles under his eyes. Danton was sure there was something bothering him. The urge to speak near screamed from the boy's very pores. Toola was up early too and Danton feared she would wish to accompany them again. He had been hard-pressed to invent an excuse to go after her the day before. He knew she hadn't bought it. Also he suspected Linel's worsened limp and bruised face today were due to her anger. How tight was this noose? The only way they were going to get away was to sneak out through the tunnel and not come back. That would take some planning. He had yet to organize the rendezvous with his men. They'd spent too much time caught up in this tangle of intrigue. There had to be another way.

Toola placed her teacup on the table, her elegantly clad body gliding out of her chair. "I must leave you to your own devices today. You'll forgive me if I don't accompany you. I have some important business. Linel will help you search."

Danton made to protest but she lifted her hand, silencing him. "I won't take any thanks from you, Danton. I could not live with myself if any harm came to you or your friends while you were staying under my roof. In such a rough part of town too. What if you were taken?"

Danton tensed. He could take that comment two ways: as an expression of concern or as a thinly veiled threat. Danton watched as Toola stood up to exit the room, pausing in front of Mandin at the door. Danton shook his head. It was hard to believe. He didn't want to believe or think that Toola meant him harm. But something was not right with her. Something had changed. With light fingers, Toola cupped the other woman's chin. "I wish you luck today, my sweet. Do not give up hope. I can always help you, where others are unsuccessful. You must trust me. I can help you and I can protect you if needs be." Then, as Mandin gaped at her, his cousin pressed a deep kiss on her lips and left the room, her sumptuous perfume wafting in her wake.

This little play revealed a few things and forced Danton to make some hard choices. This would be the last time he would go with Mandy to search for her daughter. He also had to change tactics with Toola, otherwise Mandy and Brill would suffer for it. His priority had to be finding the wine and his men and getting himself and Brill and Mandin out of Toola's clutches. The dragon wine had drawn them all here to Sartell in the first place. Also he decided that Brill would have to come with him on his next outing and not return. He needed the boy safe. As he examined Brill's face and posture, he realized that this place was having too great an effect on the young man. Danton had wanted a slight loosening of his morals, not the total disintegration of his personality. That meant installing Brill with his men, and putting him to work again. Not so easy now that Toola knew him by sight, name and pedigree. His frustration made him grind his teeth. He scratched under his eye patch as they filed out of the brothel and into the bustling, filthy streets of Sartell.

A cool breeze sent the various street smells in every direction. Litter and dust swirled in tight cones, sending grit into his remaining eye. Mandin held a borrowed veil close over her head and Brill used his forearm to guard his vision. Linel limped forward with great energy that belied his painful stride, unhindered by the wind-borne debris. Perhaps his heavy brows served as a shield. This early the streets were relatively deserted except for huddled shapes on the pavements and nestled against buildings. Occasionally one moved, disturbing the pile of rags that served for clothing and blankets, revealing disease or gross deformity. Danton shook his head. The world was a nasty place. Seeing this made him doubt whether goodness could ever come again. He had to turn his back on the violence around him, the poverty and the abuse. He had to think of the people at the observatory, of Salinda and Garan. Those who had light in their hearts.

Brill missed nothing. To the lad's credit the people on the streets and their condition visibly shook him. Brill had grown quite a lot in these last weeks. He was no longer a boy but a man—and one who had seen too much of late. The shades of light in him were tempered with gray. Brill had peeped into the dark places where Danton had once dwelled. He did not wish any of those experiences on the lad. Brill had spirit and cunning, but could he survive what was in store for them? Danton was sad in a way. He had not deliberately set out to make the boy a model of himself. Yet like some prophecy, he could see it unfolding.

They turned into Slaver's Lane. Already the market had some trade with a few potential buyers around, peering into cages or running hands down bodies to check for malformation. The instinctive revulsion against any who did not fit the mold held sway here in the city, even more so than in any backward town. A universal trait, perhaps.

The wind was no less bitter in the slave cages. Would-be merchandise sat huddled into balls, trying to keep the treacherous debris from flaying their skin. Bisma was still in the process of opening up his stall, directing cages out of storage to be put on display. Men worked at winching up the cages to form stacks. Danton knew when the slaver noticed their approach. He saw the man tense. He recovered quickly, and then pretended indifference as they walked up to him.

Mandin reached for Danton's arm and squeezed. He could sense her excitement. This could be the moment when she found her daughter. His hopes were with her as he patted her hand. If there was no success today, he was sure it would flatten Mandin. If she found a lead to her daughter or the actual girl herself, he didn't know what would happen next. Danton had not thought beyond that point. He had avoided thinking about Mandin on a personal level at all. He had never been in this situation before.

He cared for her and obviously desired her, strange as that seemed to his rational mind. But he could not keep her as part of his rebel band and continue their relationship. It would go against everything he believed in, and he knew the effect it would have on his men. It would change the dynamics, cause friction. That would not be good for morale or his leadership. If she found her daughter then they must immediately part ways. The child would give him way too much grief, if she was to be cared for as part of his rebel band. Suppressing a sigh he saluted a greeting to Bisma.

"Well met," Danton called above the wind and the noise of men working.

Bisma's gaze passed over them, lingering for a moment on Linel. "Well met. Come to consider my goods again? You are eager. Did you bring money?"

Mandin stepped forward and shifted the veil from her face. "Yes, I have come to see a particular slave. May I look?" She dumped the coin that Danton had given her on the man's counter top.

Bisma raked the money into an apron he was wearing. Danton was determined that Mandy be left alone with Bisma. He would take Linel to the ground if need be. But a shout from behind made them all turn around together. Squeezing through the tight lines of slavers was a troop of uniformed men. Danton turned back to the slaver in time to see the fear in Bisma's eyes. "What have you done?" the slaver hissed at them.

Danton shrugged. "Nothing. Why? What is it?"

Bisma was backing away from them, fear watering his eyes. "It is the customs officials. They are coming for me."

Danton turned back to the entry to the lane again and the uniformed men did appear to be heading straight for them. A ripple of fear spread through the other slavers. He saw relief in the ones that the troop passed by. Bisma began shouting orders to his staff, waving his hands to chivvy them. Danton stepped forward and touched the man's sleeve. Bisma started and brushed him off. His gaze flew once again to the approaching men and then he grabbed onto Danton's shirt and pulled him closer. "Flee," he hissed into his ear. "You will be taken too."

The slaver gave him a shove. Danton backpedaled, dragging Brill by the collar. Mandin had heard and lurched forward even as the troop of customs officers began smashing cages and dragging slaves out of them by the hair. Before he could stop her she ran forward and pulled on Bisma's cloak. "Please!"

In the confusion, Bisma pushed something into her hand before he shoved her roughly to the ground. Then he ran for his office, dragging the ledgers out from under the counter. Mandy ran back to Danton and Brill and they slunk into a corner to observe the proceedings. Linel crouched, his large body guarding them from view, but it was as if they weren't there.

The commanding officer strode through the chaos his men were wreaking on the slaver's stall. All the slaves were being lined up and forced to kneel. In among them were Bisma's staff and personal slaves. For a minute or so Bisma was not to be seen. He had disappeared through the back of the stall. Hopefully he had a secret exit.

A shout filled with triumph arose in the air around them. A few minutes later Bisma was brought struggling out of his stall to be thrown at the officer's feet, the pages of his ledgers flying loose in the wind. Danton had a bad feeling about the scene unfolding in front of him. He glanced sideways and saw Linel's face, which was a cold, hard mask. This had to be Toola's doing. It was too much of a coincidence.

Mandin cried out and then buried her face in Brill's shoulder. Danton could guess what was going to happen. One flick of his gaze confirmed it. All the slaves were being executed, their throats cut without mercy or thought. Bisma was trussed up with wire. Already his blood was leaking onto the paving stones. A kick in the guts made the man vomit. This was the price Bisma paid for daring to help them. They stayed quiet and calm in the corner where they hid, ignored or unseen by the customs officials, Danton wasn't sure. He was grateful, though, not to be caught in this net. When Bisma was carted away along with the remains of his slaves, the remaining slavers swooped down on the shell of his stall and stole whatever was left behind.

Within half an hour the only sign of Bisma and his stall were the bloodstains on the pavement. Feeling cramped, Danton emerged from the corner, bringing the others with him. Linel appeared unmoved by what had happened. As he took a step, Danton could see that the man's limp was worse, probably exacerbated by crouching down when hiding. Danton longed to ask him if what had happened was Toola's doing, but he recalled the blind look of devotion Linel had for his cousin. There was no way he would betray her or say anything against her. He would find no help there.

"Let's go back to the brothel," Danton said with false calm. "There isn't much more we can do now. We have to hope that Toola finds out something for us. My cousin will do her best, I know."

Toola had outmaneuvered him. He needed to regroup. He needed to extract Brill, Mandin and himself before it was too late. He had to alert Squab and make arrangements. It was all so delicate. If Toola did have the influence to crush Bisma and was no longer a friend, then Danton was in big trouble. Mandin nodded, though her face was gray and her expression sad. Brill nodded, too, although the lad appeared numbed by shock. He hoped they understood what he really meant. Danton was intending to get out when they got back.

He needed to talk to Mandin. From what he understood from her, she thought Toola was her best chance of getting to Eneit and providing protection. Mandin had no wish to go after the wine. Not without securing her daughter and getting her to safety. That meant she had to stay behind in Sartell. Danton respected that. Mandin could serve as his insurance, particularly given their pretended romantic liaison. She wasn't ready to go anywhere yet.

If Toola had sold him out, then leaving Mandin at the brothel would allow her to keep on believing he would be back, that Toola had leverage. Danton had to contact Squab and meet up with the rest of his men.

Once back in their room, Mandy opened the note that Bisma had given her. It had one word on it in a hastily written cursive script— *Eternity*.

"What does it mean?" she asked him, a sob escaping before being muffled by her shaking hand.

Danton took the note and studied it. "I don't know. Destroy the note, but remember the clue. We made need it before the end."

Chapter Twenty-three

THE REACH OF ONE'S WINGS

Gercomo flew long and hard over the barren plain in search of food. Sources of nourishment were hard to locate in close vicinity to the hatcheries. This herd of dragons was situated in the most barren region Gercomo had ever seen. Water meant life, but even a water source was hard to locate. The other two bulls kept him in close sight. He wondered if they were going to attack him if he didn't find anything.

Ahead and slightly below him was a number of rocky hills. He angled down, looking for a place to land. The other two bulls kept circling. The human part of him deduced the formation might hold water. On landing, Gercomo sensed some small life there and smelled water. Surprisingly he wasn't tired yet. Even though he was hungry, he had strength. He had not forgotten how energizing the sun's rays were.

A movement to his left alerted him to the life form scrambling to safety. Yet he anticipated the move and intercepted, swallowing the wild horneger whole. It wasn't enough to fill the emptiness inside but it was better than nothing.

There was a pack of them. Gercomo swung around and arrowed his snout after another one, and he gulped that one down too. The bulls landed and gulped the remaining six between them.

A horneger was not sufficiently large to be worth carrying back. He needed to locate a couple of burden beasts or a wargnu or three. When he had been stationed at the vineyard he had hunted on occasion. Wargnu were difficult prey. They liked to lie in soft pits of sand on the plain, waiting for the insects, the snakes and the slugs to slither by.

They would be hard to spot from the air. Yet, casting his mind back to his hunting days, he remembered they left particular wave patterns in the sand, a trace of where they dug themselves down. From the ground the waves looked like ridges, but from the air they would resemble a fan pattern.

With his hunger slightly sated, he spread his wings and leaped into the air, letting the breeze lift his wing membranes. The bulls accompanying him did the same. One bellowed something at him. Reaching out with his newfound dragon sense he detected their wariness even though he had led them to food.

Gercomo glided in an ever-widening anti-clockwise circle. It allowed him to survey the ground and conserve energy. He had to concentrate but he could see no sign of any wargnu. He changed direction and now he circled clockwise, but starting on a wide angle, contracting inward with every pass. It was going to take patience. The sun was tracking lower in the sky. Finding food in the dark would be harder as the sand would disguise the life force and the patterns would be hard to see.

Near the center of this contracting circle, Gercomo saw the familiar markings. He circled again and then chose a place to land. The other bulls landed, too, and between them they had three points covered. Now to rouse this beast from its nest.

Gercomo thumped his foot—once, twice. He looked at the other dragons and they understood. They brought down their clawed feet and the ground vibrated. Gercomo's lesser weight and size could not produce the same effect and would provide no incentive for the wargnu to stick its head out. However, the bulls' greater mass did the trick. There was a faint ripple in the sand pit. They had caught the beast's attention. Unfortunately it did not raise its head or move again.

Gercomo had to think of something else. He began to claw through the sand in an attempt to uncover the beast. The bulls continued to thump and the beast, feeling the removal of its protective layer, began to squirm. Sharp thrusts of fear emanated from the beast. Such fear tasted good to Gercomo. He would enjoy slowly killing the wargnu.

The other bulls began to uncover the beast, scooping large drifts of sand clear. The turmoil within the pit increased. Gercomo reared back, wary of the beast's triple-pronged head. One bull did not pull back in time and was struck in the neck. Shaking its head, it bellowed and lashed out instinctively, effectively stunning the wargnu. Gercomo, disappointed that the beast would not suffer, took the opportunity to aim the killing blow. There would be other times, he thought, as the beast fell back to rest against the side of its pit.

The three of them bit off sections to eat and divided the remainder to be carried back between them. The other two bulls took larger portions. Gercomo was not sure he could manage a load as well as fly. He put the section of carcass in his mouth and then ran to get lift. It wasn't as difficult as he had supposed.

The bulls led the way this time, homing in on their nest. Gercomo reached out with his senses, wondering if he could do the same. But the pull of the hatchery was not there. He would have had to deduce his way back from his hunts by retracing his path. When they drew closer, the familiar scent of the place was recognizable. Perhaps these beasts were drawn here because they were marked by the place where they were hatched.

Upon landing, dragons crawled out of their sleeping holes and out of the pit. The herd leader thumped his way down from his perch. The smell of warm, fresh meat rippled across them. Gercomo and the bulls marched up the flight track and one by one dropped their bundle at the alpha's feet. Then slowly they crept backward. Stomachs full, they did not need to partake of the meal but could bask in the glory of finding a kill. The bull bellowed loudly then took a large bite. Then he stepped back as the others took turns to take a portion of the food. The bull turned away and went back to his roost.

Gercomo had been expecting something more, some acknowledgment, but there was none. He looked sideways at the other bulls; they too had been ignored. Did that mean that this herd was finally accepting him? Then he understood that he would be free to roam. He had proved himself. He grinned a toothy grin. There was something he was searching for—a girl with power.

Chapter Twenty-four

POWER UNITES

Garan had practiced the exercises Salinda had set him to do until he could do them in his sleep. Except he wasn't sleeping now, because in the morning Salinda was going to transfer the cadre to him. It wasn't the worry so much that was keeping him awake; it was the contemplation of all the possibilities. He did not fully understand his own abilities. What responsibilities did this new power bring? Would he still be Garan or would he change?

Salinda had changed. He had seen it. Her eyes glowed all the time, something she would have to work on because such a characteristic could be dangerous out in the real world. Looking at them reminded him of Laidan and the terrible flight from Vanden. But she was different in other ways, too; there was an even more faraway look in her eyes. It was as if she had seen things more profound than she could put into words, and the aura emanating from her was tangible to him. Laidan had noticed it too, but she said she thought it was her cadre reacting to Salinda's.

Salinda had tried to explain what she had done while alone on the island but she could not articulate it well. Garan guessed that much of it he would never know or understand. It was all she could do to concentrate on the transfer and provide him with instructions. Time would allow her to calm down and digest it all and then maybe explain it in a simpler way.

Garan sat up in bed and ran his hand through his hair. It had been three days since he had rebuffed Laidan's advances and still she was being nice to him, smiling at him as if he was the center of the universe. His first thought had been that she would revert to hating him, but that had not happened. That made her behavior all the more intriguing, and he found that he was still susceptible to her wiles. His feelings were aroused when she accidentally touched him or smiled at him.

Now he was even more convinced that he loved her. Truly loved her to the point where he could define his choices by her desires. Then he was faced with a hard question. Would taking the cadre change that feeling? He did not want to lose that love he had for her or the love he was certain she felt for him. Surely her desire for intimacy was driven by love. Her love was something he treasured.

What of Brill? He could not ignore the other man's existence. Did she no longer care for him or he for her? Could she lose such a strong feeling so quickly? He could not make sense of it, so he got out of bed and began to shave.

Light from the shuwai and the newly replaced streetlamps flowed in through the window. Living underground was unnerving most of the time. Because the space was so large it did not feel closed in, but the absence of wind was noticeable. More disconcerting was the absence of Belle moon and Shatterwing, which he was used to seeing every day of his life.

Thoughts of the observatory came to mind as he paced in his small living area. How was Elder Wylie getting on? And that new boy who found it hard to fetch crystals quickly? His thoughts also strayed to Vanden and the changes needed to help the people get back on their feet. There would be new tenders at the observatory and old friends now living in the town.

Finally, as he sat on the sofa staring into space, he thought of Thurdon and all that he had learned. The old man had not abandoned him as he had supposed; he had even wanted Garan to take the cadre after his death. These two facts helped Garan go back to bed and rest. He would need all his strength for the morning.

A few hours later a knock on the door woke him. Still tangled in his bedclothes, he was sitting on the bed when Salinda came into the room. "Still asleep?"

"No...yes...I found it difficult to rest. I am sorry."

"Understandable. Are you ready?"

He nodded.

"Good. Now, would it be easier to do it in here? You seem comfortable and Laidan is outside. I could ask her in."

Finally removing the bedcovers from around his legs, Garan stood up. "In the sitting room is good. Please be welcome."

Salinda turned away to sit on the sofa. Garan dressed quickly and joined her as Laidan came in and sat down opposite him. She gave him a nod of acknowledgment without her brilliant smile. Garan was grateful to do without the distraction of his attraction for Laidan. Surreptitiously he searched her face for anguish and pain and found none. Her visage was as serene as he had ever seen it. He comforted himself that she was not too upset by the impending loss of the cadre.

Laidan's blue eyes were glued to Salinda, who sat with eyes closed. Salinda's strangeness was even more apparent at this moment. Garan didn't completely understand what had happened to her, and he was slightly afraid of it and hoped that it did not happen to him.

Without physical contact, Garan sensed Salinda reaching out to Laidan's cadre. It was like the feeling of energy discharging during a thunderstorm. Otherwise there was no outwardly visible sign of what Salinda was doing.

Her voice broke into his thoughts. "Now, Garan, make the tendrils in your mind that I told you about. Spread them out and make sure you are ready, for they are the anchors."

Garan did as she bid. It was easy, though he could see no tangible results of what he was doing. The tasks she had set him had been mental exercises. Now as he watched he saw the cadre, now visible, lifting away from Laidan. It was an oval shape and it sent out blue-tinted shafts of light in all directions. He squinted against the brightness and his eyes watered. It was not possible to take his eyes off it. "Keep those tendrils ready, Garan."

His gaze flicked to Salinda. Her eyes were alight with the flame of her power and they were latched onto the beauty that was the cadre. It was moving closer to him. He detected it passing through his forehead; its touch like a cold razor cut, short, sharp and then gone. The thudding of his heart gave him sudden discomfort. "Secure the anchors now. Make the tendrils grasp the beams of light and bind them."

Garan did the best that he could. It was as if there was a block of ice inside his head. He was mesmerized by the cadre. As the tendrils of his own mind connected with it, his body jerked, and alien emotions and thoughts pierced his own mind. He heard screaming and knew it for his own voice. He could hear but not see Laidan slipping away quietly, though he could sense something like grief in her. Or was that in the cadre? Salinda was next to him, whispering to him. "It is a success. We did it." Her voice sounded awed and distant, two of her new characteristics. "Garan, do you hear me?"

The cadre in his mind reacted to her presence. Her being so physically near made the cadre try to rise out of his head. He fought against the pull of it. "Yes, I hear you. It wants to be with you."

Salina edged away from him. "Is that better now, Garan?"

The cadre subsided and no longer fought against his hold. Light filled his mind, turning everything white. The breadth of it was daunting. He was distracted by this inner force.

"Rest now, Garan," she said softly. "Lie back on the sofa. You need time to adjust to the cadre and it to you. Remember what I told you. The visions will be strong at first and then they should die down. Don't be surprised if you have a hint of Laidan in there, for I believe she will have left a small impression. While each holder adds to the whole and joins with the cadre at death, making it something more, Laidan never accepted the cadre and held it but a short time." He heard her move away but before Salinda left she spoke again from the doorway, the tone in her voice tinged with certainty. "You will be one of the greatest holders of the cadre, Garan."

Garan eased back onto the sofa, gently raising his feet. Then he lost touch with the moment and had no idea how long for. The normal everyday sounds of Nils talking to Salinda filtered through the door, bringing him to the surface, and then faded as they went away and he sank back into the cadre. He kept his eyes closed, hoping that would help him settle the cadre into his mind.

For a while it sat there like a lump and then gradually it began to warm as it settled into his mind. He could touch it, like touching a raindrop without breaking it. The outer layer was more like a skin, with light rippling underneath. Then he could feel the strands poking through the layer. He probed one and Thurdon sprung out at him. Garan gasped at the strength of his old mentor and the vividness of the images flashing through his mind. The flavor of Thurdon was strong. It was as though Garan could smell him, see him, feel his words. Like he himself was Thurdon.

As his surprise lessened, he experienced more. He sensed the old man's relief that finally the cadre rested in Garan. So Thurdon was aware within the cadre? He was not truly dead then. That realization gave Garan comfort. Salinda had told him that before, but now he had it directly from the old man. Well, the old man's essence, anyway. The sense of relief and happiness that Thurdon exuded turned a whole lifetime of Garan's feelings of unworthiness on its head. This was meant to be. He was meant to hold this power and knowledge. He was worthy.

With this inner acceptance, the cadre connected to something deeper within—something that was him but not him. The cadre reacted and appeared to flash mauve, like a crystal from the observatory. Power surged through him. Salinda had not mentioned this feeling. In reaction to the strength of the power, he yelled and unknowingly leaped to his feet.

Sweat soaked his clothes and his voice came in short, raspy pants. Salinda raced into his abode, eyes wide and still showing the glow of power. "Wing dust! What was that?"

Garan's hair began to lift and then stand on end as power discharged like thousands of minute, forked lightning strikes. His hands glowed mauve in front of his eyes. Small flames leaped from his fingertips, discharging into the air. Nils came in behind Salinda and his mouth dropped open. Without a word he rushed back out again. Had Garan scared the Hiem? Garan was able to pass the power like water from hand to hand, pouring it from one to the other. As he continued to do so, Salinda stared at him, saying nothing. Yet there was calculation in her eyes.

"What does this mean?" he asked her.

She shook her head and then licked her lips before she answered. "I can't say. It is good, whatever it is...and unexpected."

Nils returned with an armful of power units, any power units. There was a slight smile on his face when he laid them before Garan. Looking up at Garan he said, "No use wasting that power, now, is there?"

Salinda laid a hand on his arm and laughed. "Oh, Nils. You are so unflappable sometimes. Normal things like dragons excite you. Extraordinary displays of power don't."

Garan did not touch the power units. He passed the stream of power over them. It was all he needed to do to charge them. Nils gathered them up quickly and headed for the door. As he lowered his frame to exit, he replied to Salinda. "After that night at Trithorn Peak when you and Garan transformed a man into a dragon, I found that nothing at all about you two surprises me. Dragons, though, are still a big unknown. I think I am much more likely to understand them than I am to comprehend you and what this cadre is."

Salinda eased Garan back down into a sitting position on the sofa. When Nils was gone she smiled at Garan. "He is wrong, you know. The cadre is much easier to understand than dragons, and much more accessible. But that knowledge will have to wait. You must relax again. Hopefully this reaction is the only thing unanticipated in all this."

Kneeling next to him, she brushed the hair from his face and soothed it until it curled around his ears and shoulders. "You should stay quiet for a few days, Garan. You need to allow yourself to adjust. You don't have a lot of time, so take what you can. I have a feeling we don't have much left before we have to take action."

He brought his gaze to hers. There was a connection of some kind that flashed between them. "Oh?" Salinda said. "How strange it feels when the cadres acknowledge one another."

Patting him on the shoulder, she stood and left him alone in the abode.

Chapter Twenty-five

A DIVISION OF PATHS AND LOYALTIES

Danton decided to stay one more night at Toola's establishment because he owed Mandin an explanation for his desertion, and he wanted to say goodbye to the woman who had become close to him. From the sad look in her dark eyes, he could tell that she knew they had come to a crossroads. Her quest was not complete but it was time for Danton to go his own way. They both shared the conviction that Toola was behind the attack on Bisma and the drying up of Eneit's trail. Danton couldn't understand it, but it had demonstrated to him that Toola was heavily involved in the dark politics of this place and that none of them were safe.

Mandin smiled, but it was a smile that knew regret. Danton embraced her. This would be their last time together.

In the dark hours of morning, Danton told her that he was leaving. He detected her nod. "Tell Toola I'll be gone a few days. If I can't find the wine I'll be back to try and get you out of here. Are you sure you will be all right?"

"Yes. I have to stay, I understand that. Toola knows something. I know she does. I have to find out what it is. I will not leave here without Eneit."

He nuzzled her neck. "I will take the lad with me. I hate to leave you alone, but..."

"I understand," she said, running her fingers through his hair and then ruffling it playfully. "Brill has done more than enough for me. I'll miss him."

"We will worry about you."

"I can take whatever Toola gives out, particularly if I know it will lead me to my daughter. But..."

"What?" he whispered, once again nuzzling his rough chin in the soft folds of her neck.

"I'll miss you too, Danton. Thank you for everything...for sharing yourself with me. Salinda made a big mistake."

Danton stoked her hair and rubbed her earlobe between his thumb and forefinger. "No, Salinda chose what is right. That much I know. What could I offer her but a wasted life, a used-up man? She is something special."

"Oh, you are a fool..."

"We are all fools for trying," Danton whispered, and then winced because he'd let out some cynicism that he'd been trying to hold back. Toola's betrayal cut him deep.

As Mandin dozed, Danton crept from the room and went to fetch Brill so they could slip out before dawn. Noises from the other brothel rooms assaulted him when he stepped quietly down the corridor. The place was at its liveliest in the small hours of the morning. No doubt the spies were following him. He found Brill's door. Brill lay on his side, sleeping with his mouth open. Danton reached out and shook him. A lamp burned low in the corner and its light reflected in Brill's now open eyes.

"Come," Danton whispered. Brill nodded, quickly donned his clothes and gathered his gear. Brill tossed one of the shrouds to Danton. They slipped them on. It was a good plan to sneak out without being seen. Even with the power turned off, the Hiem shrouds helped them blend in. After checking the corridor, they left the room. Danton touched Brill on the shoulder and whispered close to his ear.

"Meet me in the lane. Leave by the roof courtyard, climb down to the street. I'm going another way. We'll be gone a few days, perhaps for good."

Brill nodded and knuckled sleep from his eyes. Danton nodded once and darted into the shadows down the corridor. Brill stepped back into his room to wait a few minutes before he too made his move.

As stealthily as he could, Danton edged his way down the corridor to the escape tunnel. Suppressing a sigh of relief when the hatch opened at his touch, he threw himself head-first into it and crawled through to the other side. Then turning his body to secure the door behind him he made his way through the pitch-black tunnel.

Now that his trust in Toola was completely shattered, he found that the short crawl through the tunnel filled him with anxiety. Every rodent's scuttle, every drip of moisture or shift of rock under his foot, kept him alert.

When he finally made the door to the lane, and checked that there were no soldiers or obvious followers, he let out a big sigh. There was no sign of Brill yet. The lad had the tougher journey. Danton drew his deactivated shroud around his shoulders and sauntered to the end of the laneway to wait for Brill.

City living had softened him, Danton thought, as he watched groups of men walk the streets. He had lost his edge. An unlicensed harlot stepped out to grab one of the passing men, a well-dressed youth. He pushed her back, hurling a disgusted epithet after her, and she tripped on the pavement. Another group was coming up the street. Danton pressed himself closer to the wall and deeper into the shadows, hoping that Brill would be along soon. Lingering there for any length of time was bound to draw unwanted notice.

The harlot called to another young man in the next group. This one was dressed in workmen's clothes and appeared intoxicated. The woman said a few words to the man, who stood wobbling while he gaped at her. Handing his hat to one of his friends he leaped on the woman, pushed her up against the wall and began rutting with her with his trousers still on. The woman grunted with animal pleasure.

Danton looked away, shaking his head with repugnance. Sartell disgusted him. More importantly, he was disgusted with himself. How easily had he fallen into Toola's trap and let the trappings of comfort and ease divert him from important things? How close had he come to destroying Brill's views of the world? The sound of a few coins hitting the paving snagged Danton's attention. His eyes tracked the men as they moved past him. The street harlot scrambled on all fours to pick up the coins and then scampered back into the shadows.

Danton finally spotted Brill. The lad was walking along the street, giving the harlot a wide berth. As he walked past Danton, whistling quietly to himself, he pretended not to know him.

Danton waited a heartbeat and followed the lad. Brill was being careful and that meant trouble; it meant he had acquired a follower. Hopefully it was someone they could deal with easily and without too much attention. Brill had a backpack draped over his shoulder. Danton smiled to himself. At least the lad had come prepared.

Brill headed into the square, where several taverns remained open, still spilling patrons onto paving stones and roadway. Burden beast dung lay in sporadic piles and a few bodies lay in the gutters. By morning, the bodies at least would be cleaned up; not so the rest of the refuse, thought Danton as he shadowed Brill across the square and down an alley. Danton detected the followers: a group of three men, who had split up and disappeared into the crowd in the square and then converged behind Danton once the lad had chosen the alleyway. This meant that they were after him. His heart sank. The last hope he had that Toola hadn't betrayed him bled out of him. Now to turn the tables.

Danton took a step into the alley. It smelled rank and was barely wide enough for a man to walk down, let alone fight in. Brill wasn't visible. Danton took the opportunity to flatten himself against a wall, edging himself into a narrow doorway. It was strange that Danton could no longer see Brill. He wished that he had been able to make himself invisible too. The knife that clanked against the wall close enough to shave him convinced him of it. Danton spun around and kicked the man who had thrown the knife in the gut. While his assailant doubled over he brought his fists down on the back of his neck, flattening him out.

Another man ran down the alley, in search of Brill, Danton suspected. That left the third. The remaining assailant was backing up to the opening of the alleyway, blocking the entrance. He had a long knife in his hand, the kind you could hide in trousers without looking like you were carrying a sword. Yet it was twice as deadly in a close fight like this. With a sharp point and razor-sharp edges, it could stab and slash.

Danton dodged the first lunge and spun around, kicking the man's feet out from under him He went down and the huge knife went flying off. Danton ducked beneath it only to be tackled by his opponent. They wrestled, and Danton punched the man across the chin. While the man was stunned, Danton was able to get free. Danton clouted him again for good measure and looked for something to gag and tie him with.

The sounds of a body hitting the ground reached him. He fervently hoped it wasn't Brill. There was little room to maneuver in the alley. Danton's gaze flicked up and around. There wasn't much he could use but his bare hands. His hurling blades were with his things at the brothel. Leaving his bags had allowed him to give the impression he was coming back, but he knew Toola probably wouldn't be fooled. Still, he hadn't expected to be sprung so quickly.

These men must be hers. Why else would they be following him?

The man came to before he could finish tying him up. He bolted upright and tried to head butt Danton. Danton lunged to one side, his boot hitting the wall to give him enough force to rebound and knock the man down. They connected. The man grabbed him by the neck and flung him backward. Danton hit the back of his head and was dazed.

A knife thrust caught him by surprise. He barely dodged it and was done for with a counter strike. Without warning, the attacker's eyes widened and blood leaked out of his mouth. For a moment he just hovered there before toppling to the side. Danton shook his head, looking at the empty laneway. Brill's chuckle reached him and then the shroud slipped off his head.

Danton gaped. "I clean forgot about the shrouds. Good thinking."

Brill squatted beside him, his eyes frequently drawn to the entranceway. "Do you need a hand? We should move now."

Despite Danton shaking his head, Brill helped him to his feet. Danton put a hand out to the wall to steady himself. "I am getting rusty."

"Or maybe we're in way over our heads?" Brill quipped as they edged to the mouth of the alleyway and joined the crowds walking across the square. When they were sure they weren't being followed, they slipped down the street and headed to the wharves. Once free of the traffic, Brill filled Danton in on what the girl Lexia had told him about Toola's connection with the Commissioner of Police. The rest of Lexia's story had him cursing roundly. Toola let Lexia's father have his own daughter? Toola beat the girl and let her pet monster violate her?

After what they'd gone through as children, he would have thought Toola would have protected vulnerable children like Lexia. Obviously things had changed. Toola had changed. Danton was staggered to hear such a detailed account of incest and abuse. He had left Mandin to that? Danton shuddered. *Magol curse me!* he thought.

No wonder Brill had been looking so downcast. Toola's brothel was not full of willing workers, but those who had been sold, those who were unwilling and had no choice. Toola could have protected them, instead she exploited them. It convinced him that Toola had slipped further into the cesspit of politics than he had first allowed himself to believe. In addition, her influence was far-reaching.

Yet if she had wanted to, she could have sold him out already—all of them. She hadn't, so that meant there was still a bond of kinship there, some final barrier that had not been broken. Yet Danton had to tread carefully. Perhaps she was waiting for the right price, the right opportunity, the right moment.

As the sun rose, turning the gray river sludge to a pale murky green, Danton and Brill entered the wharves. Squab was waiting for them. She didn't look happy. They were three days late.

Chapter Twenty-Six

BAIT

Mandin awoke alone in the room. And for the first time since arriving in Sartell she felt truly alone. Danton had said he would try to come back, but Mandin was smart enough to know that this was not a given. If he found a trace of the wine, he'd be after it with no time to come back for her. It was now up to her to take charge of her search for Eneit—if she could. With Danton gone she had lost his protection, which meant nobody stood between her and Toola. Nobody stood between her and the rest of Sartell. Just the thought of ending up in one of those slave cages made Mandin's hands shake and her body sweat.

Whatever Toola had planned, Danton and Brill leaving without her knowing about it was going to stymie those plans. Mandin did not have to be an intellectual or a great strategist to know that there would be payback for Danton and Brill leaving, even perhaps for her taking Danton to her bed, and anything else Toola decided needed repaying. It was the simple way of human nature, as natural in a small town as it was in this vast city and this brothel.

Yet Mandin could not blame Danton for using her as security. Time had run out for him. Just as time had run out for Eneit. Mandin knew it in her bones that Eneit was in Sartell now. Any moment, her sweetness and innocence would be extinguished. Mandin brushed tears from her cheek. Toola knew something. Mandin was sure of it and her best bet at finding Eneit lay with the brothel madam.

The problem for Mandin was how to tie herself to Toola so she could be there when the moment came. In a half-doze Mandin lay there for a while, thinking about her options, mentally preparing herself for whatever the day would bring. She was more resilient since arriving in Sartell but was she resilient enough?

There was no use delaying the inevitable any longer, so she threw off the covers and climbed to her feet. Mandin chose to face things on her own terms, which was the only way she found acceptable. She had to pretend more courage than she felt. She had to be confident.

With an exaggerated sway to her hips, Mandin walked down the corridor past the baths. The damp scent hit her as she pushed open the doors. A few clients were reclining in the baths, towels wrapped around their heads, shoulders being massaged. All normal for this place.

She knocked decisively on Toola's kitchen door. The door snapped open and Linel stood there, his face expressionless. He stood back and she stepped in.

Toola looked up, holding her cup of tea midway to her mouth. She leaned back and lowered it. "Well, good morning."

Mandin inclined her head. "Good morning to you. I have come to talk business."

"Business? Is that what you call it?"

She leaned back to the cupboard and brought down another cup and placed it on the table. "Sit if you please."

Mandin flashed a nervous smile and took a seat.

"Danton and Brill have deserted you," Toola observed after pouring the tea.

"Our paths have diverged. Yes."

"Diverged?"

"I chose to stay here with you because I believe you can help me."

"Help you? But you threw my friendship in my face. You thumbed your nose at what we could have had to be Danton's tart."

Mandin flinched. "It wasn't like that. I had a loyalty to him and a common purpose. Things have changed."

Toola leaned back. "They have indeed."

Mandin lifted the cup and sipped. This meeting was not the easy camaraderie that had existed between them at first. There was tension, a battle of wills. Mandin bit her lip, wondering what to say next.

"You have nothing to offer me," Toola said bluntly. "Nothing with which to pay me for helping you find your daughter. Previously I offered friendship because of Danton's relationship to me. Now that he is gone..." She opened her hand to signify emptiness.

"He said he would come back," Mandin said.

"Really? He has left some of his belongings, so you could be right. Do you know where he has gone?"

Mandin shook her head. "No. He never took me with him and never talked about it either."

Toola smiled. "Does he genuinely care for you?"

Mandin nodded. "Yes, I think he does."

"So if you were in trouble he'd come for you?" Toola lowered her eyelids, studying her.

"If he could. If he knew about it perhaps." A feeling of unease grew in her gut. There was a trap here she could feel but not see. Where was this leading?

"Linel?" Toola said peremptorily. "Bring a contract for Mandin to look at."

Mandin had jumped at Toola's command and spilled some of her tea. She put the cup back on the table. "Contract?"

"Yes. I will help you Mandin. I will find your daughter. But as you have nothing but yourself to offer me in payment, I require a contract."

Linel put the document in front of her and laid down a pen. "What kind of contract?"

"One where you owe me your life." Toola's mouth lifted on one side. "You did say you'd give your life for your daughter. Well, now is the time to prove it."

Mandin stood up, ready to walk out. She was not signing her life over to Toola. Linel blocked her path. "Stay. Where. You. Are." Toola launched out of her seat and prowled around Mandin. "You've become much more worldly since we first met, Mandin. Fornicating with my cousin has been good for you. There is a bloom to your cheeks, more confidence in your walk. You hold your head up higher."

Toola rested her rear against the table, arms crossed as she assessed Mandin.

Mandin faced the other woman, eyebrow arched in a mockery of Toola's well-used gesture. Mandin could see that Toola was fuming and doing her best to hide it.

Toola's head tilted a little to the left. "You are taking Danton's desertion well. Seeing as he left you unprotected. I offer you protection and you spurn it. Why is that? I thought you wanted to see your daughter." Her tone was more normal now.

Mandin didn't think the woman was any less dangerous but her choice was to deal with her. "I do, by my life I do."

"I did hear something yesterday. I am going to follow it up, but what good is it for me to do that? You don't want to know about it."

Caught, Mandin blurted, "I do. I do want to know."

"Then agree to my protection." Toola tapped the contract with a forefinger.

Mandin's gaze drifted back to the document. Words, words, words that would twist the cord of slavery around her so tight she would lose all hope. But in agreeing to this she had a chance to save Eneit. Tears rolled down her cheeks and she wiped at them, ashamed to be crying in front of the other woman. "You were so generous to me before, I can only ask your forgiveness for any offence that I caused—"

Toola slammed a hand on the table. "Enough. Sign it or get out. See how long you last on the street on your own."

Mandin picked up the pen and signed her life over to Toola.

After what seemed like an age, Toola spoke. "I did hear of a shipment. The kind we were talking about. Three girls: whole, young virgins. They are to be sold and the price will be very high."

Mandin could not stop the look of hope that leaped to her face. She bounded from her seat and threw herself at Toola's feet. "Please, please help me. Please help me save my daughter. I will do whatever you ask."

"The price will be high. I am not sure I can afford it."

Mandin knew the woman had her. All her plans, all her bravado fled. There was only need. Her eyes pleaded as she gazed up at the woman. "I will pay you back for everything. What can I do to prove my loyalty?"

Toola grinned, stood up and then headed for the door. Before leaving, she paused and her gaze flicked to Linel. "Beat her publicly, in the bar. That's the best place. The entertainment factor may increase the morning's takings. Make an example of her."

Mandin swallowed and gaped at Linel. His normally expressionless face held a nasty grin. "But..." It was too late. She'd signed the contract and Toola could do what she wanted with her

Chapter Twenty-seven

A DEAL UNDONE

Nils had had a lot to deal with, and he was coping rather well, Salinda thought as she left Garan alone in their abode. There was an excited gleam in Nils's silver eyes when she caught up with him on the main thoroughfare. It unnerved her. She had gone away and come back changed and now Garan had discharged violet-colored flame in the Barr family node. Surely there would be repercussions. Surely Nils would object to this upturning of his usual routine. She attracted his attention and waved hello.

"Why did you make me leave when things were becoming so interesting?" he asked, towering above her.

Salinda did a double take, surprised by Nils's reaction. "Because Garan needs to be quiet for a while. You getting excited about what is going on is not good for him."

"Me? You take me away from happenings that should be recorded. This is not appropriate."

"I know, Nils. But sometimes things just have to happen as they happen. I am curious about what is going on too. But he needs time. Later you can interrogate him, and I'll be happy to listen in. You forget that that little episode with the flame was unexpected."

"All the more reason for us to observe and record."

Shaking her head, she moved away, feeling his gaze on her but unable to continue to argue. She was exhausted from performing the transfer and also excited by her success. On top of that she was in awe of what had transpired with Garan. Processing what had happened had become a priority for her.

The cadre she had transferred had changed already. When she had glimpsed it within Garan's mind, she had seen that it was no longer bluish white, but mauve like the power released from the crystals. It was reacting with the essence of Garan, the inherent traits in him that made crystals respond and throw off power. She wondered if Thurdon had known that such a thing would occur. It was too late to ask him as the cadre he dwelled in was now in Garan. And if the process had gone as it should, contacting Thurdon again would be difficult, if not impossible. Garan's mind would have taken the cadre and soaked it up.

Perhaps the memories and essence of the last person who held it would still be on the surface. That would mean that something of Laidan could be there in the cadre and Garan might have easy access to her recollections. With a sigh of regret at the lost possibilities for exploring Thurdon's knowledge, she nonetheless knew it had been the right thing to do, and just in time too. She hoped that Laidan's residue would be slight and perhaps pass by Garan unnoticed.

⏾⏾⏾⏾⏾

The flare of power exuding from Garan's eyes after the transfer of the cadre lessened after a few days. During that time, Garan found little rest as he was bombarded by visions and physical discomfort as the cadre nested within his mind.

After each dreamed-filled night where Garan was assaulted by the lives of those who had previously held the cadre, he would wake exhausted and drained. Yet after a few days, he recommenced working on the city lights, as that allowed him to relax his mind and channel the excess of power into the power units.

On his first trip down, Nils had shadowed him, claiming that the lamps brightened noticeably when he passed them by. Garan found the phenomenon as disconcerting as he did Nils's increased interest in him. Luckily, Salinda had come at a run and urged Nils to leave Garan alone.

In something of a daze, Garan took note of what was happening around him, but was so absorbed in the cadre's side effects he did not have the capacity to react appropriately. He was vaguely aware that Nils had descended into the archives at Salinda's urging and then she too had faded away from his notice. Garan did not encounter Laidan in those first few days either, and that did not seem to matter to him. The changes in his mind and body consumed him.

As the visible display of power ebbed from his hands and skin, he found he could still re-energize mechanisms without touching them, but he had to be in close proximity and concentrate on them. However, making the effort to concentrate was difficult due to the cadre's presence in his mind.

Traversing the city, even in his post-transfer haze, Garan could see that his task was almost done. The city was bright with light. What would he do when the task was completed? He could barely think about the future, caught up as he was in the lives of those who formed the cadre. Still, the thought of Nils and what a fully lit city would mean to the Hiem warmed him and comforted him. Hopefully the cadre would settle and he could light the sacred flame in the Hall of Elders and reward Nils for his assistance and friendship. Garan had come to know Nils of late and he was moved by pity for his circumstances. The cadre echoed his sympathy; at least, he thought that is what he could sense.

Would the lighting of that one last flame signify the end their sojourn in Barrahiem? He could not stay away from the observatory too much longer; he knew they needed him. And even more so now that his power was enhanced. The thought of how many meteors he could shoot down made him sweat with anticipation. This power gave him a means to save the world, or at least to protect it from meteors. Would the cadre assist in repelling the last of the moonfall? Hunching his shoulders, he realized that it could not.

On his return to his own abode, he found Salinda lingering at the entrance to the node. Gently, yet deftly, she quizzed him on how he was going and what symptoms he was experiencing.

"I am well so far," he answered as if from far away. "Soon it will be time to leave."

Salinda put her hand on his forearm, preventing him from entering his abode. "I counsel you to wait," she said. "There is much to be absorbed from the cadre: memories, knowledge and power. It will take time to sift through those that come easily. Later, I will show you how to go deeper and delve into the greater knowledge hidden there.

The time of need is upon us. We can no longer be passive recipients of knowledge. We must seek it out. I, too, must sift through the things that have been revealed to me and place them in perspective. Knowledge can be a blunt instrument if you have not the wit to apply it."

He nodded, acknowledging her greater wisdom and experience, but more than that he trusted her.

"And when you are ready, we will talk more about the origins of the cadre. I think you will find that the most interesting thing of all."

Garan went inside his abode. Food had been prepared for him, perhaps left there by Salinda. Physical tiredness weighed him down so he ate quickly and went to bed.

The next morning he was more rested. The dreams and memories were there, but less virulent, less intrusive. He had finally slept a full night. Once again he headed out into the city to continue the task of repairing the lamps. He came to an intersection. All the lights were working. He must have passed this way before. The city was becoming so bright that it would keep them awake at night. Garan realized that he did not know if it was truly night. Without the sun, moon and Shatterwing, Garan was adrift. He reached out to the comfort of the cadre easily, realizing that it was becoming a part of him.

Laidan sat on the threshold of a cluster of abodes. Though she hadn't yet seen him, Garan gazed at her and found an image forming in his mind, a recollection, hazy, obscured and tinged with bitterness. Was that Thurdon? Was this what Thurdon experienced through the cadre? No, not Thurdon, the cadre as a whole. Not even that; it was an echo of Laidan's presence in the cadre. Salinda had warned him. He stood stock-still as the vision of Laidan and Brill together unfolded.

His knees went weak so he sank to the ground, bracing himself with his hands to steady himself. He was totally absorbed in what he was seeing, not quite believing, yet knowing it to be true. Laidan's intent was writ heavily through the images—she had wanted to seduce Brill, to bind him to her—she had deliberately worked on him and led him to betray his own ideals. There were traces of her recent behavior with Garan himself. She had been seeking to lure him, too. She had been obsessed with gratifying herself, disregarding everyone else, particularly Garan's own feelings for her. They meant nothing to her. He was nothing to her but a tool, an instrument to be manipulated and then discarded.

Garan was shocked. He fell backward and sat heavily on the ground, mesmerized by the scene replaying in his mind. He really didn't want to see it anymore but he couldn't shut it out. He thought of how he felt about Laidan, the tender regard he had had, and how she had spread horrible rumors about him. Her heart was dark. She was tainted. She had given her body to Brill, wantonly, against her upbringing, against the beliefs of those who had harbored her. It was not only the seduction, but the complete focus of her mind, as if it had been possessed by the desire for sex, for adoration, for being the complete central focus of others. When had Laidan become so needy?

"Are you all right, Garan?" Laidan stood over him, her hair brushed to shining, a smile playing around her mouth and crinkling the skin around her eyes.

He bolted to his feet, towering over her, unable to suppress his anger. "You gave yourself to him," he hissed. The harsh words burned out of his throat. Never had he spoken to her in such a tone. He was disgusted by her and could not hide it. The cadre was disgusted by her, particularly Thurdon. How could she have borne the ill feeling the old man exuded in the cadre?

Laidan jerked backward as if he had struck her, the expression on her face changing from puzzlement to awful understanding. "I..."

Backing up, she hit the wall. He bore down on her. "I saw it all," he said in a low voice, pointing to his head. "What you did, what you felt, and what you intended. You have a whore's heart."

Laidan's skin darkened to a deep red and her hands were clenched into tight fists that she held close to her chest. "How dare you speak in that way to me? You can't mean that." She pushed against him, pounding her fists on his chest, and when he backed up she then slid sideways along the wall to get away from him.

Grabbing her shoulder, he swung her round, forcing her to look at him once more. "How can I not mean it? 'Tis enough that you disregarded me and how I felt about you. That is nothing. What about Brill? You used him. You wanted nothing but gratification and adoration. You manipulated him to get what you wanted. What about those who care about you? You had no thought for them. Pleasure is all you thought about, and getting your own way." Rage swelled inside of him. "You disgust me."

Laidan shook her head, and tears dampened her crimsoned

cheeks. "No!" she said breathlessly, shaking her head. "No, you don't understand. It wasn't like that at all. I love Brill." She put her fist in her mouth to muffle a sob.

"But I do understand." He tapped the side of his head. "'Tis all in here. You thought there were no witnesses but you forgot about the cadre. Every sordid detail, every wayward, lurid thought is in here, replaying in my head. Thurdon's essence witnessed it, Laidan. Thurdon knows it all. I know it all. Shame, Laidan. That is what you should feel. Shame!"

Laidan screamed and lunged for him. "Stop it," she cried. "It's not right that you can see inside of me. It's you who is disgusting." She repeatedly thumped his chest and then she lost control and attacked him by every means. He did not try to restrain her, except to guard his eyes where her nails were aimed. She was frenzied. When she began to tire, he eased her back against the wall. He gave her one steady look and she turned her face away, chest heaving with emotion. When he took a step back, she scrambled away. Crying out, she sobbed the words, "No, no! I can't bear it."

Garan hugged himself, suppressing a shudder. He needed to put some distance between himself and Laidan. He had to process what this meant for him and how he could deal with her in the future. It was all too raw, too new. It was disconcerting to be in another's mind, even an echo of a mind of someone you cared for and loved. Leaving the bright streets of the city behind him, he ran down to the lake. There, with the dark water filling up his senses, he stood on the bank and stared out into the fathomless black. The brooding presence that had touched him previously hovered out of reach. It could not distract him. Laidan had given herself to Brill, and Garan could not work his way back from that. All his dreams with regard to her had been shattered. All the possibilities came flooding back. If the Master Elder hadn't intervened perhaps they would have been husband and wife now. There would have been no Brill. Was it his fault, then, for killing Turnet and being incapacitated so that he could not argue for their relationship, which had been on the cusp of becoming something?

Yet Brill had still been in the equation. Educated, well-mannered and a prince—what chance did Garan have? He did not even have the glory of a rescue because Danton and Brill had helped. Now he was being self-centered and selfish. What right did he have to accuse Laidan when he could not control his own base desires?

Where had all that potential for love gone? He knew Laidan was not responsible for his own dreams; they were his desires, not hers.

In that he had wronged her. His anger had been based on his own thwarted desire and the vividness of the experiences he had re-lived.

He lowered himself to the ground, letting regret wash over him like the moist droplets rolling in from the lake. Had Salinda known and kept it from him?

Even now he could feel Salinda approaching and knew that the sound of their argument had reached her. An empty city threw echoes, and thus he had ruined the reverent calm of the city with his anger.

Now shame washed over him. Misery filled up his heart. What would Nils say? Would he understand the difference between a whore and a bonded love? He had no right to speak that way to Laidan. He scrubbed his face, wishing he could change what had happened, wishing he could unsay what he had said.

"Garan?" Salinda stepped softly up to where he sat.

Garan rubbed his hands over his face and washed away the beginnings of tears. Salinda needed him to be strong, not a young, heartbroken fool. He glanced at her, giving her a light smile. "Hello."

She sat down next to him and rearranged the folds of her gown. She stared at the lake, saying nothing. Even now her eyes still glowed against her will. Not bright and dazzling as Laidan's had been when she had received her cadre. Salinda's glow was more tempered and reducing gradually every day. His eyes glowed too. He sniffed.

Garan couldn't bear the silence Salinda brought with her. "I am sorry. Our voices disturbed you."

Salinda turned her face to him, her faraway gaze passing over him, even through him. "Not at all. I wasn't quite certain if the cadre had retained the knowledge of her deeds. She was so disconnected from it, I thought perhaps they would go unnoticed. Had she done something very bad?"

Garan nodded and then shook his head. "I had no right to speak."

"Brill?" she asked.

Garan laughed hollowly. "Yes, with Thurdon looking on. Even though you had put him to rest, he watched her and felt extreme frustration and betrayal. He could no longer influence her. And the deed is layered with her emotions, her motivations, her desire...all of it. Nothing hidden."

Salinda frowned and let her gaze be drawn by the lake. After a time she said, "It goes deeper than that. My theory is because

Laidan was thrown in amid some lecherous and devious men when previously Thurdon had sheltered her, her mind has been overset. Just recently she had come into her womanhood, her beauty and thus her vulnerability were many times amplified. She had no mother to warn her, no friends to protect her, no barrier to guard her fragile youth."

Salinda directed her gaze on him, seeing him this time. "Laidan was on the cusp of understanding the world around her, the impact of her beauty and how she could protect it, when her life changed. Thurdon was going to leave her at the observatory, you know. Leave her there with you. Yet it was not to be. At the moment when she was focused on herself Thurdon died, and you know the rest."

Garan wiped the tears from his cheeks. "You sound as if you want me to forgive her. I have no claim on her, and she no longer has any hold on me. I have nothing to forgive."

Salinda smiled, dazzling him with the light sparkling in her eyes. "I did not think you a fool, Garan."

Garan ground his teeth together. Salinda's words were simple yet true. The love was there, even though he wanted to deny it. Now that the anger had gone, he found he still cared. Source preserve him. How was he going to bear it?

Salinda climbed elegantly to her feet and brushed sand off her robe. "If you find yourself able, some exercises may help to settle your mind and the cadre. I hate to pressure you. We do not have the luxury of time. You have taken well to the cadre and it appears to be undamaged from its adventures. But there is much we do not understand and much I have to tell you."

Garan climbed to his feet and hurried after her. Salinda had already reached the steps and was ascending to the park they had worked in previously. In preparation for the exercises he tried to clear his mind.

Try as he might, Laidan kept returning to his thoughts. Remorse at his angry words flowed over him. He wished to run to her straight away and beg her forgiveness. Yet his duty was with Salinda for now. Would that he had not been so hard on Laidan. There was sweetness in her still. That much he knew. Later, he would make it up to her. There would be time when he had finished this new round of exercises.

❧❧❧❧

Salinda watched with pleasure as Garan successfully completed the new series of exercises. The cadre would settle in record time, she was sure. It had melded well with him, despite the rather explosive meeting of two types of power: the cadre and Garan's own inherent one.

His ability amazed her. She had not been as quick or as deft as this young Skywatcher. She could sense the cadre ordinarily enough even within Laidan. However, in Garan's possession its presence was amplified. Then again, her own excursion into the cadre had changed her, made her more attuned.

While she watched him repeat the exercise, she tried to gain a sense of the other power within Garan. She wanted to observe whether the interaction of the powers was discernible. Would Garan provide a lasting and unsurpassable addition to the cadre? Or was this the time when the cadre would be used one last time? Was that rogue asteroid the final heavenly stroke for Margra?

When she looked at Garan and considered him, his power, his youth, his pure heart, she thought that it was time. Too many things were falling into place. *Is it so?* she asked the cadre, and the answer she received was*: The pieces are not all in place yet.*

All she could get was confirmation that she had done the right thing in transferring the cadre, and that somehow Nils was important. The time was approaching. It would be here soon. She didn't know what she was to do. She let the tension slide away. The cadre always worked better when she wasn't wrestling with it. Then the image came to her. The image of the Inspector transforming into a dragon. Was it a warning or was it important?

Salinda had lost track of time when Nils strode into the park where she worked with Garan. At his approach, Garan ceased manipulating the power of the cadre, letting the fireball dissipate into the air around him. "Has something happened?" she asked Nils.

He stilled, realizing that he had disturbed them. "I...I..."

Salinda walked up to him and placed her hand over his, holding it gently. "Be at peace, Nils. We were finishing soon anyway. Tell us what troubles you."

Nils gaped at her. Salinda blinked and fell back a step. Was he learning their ways or had something bad happened? Her gaze shifted to Garan then back to Nils. The silver of his eyes dimmed. "Did you give Laidan permission to enter the Travel Ways?"

A rock landed in Salinda's gut. The baby kicked at that moment and she placed her other hand there. "No, Nils. We have no need to enter the Ways."

"But she has entered them. I felt her. She's gone!"

Garan rushed past her. "No! Laidan! By the source! She has run away. 'Tis all my fault. We must hurry."

Nils regarded Salinda. "Why has Laidan disregarded her promise? Why would she leave the safety of the city?"

Salinda's grip tightened on his hand. "Forgive me, Nils." She leaned around him to call after Garan, who was taking the steps two at a time and was nearly out of view. "Wait, Garan. You cannot follow. Stop!" She saw Garan pause and turn back, saw the look of anguish on his face and sighed. "Oh, Nils. I have been stupid. Do not blame her for this. It was my doing, my mishandling of the situation. I should have known her affair with Brill was more serious than first appeared. Garan found out about it and they quarreled."

Blinking rapidly, Nils looked to Garan who had come back to where they stood. "You told her to go?"

"What? No, of course not—but I said horrible things to her. It's my fault she has run off. We must go after her."

"I agree. There is much danger for her in the Ways. She has no idea how to navigate them," Nils said.

Salinda grasped Nils's arm. "Worse still, what if she leaves the Ways and goes into greater danger?" A wedge of fear lodged in her gut.

Nils opened his mouth and shut it quickly. "Indeed," he said. "It is much more dangerous out there unprotected."

"We must prepare and follow," Salinda said. "Nils, can you prepare maps? Garan, you pack some supplies. It might take a day or two to find her."

A wail of misery escaped Garan as he turned and ran for the stairs. "'Tis all my fault."

End of Part Two

The story continues in *Bloodstorm* Dragon Wine: Part Four

Chapter One

A FOOT UP THE LADDER

After returning from a long foraging trip, his belly full of a human snatched from a river, Gercomo saw the female dragon again, the one who had laid the eggs he had so enjoyed eating. She hissed at him as he drew near. Gercomo found her behavior amusing because with her bulk, she could do some serious damage to him. Jagged fangs. Razor-sharp claws. Yes, she could shred him without a thought. So why hiss? Why not strike? The fact that she hadn't intrigued him.

He angled his head toward her and lathed his tongue across her snout. It was a daring tease. Her body tensed but she didn't strike back, just hissed again and then turned away and ignored him.

Gercomo sauntered away to settle down into his burrow, belching up human aftertaste as he did so. He caught a glimpse of her scrabbling toward the egg pit.

Gercomo smiled inwardly, tempted to peer down after her to see her reaction to her empty nest. But that would require more daring than he possessed, and he had to be careful to keep his thoughts small or all would know that he had been the one to destroy the clutch of eggs. The dragons might not use sentences and concepts like humans, but they sensed strong emotions like guilt and fear. Gercomo would bet they could read intentions too.

A few minutes after the she-dragon had disappeared from view he heard a commotion. A few dragons who were slumbering among the rocks lifted their heads in response but were not interested enough to climb out of their burrows and investigate. Gercomo turned his head and noted that the head bull slept on, blissfully unaware of the female's distress.

More intense screeches echoed from the hatchery below. It wouldn't take long for the bull to react now, for it sounded like a fight had broken out. A grunt came from the bull's resting place.

It was time to distance himself from the action below, to remove himself from blame. Gercomo crawled out of the sand, which fell to the ground in a warm shower. The morning sun was strengthening as it rose and the scent of sulfur was on the air. Gercomo breathed deep.

Warm pools littered the area where he walked. Steam vents spewed vapor into the air, giving it moisture and warmth and releasing pungent aromas. He was tempted to lick the rocks for salt like the hatchlings did. He wandered further in. In the thermal area, he sampled different scents and tentatively tasted the mineral deposits that rimmed the ponds and vents. The purple salts were like hot spice and the yellow more like rotten eggs, or what he remembered of rotten eggs. Food did not taste as it once had; the crunch of bone and the slurp of blood gave him much enjoyment now, as did the quenching of the lilac-colored glow that centered on living things.

The sound of rock hitting rock alerted him to the presence of another dragon. He inhaled and knew it was her, the she-dragon who had so humiliated him and who he in turn had punished. She had come to challenge him over her eggs, the ones that had filled his belly with delicious energy.

Vengeance spewed from her mind. Turning her head sharply, she fixed her gaze on him, fangs dripping, ready for the kill. Gercomo could taste the hot emotion, like some strange sauce caught at the back of his throat.

She'd come alone, without her mate.

He had barely turned to confront her, when she lunged for him, swinging with her head to knock him down. Although he was taken by surprise, he was able to duck, avoiding the full force of the blow. Before she could strike again, he bit her on the neck, ripping the skin with his broken tooth.

Her screech near deafened him. She clawed at the ground and at him until he released her. He backed up and circled, trying to devise an attack strategy. She was a female, hence smaller than the bull, and yet larger than him by far. She lunged again, catching him a glancing blow across the head. Violet-tinged blood leaked down her neck.

He had wounded her. His grin could not be suppressed. *How interesting.* Although physically larger than he was, he could outmaneuver her and he was smarter, of that he was sure. The blood glowed temptingly with that violet-colored energy; her life force. His tongue lolled. He wanted to drink it.

Feinting left, she went to block and then he was on her, overbalancing her so she fell. The blood on her neck drew him closer. He sniffed and licked tentatively, pretending at first to be considerate and caring. She did not throw him off. The taste of blood on his tongue sent ripples of ecstasy through him. What was that? He had to have more.

He licked again, savoring the blood, and then bit down hard into her leathery flesh. The female tried to break free but was paralyzed by his grip. He sucked the blood in, drew it down his throat. It burned and singed its way into his stomach. Then the strength of it hit him. He let go of her and reeled, staggering backward.

Power. The raw power of dragon blood tore its way through his flesh and mind. The world tilted. He had a vague sense that he was on the ground before he lost consciousness.

When he came to, the female was sniffing his penis, gently probing it with her tongue. He growled a warning, but she put her foot on his torso and held him in place and licked him in earnest. Despite his revulsion, he was aroused by her ministrations. His cock hurt, though. Curling in on himself, he saw it was large, too large for his stature.

The power of the blood was still inside him, bursting to escape through his skin. He roared at the female. She withdrew her snout from between his legs and retreated. A shaft of pain hit as his hindquarters grew in size, first one leg then the other. It hurt but he was growing, stretching, being more. Giving himself a shake, he realized he was a good foot taller.

It must have been the dragon blood.

What else could account for this power roaring inside him and this sudden growth?

Climbing unsteadily to his feet, he checked himself out. He had definitely grown, but was still a runt compared to the rest of the herd. His tail swished across the loose stones littering the ground.

The female abased herself before him and whimpered. Alert, he studied her. Was she seeking to mate with him? He blinked and then she arranged her tail so that he could have access. Could he? Should he?

He circled her and her scent filled his nostrils, potent and overwhelming. Gercomo's erection quivered and burned in reaction to the chemicals hitting his brain. He wanted—no, needed—to copulate with her. It was all that was in his mind at that moment.

He climbed atop her and she opened for him. As he pushed into her, she moaned—a sound of pleasure. Gercomo just had to move, just had to ejaculate as fast as he could. The thought would not leave his mind. It possessed him, made him mad with lust. He thrust into her vigorously. She yipped and growled. The sound of their coupling echoed around them. There would be no doubt about what they were doing.

Unsought, he had made an impression on the female. Tactically, this was a good thing. Fucking a normal-sized dragon would give him status. As a normal-sized dragon, she would be a powerful ally, a powerful mate.

His seed spilled into her, though he wondered what sort of semen he had made with his stunted dragon form. Surely he could not fertilize dragon eggs. Utterly spent, he withdrew from her. His cock, now flaccid, was still large in comparison to his body. She turned and licked his snout, nuzzling him and nudging him gently.

Let the rest of herd mock him, but this female was well satisfied with his performance. He growled at her, thinking pleasurable thoughts. It wouldn't hurt to keep her on side.

Ambling back to his nesting place, he burrowed himself in the sand, conscious of the other dragons' attention. The bull looked up and roared once. The female he had coupled with roared back. A sense of merriment filtered through his dragon sense. Had he unwittingly climbed up the pecking order by mounting that particular female?

The female grunted behind him. She had followed him to his burrow. He opened an eye and regarded her. Lowering her snout, she sniffed him and licked the top of his head. Then she turned to descend into the hatchery. Curiosity got the better of him. Disregarding his intent to hide away in his nest, he scrabbled across to peer over the lip of the pit. There she was, laying eggs. The process was stomach-turning. He was human enough to feel that. Yet, he wondered whether he had actually fertilized them.

What would his offspring be like? Would they be dragon or part human? It hurt his brain just thinking of it. He quieted his thoughts. No point in drawing attention to his strangeness. Not when everything was going along so well just now.

After pushing sand over her eggs, the she-dragon scrambled up the side of the hatchery. Before she emerged, Gercomo went back to his nest and feigned sleep. He had no idea what was going to happen next.

Through a crack in his eyelid he saw that she chose a piece of ground close to him and made the sand soft for her burrow. It appeared she had staked him out as territory. Odd, but it looked as though he now had a mate. As he dozed off, he realized this meant he had someone at his side, someone of normal dragon stature. If he kept her happy, she would do his bidding. Then he remembered the bite, and how her blood had tasted and the power that had surged through him. Her blood would give him greater power, make him stronger, larger. Maybe now he had a way to influence the herd and its head bull. Despite his misfortunes, everything was falling into place. Nice thoughts of revenge settled in his mind. *Salinda.* That blonde chit with her hidden power. *They will pay. They will.*

After a short rest, Gercomo shook the sand from his hide and lumbered off. He would fly about, test his luck. If there was prey to be had, it would be his.

Author's Note

First of all I have to say thank you to the fans of the Dragon Wine series who have asked for more of the books. Your support has made me revisit the drafts of *Deathwings* and *Bloodstorm* and decide to publish them. I wrote them years ago, well before *Shatterwing* and *Skywatcher* were published, and it feels so good to revisit them and to publish them. The final two installments may take some time, but rest assured they will see the light of day.

I hope you like the new covers! I do and I'm so excited to be working with Frauke at Crocodesigns.

I have to say a heartfelt thank you to Brianne Collins. She edited the first two books so it was good to get her for these two. She makes me sweat and tells me what she thinks. Also, a big thank you to Jason Nahrung who made time in his busy schedule to proofread *Deathwings*.

I also have to thank Craig Cormick for some valuable feedback and insights into the story. It is wonderful to have an author you respect and look up to praise your work but also take time to give you some difficult feedback. It is wonderful too to hear from fans of the books and also see reviews. I am dealing with a sensitive subject matter here. One that is not easy to look at. The premise I explore in the books is something I think about when I see bad things happening in the world—*no matter how low humankind can go, they are worth saving.* To those of you who see light in the dark spaces, I heart you!

Lastly, many thanks to my partner, Matthew Farrer, and my children, Taamati, Shireen, Erana and James, and the grandkids (who should never read this book), Madelyn, Yumi and Alexander.

Donna Maree Hanson

May 2017

www.ingramcontent.com/pod-product-compliance
Lightning Source LLC
Chambersburg PA
CBHW022031120726
47899CB00007BA/2172